TALES OF *Modern* INDIA

# TALES OF *Modern* INDIA

## Eight Stories by Tagore

Translated by
**Soumitro Das**

Vitasta

Published by
Renu Kaul Verma
Vitasta Publishing Pvt Ltd
4348/4C, Ansari Road, Daryaganj
New Delhi - 110002
info@vitastapublishing.com

ISBN: 978-81-991712-2-0

First Edition 2025

MRP ₹ 525



Edited by Soham Debsarkar
Cover Design by Rohit Gautam
Layout by Shubhpreet Kaur
Printed by Vikas Computer and Printers, New Delhi

# Contents

# Preface

Tagore never mattered to me.

Growing up as a child in New Delhi, surrounded by Punjabi Hindu refugees from West Pakistan, I only knew, like them, that Tagore was a winner of the Nobel Prize and that he had written the national anthem. That's all. I also knew that he had a certain place in the culture of my parents, but even at that age, I had very little respect for my parents' opinions about the world. I learnt no Bengali at school and did not read or write that language. The only Bengali text that I could claim to know to some extent was Sukumar Ray's *Abol Tabol,* because my mother read out some of the poems from the Signet Press edition of the book. I found the poems very funny.

Of the two languages that I used most frequently in my childhood, Bengali at home and Hindi outside, I knew nothing of their written culture, except what was taught in school. My written culture was wholly Anglophone. I devoured books and comics in that language voraciously and on one occasion, remember having read three books in a single day. My hunger for books was endless, and there were no good books in the house. So, I relied on the library—public, circulating, and school. And that was not enough. My parents, instead of encouraging my reading habit, were, on the contrary, alarmed by my social and cultural health. They thought I would turn into some unrecognisable spectre with no practical instincts of any kind.

Though there was no Bengali culture in my childhood to speak of, there were areas of Bengaliness. For instance, football. My father used to take me to watch Durand Cup matches featuring our team, East Bengal. I remember the thrill I felt when I saw the East Bengal red and yellow jersey emerging from the tunnel onto the field for the first time. I wanted to be a footballer.

There was Durga Puja, but then, I lost my faith when I was thirteen. I looked at the idol of the goddess and asked myself, 'Does God look like that?' The answer was 'no,' and that was the end of the faith of my ancestors as far as I was concerned. It was at the same time that I had started reading the Bible, and I remember being deeply impressed by the personality of Jesus Christ.

And then there was Satyajit Ray. I took to him immediately; even as an adolescent, I had no problems in relating to the world I saw in movies like

*Kapurush o Mahapurush*, *Teen Kanya,* and, of course, *Goopy Gyne Bagha Byne*.

The food we ate at home was Bengali, East Bengali to be precise, and it is a cuisine I have enjoyed all my life.

Also, my father was an actor in an amateur theatre group, and I enjoyed watching him on stage, mostly. He would, at times, take me with him to his rehearsals, and I would be fascinated to watch him bring his role to life. He also took me occasionally to the Ramakrishna Mission in Delhi, and I would be bored to tears.

Thus, there was no occasion for me to deal with Tagore directly or indirectly anywhere, and my Bengaliness remained superficial throughout my life. Nevertheless, I was brought up to believe that the Bengalis were an exceptional people. Why, I never bothered finding out.

It was only when the family shifted to Calcutta in 1979 that I came into contact with people who spoke no language other than Bengali, and I began understanding that Tagore was a social and political force among the *bhadralok*, who, at that time, were the dominant elite. There was not a function or a programme anywhere without some element of Tagore in it–usually the songs, bits of recited poetry, and what are called, among Bengalis, dance dramas. Tagore was everywhere. He was claimed by everyone: all political parties, all classes, all castes, all communities, everyone everywhere. Today, I ask myself whether any other writer in any other culture has almost monopolised the cultural space the way Tagore has done. Goethe? Shakespeare? No, not really. They may loom very large, but they do not occupy as much space in the English and German minds as Tagore does in the Bengali. I was slowly learning to recognise the contours of a myth, a myth that overshadows Tagore the writer. This myth contains, very broadly, four mythemes:

Tagore represents the totality of Bengali culture. In other words, had there been no other poet, musician, or philosopher but Tagore, Bengali culture would still be great.

1. There has never been anyone like Tagore; there is no one like Tagore; there will be no one like Tagore. This is what has turned Bengali culture into a closed culture.
2. One cannot define oneself as a Bengali without reference to Tagore.
3. And that it is sufficient to subscribe to the mythemes above to qualify as a cultured Bengali, even if one has not read a single line written by Tagore.

Given the myth, how does a Bengali writer in 2025 wanting to write outside of Tagore, approach his task?

In the first place, he must tackle the proposition that Tagore is universal. *Vishwa Kavi*. Let us look at this more closely.

It is clear to everyone looking at it with non-mythical eyes that Tagore was received in the aftermath of the

Nobel Prize as an oriental sage, rather than as a poet. He looked the part. He did nothing to dispel the notion that he was a representative of the mystic East. He spoke continuously about the *Upanishads* and the *Bhakti* poets. For him, it was these texts that were universal, and his own poetry participated in that universality. In any case, nobody then had the tools necessary to gauge Tagore's worth as a poet. Nobody knew Bengali, and there were no good translations available. Yeats had to make do with the translations that Tagore himself had done, and these were not high-quality translations. Part of Yeats's sympathy for Tagore was based on the fact that he was presented as a symbol of India's native genius, just as Yeats himself was considered a symbol of Ireland's native genius. In fact, with the notable exception of Pound, the enthusiasm around Tagore was due to the fact that he was totally unlike a Western poet. This is what Per Hallstrom, member of the Swedish Academy, had to say about Tagore: 'The intense and loving piety that permeates his every thought and feeling, the purity of the heart, the noble and natural sublimity of his style, all combine *to create a whole that has a deep and rare spiritual beauty*. There is nothing in his work that is controversial and offensive, *nothing vain, worldly, and petty;* and if ever a poet may be said to possess the qualities that make him entitled to a Nobel prize, it is he.' (Our italics) He was given the prize because he was a saint. Think of Baudelaire, think of Rimbaud, think of

Mallarmé, and you will see why Hallstrom was so thirsty for purity of feeling and wholeness. It was not Tagore's universality but his specifically Eastern traits that led to the prize. Ezra Pound wrote in vain that Tagore was a poet first; nobody listened to him. The public at large responded firstly to Tagore's appearance and his demeanour, and then to the substance of his lectures, which were all centred around India's spiritual greatness.

In order to be universal, you have to keep yourself ready to understand deeply and profoundly the creative spirit of other cultures. It is not clear, from what his biographers say, how much Tagore had read of Western literature. Or whether he read any at all. He didn't ask to meet anyone when he went abroad and left it to his various impresarios to arrange meetings with poets, if any were available, and with notables, kings, presidents, and so on. He did read Yeats, perhaps more out of courtesy than genuine interest; one doesn't know whether he read Pound or Gide, who had rendered him service. He had an exchange of correspondence with Romain Rolland, but Rolland had an interest in Eastern religion and spirituality that pre-dated Tagore. He also met the Countess de Noailles, Jean Cassou, and other minor poets when he went to Paris for his exhibition, organised by the formidable Victoria Ocampo. But he didn't meet any of the modernists or of the avant-garde–Surrealists, Dadaists–he remained content to meet whoever wanted to meet him. Who indeed were James Pond, Vaughn Moody, Harriet Monroe, etc., who milled around him when he went to the US? These names do not figure in the history of Western literature.

A world poet who knew nothing or very little about world poetry.

The myth is intact. There is not a cultural event, local or global, in which Bengalis do not celebrate some aspect or the other of Tagore's voluminous oeuvre. But for how long? As long as the *bhadralok* survives in a climate that is changing rapidly, even in Bengal. Two things have happened in the last 30 years: the rise of the Hindu Right to power and the introduction of naked, competitive, profit-motive capitalism. Both herald India's entry into the era of modern nihilism, a nihilism defined by Nietzsche as the devaluation of all the higher values.

Capitalism has introduced a complete dichotomy between the public and the private. The world of work is run according to one set of values—rationality, progress, competitiveness, ambition, individualism—while the domestic sphere is dominated by values derived from religion, primarily by the religion of the majority, i.e., hereditary hierarchy, myth-making, magic, and the submergence of the individual by the community. There is a cultural schizophrenia that lies at the heart of the order of things defined by capitalism.

On the other hand, the Hindu Right regime

swears by modernity and technological advancement while espousing reactionary and obscurantist ideas simultaneously. One has witnessed the cynicism, the hypocrisy, and the mean-mindedness of this quasi-fascist ideology on a daily basis for over a decade. All the higher values are degraded, and what has taken their place is an aggressive, religiously-coloured nationalism based on a projection of brute force that often brooks no dissent.

How does one fit Tagore into this scheme of things?

For Tagore, the higher values were not degraded; they were intact. Love was love and not, as the noted French psychoanalyst Jacques Lacan put it, love-hate, where love is the mask that hatred wears and hate is in fact a concealed longing for the thing one desires the most but cannot possess. Tagore understands modernity as a psychology; he can describe it intellectually, but he cannot feel the dilemma of the modern artist. The stories in the present collection speak of modernity from the outside and, therefore, seem rather artificial. He doesn't get inside the skin of the modern poet as Eliot, Auden, or Larkin would. The latter were conscious of the degradation of art itself, and it is only their brilliance that, despite the flaw in their humanity—from Tagore's point of view—brought about a revaluation of art as the capture of their own inner conflict. In such a world, a person reading Tagore may well ask himself—How does a person feel the way he does about things? It is this emotional incomprehensibility that threatens to marginalise Tagore in the future, even in Bengal.

The other factor that determines the climate in which modern writers function is anarchism, that is, absolute disrespect for all forms of authority that do not justify each of their actions morally. By a capillary effect, this has an impact on the author's authority over his work. As Barthes puts it in his famous article on "The Death of the Author," the meaning of the work is not dependent on the author's intentions anymore. That's because the narrator in the Western tradition has undergone a metamorphosis.

In the classical narrative, the narrator was God, and in his fictive universe, he was omnipresent, omniscient, and omnipotent. He knew the name of every flower, every bit of furniture, and every thought or feeling of his characters. To produce this effect, he often endowed himself with an encyclopaedic knowledge of the world. In Flaubert's *Bouvard et Pecuchet*, the pair of characters try to establish mastery over reality by reading up on one discipline after the other and remain unsatisfied in the end. Flaubert's novel *Salambo*, set in ancient Carthage, was based on voluminous research into the Phoenician culture to produce what Barthes calls the reality effect. The narrator was all-encompassing and classic. Joyce was the culmination of this trend. He ensconces his narrator inside the heads of his characters, where it registers every emotion, thought, and fancy of his or her consciousness.

For this, his knowledge of Dublin is detailed and thorough. There are no cracks.

With Kafka, things change. The protagonist grapples with a world that is lawful, apparently, but whose law functions in utterly mysterious ways, unknown to anyone. There are institutions and regularities of behaviour, but these institutions and regularities do not reveal their mind or their motives, or their meaning. They baffle, harass, and persecute the protagonist. Already with Kafka, the narrator God is incomprehensible and arbitrary.

With Beckett, things get worse. The narrator, God, can no longer rely on the evidence of his sense perceptions, except for his hearing, which he says is fine. He doesn't see properly or in an ordered, coherent way; even his judgement is affected. The first book of the trilogy, *Molloy*, ends with the words—It was midnight. It was raining. It wasn't midnight; it wasn't raining. If the narrator is god, then this god is apathetic, careless, and randomly cruel. He forms his judgement without really knowing what his creature has to go through or, worse, despite knowing. The law makes no allowance for human debility. The narrator's world goes on shrinking until it is reduced to being a disembodied voice relentlessly asserting the impossibility of continuing with the narrative and the necessity of continuing with it.

After Beckett, in at least the Anglo-Saxon world, the mainstream has become classical again because you couldn't go any further. There was Garcia Marquez, of course, who created a world in which things defy the laws of nature all the time, where the mythic and the fabulous rub shoulders with the commonplace in an easy familiarity, where magic exists within history and determines it. But Garcia Marquez created a school, not a reinvention of the novel in its philosophic roots. People have, after Flaubert's example, undertaken to extensively research their subjects in order to lend authenticity to their fictive universes. Their work occupies the terrain between fiction and a book of scholarship, with the underlying admission that for true knowledge of the human world, one has to investigate reality separately through the tools provided by the social sciences. Many people would take that to be an admission of defeat. But it may no longer be possible to produce a work of pure fancy.

Where does one situate Tagore within this narrative evolution? He is a classicist, pure and simple, who was exploring the hitherto untold. He was the inventor of the Bengali short story and had the whole terrain open to him. He had to just look around himself to find stories to tell. He probably never read Maupassant or Chekhov, the two outstanding modern exemplars of the form. But Tagore's judgement is sharp, his enunciation clear, and his understanding, well, god-like.

The overwhelming majority of modern writers would swear by materialism; they would acknowledge that the universe is mostly matter and perhaps some material antimatter as well. They would expect science to provide finite explanations of material phenomena. Where most of them would baulk at is the nature of the mind. If the mind is coextensive with the brain, if the mind were only matter, as some scientists have claimed, then it would be possible to manufacture life in a factory complete with memories and fantasies. But most modern writers would also baulk at considering that as a sign of the presence of some spiritual force in the universe, because that would drag them into untenable disputes and contradictions with themselves and their artistic practice. What the modern writer does is to say, "I don't know."

Tagore didn't have a problem with God, whom he calls the Creator and whose living representative on earth is the creative artist. He looks after the universe. Indeed, Tagore's critique of modernity centres around the problem of atheism and the moral ambiguity that it produces. This is very evident in the story called "Sunday" (included in this volume), where Avik, the modern artist, tries to sell a watch gifted to him by his ex-flame, embezzles the money raised for a *Puja* and donates it to a scientist so he can go attend a conference in Copenhagen; steals a necklace belonging to the woman he loves because she was on the point of selling it to raise funds for the same scientist and because Avik believed that it belonged to her and to their future together alone. But all this is captured by Tagore from the outside, like some god, whereas the modern writer is afflicted with this ambiguity to the depths of his art. In "Child of God," Cormac McCarthy tells the story of a lunatic, cross-dressing, necrophile serial killer in such a way that, towards the end, he asks the reader, sarcastically, 'Aren't you sympathising with this man; aren't you having pity on him?'

Tagore is very sure of his moral categories. He has no hesitation in distinguishing between good and evil, between right and wrong. God exists. But, for the modern reader, Tagore risks being dated, being taken for someone who belonged to a certain narrow band of time and whose usefulness is not thoroughly exhausted. In any case, nobody reads novels anymore to know what is good and evil. That moment has come and gone. What the novel or the short story does is to analyse the human condition, or the human dilemma, and seek a path through it, out of it, through an exercise of intelligence.

So, if I don't like Tagore and think him dated, why have I translated some of his longer short stories into English? Well, first of all, curiosity. I just wanted to see what Tagore would read like when translated into the idiom of modern English fiction. Tagore's own translations are so poor that they come across as pious, sanctimonious humbug. Tagore was, on the contrary, a shrewd man who understood the way the modern mind works and traditions crumble under pressure from modernity's inexorable march apparently forward. In other words, I have also translated Tagore for the content, which, though dated, throws light on the predicament of a thinking individual who was dealing with unprecedented realities.

I believe that the encounter between the reader of modern English fiction and Tagore is a worthwhile one.

Let's see what it produces.

# Introductory Notes to the Stories

There is a clear symbolic split, in Tagore's short stories, between the world of nature and the world of ambition. This split works over a certain number of equivalences: under nature, we can place the following semantemes: religion, rural Bengal, women, an overwhelming sense of duty as defined by custom and tradition, and ordinary human solidarity within the limits placed by caste. Under the world of ambition, on the other hand, we derive the following semantemes: urban setting (especially the great city of Calcutta), men, the primacy of reason, as in science, but also as in respect for social hierarchies and cultural differences, lack of scruple, and individuality.

Nature is powerful and uncontrollable, but essentially benign. The class that best represents nature is women, often from the countryside, often from traditional milieus. Even when they are transplanted in an urban context, women continue to go back in memory to the community of origin. Thus, Charulata, when she writes, writes about her native village, while Mrinmoyee is a child of nature in her totality, free, uninhibited, and uncontrollable. Achira emerges from the jungle, where she is shown to feel at home.

Nature is also, for Tagore, a manifestation of God, a living realisation of the power and rule-breaking potential of the entity referred to by Tagore most often as the Creator. If the world of ambition is immersed in Western rationality and science, the world of nature, more often than not, is moved by forces that are unfathomable from man's limited view. For instance, Tagore often gives no explanation for why certain women undergo certain emotional changes all of a sudden. The language of emotions is the language of God. It has perhaps its own rationality of the heart, but it is not reducible to the calculating reasonings of the urban and/or male mind.

The world of ambition is also a world of vanity and of hopes belied, of the frustration of human endeavours, and the futility of human achievements. The dichotomy of nature/ambition is also an ethical one: nature is good; ambition is necessarily dishonest, if not downright bad. The world of ambition is often dominated by greed; it may be complex, but it is crass and vulgar in its very complexity. Finally, the world of ambition is open only to men; women are excluded from it, and women exclude themselves from it.

Men belong to the world; they are creatures of history. Their being and action are in the world.

Women are not part of the world, at least not directly. They are outside history. They take their place in a private sphere, ruled by the exigencies of running the house, bringing up children, and guarding customs and rituals. They have no access to the world except through men.

This was true, by and large, of the Tagore household.

Bhupati is a man of history, of ambition. He is a creature of public attention driven entirely by vanity.

Men don't need to understand women. There is nothing to understand.

Bhupati says the narrator of 'Broken Nest' (*Nashtaneer*) does not notice when his child bride turns into a woman. His wife does not even register in his consciousness as a sexual being. He pays almost no attention to his wife. In his scheme of things, dominated by a wholly masculine concern for public affairs, sex has no place. Tagore notes the fact and moves on. He doesn't develop it any further.

Charu, for her part, attaches no importance to Bhupati's world either. The two worlds, male and female, exist separately. The women are physically confined to the space that has a name–'*andarmahal*'–the inner quarters, beyond which women are not expected even to be visible. Charu instinctively understands the male vanity. That is her intelligence.

Bhupati understands that his wife is bored for lack of

occupation and company, just like other women of his set. He sees no individual worth in Charu, worth dwelling upon more than casually. He requests his cousin, Amal, to nurture Charu's taste in literature. Bhupati thinks literature is of no consequence in the world. It is not a manly concern. He deals with Charu as a superior would deal with an inferior.

Amal, on the other hand, is interested in literature, but, as Tagore shows, it doesn't sum up his being; it is a vain pursuit, a dilettante's preoccupation.

Charu is pleased that Amal demands her services. Feeling wanted seems enough for her. Their relationship begins with playfulness, at least on Charu's part. The word used by Tagore is complicity. For Charu, she and Amal have their own little game, played away from and, perhaps, also, against the more serious world of Bhupati, against its exclusivist male solemnity. Charu and Amal live in their own make-believe world built out of imagination. They are like children, investing their own childishness with the seriousness of their own imagination. They are ruled by the pleasure principle.

Their plan to convert a pond into a lake, complete with a marble staircase and a deer park, and lay a garden around it fails because their means are short. Charu doesn't want to involve Bhupati because it would destroy the element of surprise. To Bhupati's world of public affairs, Charu opposes the world of feminine intrigue and imagination, and beauty.

Charu wants a world of her own, not defined by the world outside in which she understands she has no place. She wants a private world not circumscribed by male limits.

She encourages Amal to write, but is not pleased that he has been published. Because Amal caters to a public to which Charu cannot relate. She is possessive about Amal. Amal is Charu's discovery, and Charu takes pride in that. For her, it is an achievement. Amal's vanity is satisfied by his public reputation. Charu sees that as casting pearls before swine. Paradoxically, when Amal writes, he produces ahistorical texts. His writing is full of preciosity. It's a snobbish, affected play on words and images. When Charu writes, initially, she imitates Amal, but soon discards what she writes. She breaks away from Amal's model and writes about her own experiences. Her writing is rooted in time and place. It is historical in a very concrete way. For Amal, literature is a pastime. Literature does not include seriousness that is derived from historicity alone, from masculine concerns. Literature is a frivolous pursuit. He articulates this explicitly when he says, after the final break with Charu, 'To hell with it'. Becoming a barrister and helping Bhupati is the proper duty of a man.

When Charu learns that her writing has been published and is more favourably reviewed by critics than the writings of Amal, she is despondent. She knows this might hurt Amal's male ego. She immediately sets about correcting things by producing a text modelled on Amal's style. She has no idea of being a female writer; it is an alien concept. She doesn't feel the need to be a woman of the world, whatever that may mean. It is enough that she is able to keep Amal with her.

Amal, on the other hand, is quick to react to Charu's success as a writer. He is miffed that someone who was under his tutelage, his disciple, should do better than he. He jumps to the conclusion that Charu is now inflated with pride.

Charu is hurt that Amal should read his stuff to Manda, a dull clod of clay with no taste or learning. She is hurt that Amal should see no difference between Manda and her, that Amal should cease appreciating her intelligence as before.

Charu's attempts to be dutiful towards Bhupati are in vain. It doesn't come from within, spontaneously. She has to think and rehearse beforehand. Ultimately, Bhupati was never a part of her world, just as she had never been a part of Bhupati's world. Eventually, even Amal abandons her as he realises that Charu is capable of giving herself, body and soul, to her husband's cousin, while Amal cannot even contemplate the thought of taking his cousin's wife. He recoils in horror. Tagore speaks of an abyss from which Amal is, miraculously for him and tragically for Charu, rescued. Charu simply does not have the cultural wherewithal to know that what is happening to her is called love in the world—love for Amal. Even literature has not given her the tools to understand her situation. She feels that as long as Amal is around, his rejection is unfair. it is only after Amal leaves for England that her sentiments hit her with full force. She can counter rejection with rejection, and disdain with disdain. She doesn't know what to do with the absence. How to fill up the gap left behind by Amal, she who has nothing to call her own.

'Broken Nest' is the story of a woman of exceptional ability brought to nothing by the world of men that surrounds her. Charu tells herself—for there is no one else to tell it to—that Amal brought out the best in her, but equally, Amal destroys that best through his ruthless rejection of not only her but also of the person he had been for her because of her. It is the story of every woman who seeks meaning only through a man.

Mrinmoyee is free, not in an adult, overtly sexual way, but nevertheless, in a way that girls of her age in her time could never be. She comes and goes as she likes, keeps the company of boys because they are free, is never at home, and is unaware of her own femininity.

Apoorba wants Mrinmoyee for two very different reasons:

i) He is hurt in his vanity as a university graduate and as someone who has spent a number of years in the great city of Calcutta, where all male ambitions are fulfilled. Mrinmoyee laughs at him, because he cannot negotiate his way around rural Bengal and its culture; he affects superiority without having any true authority. Apoorba feels this girl should have some understanding of who he is, who he really is, i.e., someone above all village hierarchies, culturally and socially.

ii) Apoorba wishes to possess Mrinmoyee's free body, because this body is rebellious vis-à-vis the values of order and intellectual superiority he represents. Having pilfered Apoorba's shoes from the house of his prospective in-laws, she restores them to him in the jungle, amidst loud laughter, and Tagore suggests that that laughter is as if of a forest deity; it is the gods who are laughing at Apoorba, gods, whose power he doesn't recognise. Apoorba's response is to physically take hold of Mrinmoyee, capture her like some exotic beast. There is very little doubt that Apoorba is sexually attracted to Mrinmoyee, and he wants to subjugate her physically and mentally.

The girl that his mother had chosen for him is contrasted with Mrinmoyee. He goes to see this prospective bride—this, in itself, is out of the ordinary because marriages are pacts between two families involving questions of status and decorum. Apoorba finds a caged marionette, and while he is in the process of interrogating this girl, Mrinmoyee barges in in search of the girl's brother. She disrupts the proceedings, pulls the veil off this girl, and marches off without so much as acknowledging the presence of Apoorba and the girl's family. She deals with Apoorba on a footing of equality, if not superiority. Mrinmoyee is freer than Apoorba physically and mentally. She represents a challenge for Apoorbakrishna Ray, B.A.

It is said about Mrinmoyee that her face is unforgettable because it is not a mask. Apoorba asks Mrinmoyee what his fault is. She says, 'Why did you marry me?' In other words, why are you compelling me to put on this mask, to play a role for which my family has not prepared me, about which I know nothing.

Nevertheless, Apoorba is willing to make the effort to be a part of Mrinmoyee's world. Here, Tagore is making a subtle point. His education and the big city experience equip Apoorba intellectually to absorb Mrinmoyee's world on its own terms. He invites one of Mrinmoyee's companions and expresses willingness to go play with them outside. Mrinmoyee does not respond, for by then, she has a good idea about the incongruity of such a thing in her present context as a married woman. Mrinmoyee's problem is not how to fit into Apoorba's world, but how to fit into the world of Apoorba's mother, i.e., the world of a Hindu wife bound by custom, ritual, and tradition.

However, Apoorba does manage to 'run away' with Mrinmoyee to her father's place, an obscure steamship station on the river. The father, absent, does not represent authority or law. He accepts and loves Mrimoyee for what she is—a wayward waif. Mrinmoyee, in her turn, can be herself—a child. She can play at being a wife to Apoorba at her father's place. In her attempts at cooking something, she ends up cooking something else altogether. She is happy, and everybody is touched by this happiness. Mrinmoyee thrives in freedom. The moment they return home, things are back to square one. In exchange for his recognition of Mrinmoyee's desire to remain what she is, Apoorba asks Mrinmoyee to freely recognise his adult desire. He asks her to give him a kiss. She tries and fails. Not out of puritanism, but because she is not sexually self-aware as an adult. These things go deep culturally. It was normal practice for Bengali men to marry child-brides. Tagore himself married someone who was ten years old, while he was twenty-three, and with whom he had a child three years later. The child-bride was usually trained to be a wife by her in-laws. Tagore must have realised in his own life the anomaly of demanding adulthood, especially in sexual matters, from a child bride.

It is only after Apoorba leaves for Calcutta that Mrinmoyee awakens dimly to what is required of her as Apoorba's wife. In this, there is an as yet unconscious admission of Apoorba's gentlemanly conduct towards her. She is changed.

Mrinmoyee eventually awakens to womanhood. How and why this happens, Tagore does not say. Perhaps it is the weight of circumstances, of tradition, of history. She willingly submits to the mother-in-law's regime, and the latter responds with some affection. And Mrinmoyee completes this process of maturation by finishing what was left unfinished—the kiss. It's an expression of free womanhood, now redefined by Apoorba's presence in Mrinmoyee's life, in his own terrain, i.e., in Calcutta.

In "A Suitable Boy and a Suitable Girl", Tagore presents us with three types of Indian womanhood seen through the eyes of the protagonist, Sanat Kumar. But before dealing with real women in the real world, there is an imagined marriage with Kashishwari, the daughter of his Sanskrit teacher, selected as a prospective bride for the adolescent Sanat. Sanat likes the idea of intimidating Kashishwari, of making her tremble, like his father does his mother, at the very prospect of displeasing him, of possessing a person completely, like a piece of property.

A few years later, Sanat is a post-graduate, and his father proposes that he marry the daughter of a wealthy businessman who also happens to be an ultra-orthodox Hindu, in whose kitchen the coal meant for cooking is washed with holy water from the Ganges. Sanat decides he is too enlightened for such a marriage. Then he makes a lot of money and penetrates the Holy of Holies, the westernised upper class. He likes a girl, but her mother will not settle for anything less than a barrister. It is the world of ambition, and enlightenment is not enough. Besides, these people are as punctilious about following English manners, etiquette, and speech as the orthodox Hindus are about their rituals. 'Same stupidity,' says Tagore. Then, at the age of forty, the pressure of his solitude telling on him, he stumbles across a girl who is the fruit of a mixed-caste marriage, who has no property, no dowry, and who carries a major risk of pollution. This appeals both to Sanat's enlightened self and his circumstances. The girl has clear notions about what she wants to do with her life. She carries herself with poise, dignity, and self-respect. Sanat discovers that she is loved by a boy who is willing to take on the world for her sake. Tagore is probably making the point that it is only women who feel the oppression who can invent new ways of being a woman. However, it is worth pointing out that a marriage between two exceptional persons cannot be an answer to caste and gender oppression. But Tagore is not a revolutionary; he is not advocating the overthrow of one value system by another. He prefers dealing with exceptions rather than with the rule.

In 'Sunday', Tagore lays out his argument against modernity. He examines the dilemma of the modern man, most acutely expressed in the person of his principal male character, Avik, a modern artist. Avik is an atheist—not the rational, humanist atheist of the European Enlightenment, but the radical, highly intellectual, God-negating atheist of the Nietzschean variety. God is not only dead, but there is also nothing sacred in the world. All the higher values are devalued, excepting perhaps art itself.

On the opposite side is Vibha, who does not understand Avik's art. She believes in God, was very attached to her father, and is a decent, normal person.

As is usual with Tagore, there is no conflict between Vibha and Avik, or the conflict is only superficial but serious. There is no clash of ideas as such. Vibha does not represent an ideology but has a strong personality of her own. Both Avik and Vibha recognise each other as exceptional people. When Vibha is heckled by a fellow student at the art college where she and Avik are students, the latter drags the guilty party up to Vibha and makes him apologise. Similarly, Vibha breaks into tears when she scores more marks than Avik in a test because she feels Avik's degree of sacrifice is greater. Avik's nihilism shocks Vibha mildly. Avik tries selling her an expensive wristwatch gifted to him by an ex-flame who is dead. Avik says he loved her back, but this object has no value for him. Vibha sees them as a devaluation of the sentiment attached to it and of the person who gifted it to Avik herself. Avik says he is not an idolater to set up an altar in his breast pocket. Tagore seems to suggest that the modern man easily finds reasons to justify everything that is base and shallow in man.

Avik has many admirers, especially female admirers. Tagore portrays them as sycophants who are prone to jealousy and suspect each other of being charlatans. "Positively vulgar" are the words used by some of them. By this, he probably wants to show that the human material produced by modernity is shoddy.

One of the words Tagore uses for modernity in the context of nudity in art, is shamelessness. Tagore is very uncomfortable dealing with the sexual fact. The moment there is a question of sexual attraction between a man and a woman, his language becomes convoluted, rhetorical, allusive, and prudish in fact. One understands where the discomfort lies. One of the defining features of modernism is a frank acknowledgement of the animal in the erotic. Whereas Tagore is a sexual conservative. Much is made of the relationship between Tagore and his sister-in-law, Kadambari, to say that Tagore was not a puritan. In my opinion, though the relationship was important for Tagore's artistic growth, I don't think he ever had sex with his brother's wife. That would have been enormous for a Tagore, for Debendranath's son.

Avik wants to buy a new car with the money raised by selling the watch so that he can impress his latest girlfriend. Sheila, whose presence he says is like a flame, not a luxury but a need. This shows the feebleness of his artistic conviction. Avik requires the adulation of beautiful women and objective signs of social success. Art for him is, therefore, just a search for worldly success, Tagore seems to be implying, not the expression of an artistic imperative from within.

Avik also says that for the modern man, women have

taken the place of God because the modernist religion is a religion of beauty. But it is also an unstable religion, given the insatiable modern appetite for the new. Beauty is just another product; once consumed, it is reduced to nothing, setting off a search for an endless series of substitutes. Vibha says modernity is a humiliation for women. Maybe Tagore thinks that deprived of traditional safeguards, sexual emancipation opens women up to sexual exploitation, to being used and discarded, and commodified. Emancipation suits the purpose of male sexual profligacy. Tagore doesn't see the other side of the argument, that the emancipated woman can walk out of an abusive relationship, she can reclaim her own body, the emancipated widows of Bengal can remarry, and so on.

Tagore is clear that modernism is a Western credo. He is not narrow–minded; he freely acknowledges the greatness of the West and its science and rationality. But that is not all. There is a spiritual element that, for Tagore, is a reality, something that India knows a few things about. That may be why Avik says to Vibha that he can find completeness and wholeness in her. He calls her his morning star, the stable point of his perennially destabilised world. Modernity is a hollow feeling inside.

Finally, modernity is dishonest. It's the old ends and means issue. On this, Tagore stands with Gandhi. There is no such thing as good dishonesty and bad dishonesty. Truth is an absolute. Whereas for Avik, the means don't matter much as long as the end is good.

Vibha calls Avik childish and irresponsible. But her lack of jealousy, of all petty-mindedness, and of sexual competitiveness means she can give Avik the ultimate prize for a man of art—freedom.

In "Laboratory", Tagore stages an encounter between male genius and aggressive feminine sexuality, a product of the modern age. Briefly, Nandakishore Mullick is a brilliant engineer, a wealthy businessman with a passion for science, who believes that Indians are not stupid, that they can be worthy men of science given the resources, both technical and financial. He builds what he declares to be the best laboratory this side of the Suez. His wife, Sohini, is a fierce Punjabi woman who is also, outside of sexual matters, a woman of integrity. Nandakishore is enough of a man of the world not to be infatuated by women. He schools his wife in science and inculcates in her a respect and love for his laboratory. After Nandakishore dies, his estate is bequeathed to his wife, who takes it upon herself to make something of his lab, to bring it to life, give it a goal and purpose. For this, she needs a man among men, somewhat like her husband. She finds Revati Bhattacharya. Sohini also has a daughter, Neela, who is a sexual bomb. Sohini's initial idea is to marry Revati off to Neela and keep the laboratory in the family. But a meeting arranged between Revati and Neela makes it clear that the man of science does not have it in him to handle her daughter. She also recognises that her daughter is a disruptor; who will bring any man of purpose to ruin. Revati, who does not even look directly at Neela, is stung by her beauty and deludes himself into believing that he can make it with her. Sohini also learns from Professor Manmatha Chaudhuri, one of Revati's mentors, that the man of science is a pure product of matriarchy. His paternal aunt is the effective head of the household, obsessed with the prestige of her family and religion. She has already prevented Revati from proceeding to the Himalayas on a scientific trip and to Cambridge on a scholarship. In other words, Revati knows nothing about women or the real world. Despite reservations and apprehensions, Sohini installs Revati in the lab and makes him, against his own better instincts, the president of the trust that runs the laboratory. He has access to money, lots of it. Sohini warns Neela against bothering Revati when he is working. Neela feigns indifference for somebody she says she considers to be a wimp. Everything goes well in the beginning. Revati gets down to research, and his genius shines, his merit is recognised both at home and abroad. But then, the Creator—in this case, Tagore—removes both the professor and Sohini from the scene. Sohini, before leaving on a family mission, posts guards all around the lab with strict instructions against the entry of outsiders, among them, her daughter. This is the chance Neela has been waiting for. The catastrophe unfolds with merciless rigour. Revati's delusions about Neela lead to their logical and bitter conclusion. What is Tagore trying to show us?

In the first place, there is a problem with science itself. Science doesn't necessarily jostle the social and cultural boundaries of our world. The exact sciences deal with matter, and there are those who say that this matter shows signs of a superior intelligence at work, but let us stick to facts. What science has done to the human world is diminish the authority of religion, without, however, occupying all the space vacated by religion. The human mind continues to be substantially outside its purview. The human mind can utter lies, make myths, behave irrationally—pursue pain instead of pleasure—and imagine worlds which resemble the real world and which nevertheless do not exist. In other words, the human mind does not behave like a machine, or else it could be manufactured in a factory. Artificial intelligence relies entirely on previous knowledge and provides normative responses to questions couched in a specific language. The human mind is capable of producing something that didn't exist before. So, in order to understand the world of modern humans, one has to rely on art, philosophy, and the social sciences, which have seen a spectacular growth in the modern era.

Revati has one foot in the world of science and the other in the world of religion. His family background is inimical to science in its totality, in its capacity to re-mould the mind of the scientist. In other words, his understanding of the world beyond his family is nil. He does not have the intellectual tools required to understand the world of ambition, into which he has been thrust and given serious responsibilities. It is possible to be a man of science and have no understanding of the world of real human beings. This is the first reason for his failure.

The second reason is that the culture he comes from has no tradition of seduction or courtship. There is no free mixing of boys and girls on the basis of equality, no sexual exploration, no knowing of the other. Neela, on the other hand, belongs to a pseudo-westernised world that adopts Western fashion, speech, and manners, without any real adherence to genuine Western values such as liberty, equality, and so on. There is, in this world, ersatz seduction and courtship. In the West, a man is expected to win the heart of a woman (within certain social and cultural parameters). In Hindu India, a bride is found by matchmakers or relatives. In this, caste is the dominant factor, but there are specific characteristics that apply to women, such as age, appearance, and complexion. This is the world Revati comes from, and he thinks he can win Neela on the basis of his scientific prestige alone. He does not understand that he is sitting on a pile of money, which is what interests Neela and her associates. The world is not what it seems. Revati has no knowledge, no real conception of human greed. He thinks he is dealing with ignoramuses. He is one himself; he is thoroughly deluded.

In the West, ambition is not a dirty word. The honest effort to improve one's given lot in life is socially and culturally accepted. Material rewards are not looked down upon. However, genius is not necessarily ambitious in the conventional, worldly sense. It imposes itself on the world, leaves its imprint on it by virtue of being what it is. Genius's attitude towards work is not one of instrumentality; work is not a means to wealth and power; it is an end in itself; it is the only thing that matters. In "Laboratory", things pan out a bit differently. Ambition in India would be a function of caste or class (the two are often the same). It consists of hanging on to the privilege one is born into and exploiting the opportunities that naturally come its way. No hard work, no ability, no excellence is required. One has to simply know how to work what Indians call 'the system', i.e., the given power hierarchies. Revati is a genius in the Western sense of the word. Yet this genius withers no sooner than Neela forces her way into his life and brings along with her the world of ambition as it exists in this country. Revati does not understand this world. He is not supposed to. His genius is innocent. But the moment Neela enters his life, he ceases to be a genius, is reduced to a quivering mass of sexual desire, and falls prey to a certain idea of masculine behaviour, becoming putty in Neela's hands. Is this because genius is fragile, or is it because it is India? Tagore seems to lean towards the latter explanation. In the West, there are institutions of impeccable integrity, universities, research laboratories, and reliable methods of discovering and nurturing talent that shelter the genius, provide him with a safe haven. Besides, the West has a more open and sensible way of managing sexual desire. Indians who ape the West only manage to be obscene and shameless (see our commercial cinema). As Tagore shows, the members of the Jagani Club in cahoots with whom Neela entraps Revati, know themselves to be mediocrities and, knowing themselves as such, use dishonest means to secure for themselves the good things of life. Revati has no defences against them, neither in the case of Neela, nor in the case of money.

So, for Tagore, the genius in India is caught between a tradition that is obsolete and backward-looking and a world of ambition that is corrupt to the core and is, for pragmatic reasons, respectful of society as it is.

Nalinmadhab encounters a girl scribbling away in a diary alone in the jungle, where he works as a geologist. He is struck by the fact. A girl alone, unaccompanied by any male, is unusual enough. In a jungle, it is even more unusual. Nalinmadhab is an unusual man himself. A former revolutionary, hunted by the police, he escapes to America, where he works for Ford in Detroit, tries, in vain, to convince Mr Ford to invest in India, then studies mining for the next nine years, and returns to India as a geologist of repute.

There is a kinship of spirit between Nalinmadhab

and Achira, the girl in question. Nalinmadhab's curiosity is aroused. He finds nearby a torn envelope addressed to Bhabatosh Majumdar, ICS, and asks his friend in Patna to make enquiries about this person. He learns that a professor of science had engaged his granddaughter to the man and had sent him abroad at his own expense to become a civil servant. The man returns and marries someone else. After which, the professor resigns and disappears with his granddaughter. Nalinmadhab is convinced that the girl in the jungle is the granddaughter in question. This confirms his initial impression that the girl is an exception.

He resorts to a trick in order to get to know the girl and, having done so, rather lamely reveals the trick to her. He learns that she has already learned about him through her grandfather and knows he is 'a big man.' The grandfather shows up and invites Nalinmadhab to his house for a meal. The girl pretends to complain and behaves as if nothing of any importance has happened between her and Nalinmadhab, and keeps up a frivolous, light-hearted banter all the way home. She denies Nalinmadhab any opportunity to strike a serious note. Nalinmadhab becomes a regular at the professor's house—and neglects his work in his pursuit of Achira, to no great effect. When the professor asks him whether he is married or not, he says, 'Not yet.' Achira immediately lets him know that she is intelligent enough to have guessed that Nalinmadhab has used his dedication to his work to resist attempts by his family to get him married. The reader is made to understand that Nalinmadhab does not think too highly of Bengali girls. Achira knows about the streak of vanity in Nalinmadhab's character. She has already previously asked him if he couldn't find a partner in the West, where the world of ambition is not closed for women. Nalinmadhab says that there was indeed someone, but that he had always planned to return to India. Achira saw this as an abandonment of love. According to her, men pursue abstract ideals and are impersonal, whereas, for a woman, the world is nothing without the personal. The more Nalinmadhab tries to do justice to Achira's exceptionality, the more she resists and emphasises her own ordinariness, her modest Bengali identity. Nalinmadhab notices that every time things risk turning serious between them, Achira mercilessly changes the context to one of frivolity and sarcasm. Confronted finally, Achira says that what she feels for Nalinmadhab is not love but devotion, devotion for the manner he dedicated himself to his work in the jungle day in and day out. Nalinmadhab belongs to the world of ambition, while she belongs to the world of nature, and that's the way things should remain, according to Achira. She does not want to be the cause of Nalinmadhab's defeat.

Love, devotion, compassion, sacrifice, and wisdom—these are the qualities that Tagore sees in the ordinary Bengali woman. No mean thing. They have permitted Achira to triumph over destiny. It is for these qualities that she refuses Nalinmadhab's advances, and destroys his male vanity and restores him to his true self.

All these qualities are of no use in the average Bengali family—Tagore rarely speaks of class—where a woman has worth only in terms of lineage, fortune, or, more marginally, beauty. Outside these social markers, she is worthless. She may be intelligent and talented, but that is of no consequence to the family. There is no intelligence required in the kitchen, in household chores, or in procreation. Intelligence is, in fact, a liability because it may clash with the primary attribute of the wife—obedience. In an arranged marriage, the individuality of the spouse is not taken into account; love, generosity, compassion, and courage are all useless. If a woman has neither lineage nor fortune nor looks, she can be driven out of the house, reduced to being a servant in some relative's house if she is lucky, and married off to the first available man, be he crippled, leperous, old, or mad. No matter what his condition might be, he has one great advantage over the woman—his gender. All this is now known, and things have changed somewhat. Someone commits suicide to escape her given lot in life, and Tagore waxes eloquent on Death the liberator; he becomes lyrical. Human life is circumscribed by God, the Absolute. He is the final arbiter; all questions are to be addressed to him and to him alone, and an answer is not inevitable. That Tagore should think of suicide as a solution to conjugal torture in

1914 is itself telling. A woman has nothing to fall back on; she has no resources. The moment she enters a household as somebody's wife, she is reduced to being a nullity. From this, it is possible to appreciate the revolution that has been wrought by the working woman who first emerged among the English-speaking Native elite, a class for which Tagore has nothing but scorn; he bitterly criticises it for its hypocrisy and ludicrousness. The fact remains that it was among the most anglicised sections of our society that the working woman first emerged. That is, those who could combat domestic violence and abuse on their own terms. Revolt, says Tagore, is possible, but then, one is exposed to the elements, both physical and cultural.

"Damnation" is not knowing that human beings are fragile, and they can break if pushed too far. Damnation is expecting toughness everywhere from everyone under all circumstances. Damnation is suppressing the youthful fancies of a child in the name of a puritanical view of truth.

A boy doesn't respond when spoken to, and doesn't do or forgets to do what he is told to do, while his way of going about his business only causes irritation. Why? Tagore does not bother to explain. Maybe because he doesn't measure up to the standards of behaviour expected of him, or because the examples before him have no influence over him, or, finally, because no one bothers to find out what is really going on with him, he is impervious to his immediate environment; that is all that seems to matter. It is his autarky, his lack of acknowledgement of the forces that ensure his survival, that irritates Satyadhan Dutta. It is his very innocence that is disturbing someone who is swindling him out of his inheritance.

Irritation turns into anger, and anger turns into oppression and systemic violence. By the time Satyadhan Dutta realises his mistake, it is already too late. He is already damned.

The world of ambition is a terrible thing because it can take us away from our true selves or arouse the demon in us. And success—what can be easily given can just as easily be taken away. Money corrupts, even while lulling us into complacency. The road to hell is paved with self-serving pretexts.

# Broken Nest

Bhupati didn't really need to work. He had plenty of money, and the country was too hot for rigorous exertion of any kind. However, the stars had willed otherwise, and he was born to make himself useful. This was probably why he had to bring out an English-language paper of his own. Once the paper came into being, he no longer complained of long days without end.

Right from childhood he had a knack for writing and discoursing in English. He would write letters to English newspapers and would not leave a meeting without making a comment or two, even when he had nothing to say.

Being a wealthy man, he was much sought after by the various patriotic factions who sang paeans of praise to his English-language skills such that he came to esteem himself highly in the matter.

Eventually, his brother-in-law, Umapati, who had come a cropper in his chosen field of law, said to him,

"Bhupati, why don't you bring out an English-language newspaper of your own? Given your writing skills... etc..."

Bhupati was excited. There was no merit in having letters published on someone else's paper; it was better to let his pen run free on a paper of his own. With his brother-in-law as an associate, Bhupati, at a relatively young age, came to occupy the chair of an editor.

Youth drinks deep and long at the cups of editorship and politics. Also, there were plenty of people in Bhupati's entourage to egg him on, on his way.

While he immersed himself in the running of his paper, his child bride, Charulata, stepped, in graded steps, into youth. The editor never really became aware of this significant development, his primary concern at the time being the expansionist temper of the Government of India's border policy, an expansionism that, in his opinion, threatened to breach the barriers of self-control.

The household being affluent, Charulata had no chores to attend to. She lacked for nothing, and like a flower without fruit, her job was to blossom unnecessarily through the long days and nights of her existence without a purpose.

Given these circumstances, and the right opportunity coming along, a wife can play fast and loose with her husband; the border policy of their conjugal intercourse can cross the line between the opportune and the inopportune, between the lawful and the unlawful.

Charulata had no such opportunity. On the other hand, it was difficult for her to penetrate the thick armour of newsprint and lay direct claim on her husband.

A relative of Bhupati drew attention to his young wife and berated him for neglecting her. Bhupati suddenly took cognisance of the fact and said, "Charu needs a companion, the poor thing has nothing to do."

He said to Umapati, "Bring your wife over. Without female company, Charu must feel solitary."

Having understood that the lack of female company was what was keeping Charu dejected, Bhupati satisfied himself by getting his brother-in-law's wife, Mandakini, over to his house.

When husband and wife awaken to the first stirrings of love, and manifest themselves, each to the other, in all their unprecedented splendour, that dawn of burnished love had caught Bhupati and Charu unawares. And instead of giving in to that novelty, they grew accustomed to each other in their old ways.

Charulata being a voracious reader did not find her days so burdensome. On her own and through various ploys, she kept her reading going. One of Bhupati's cousins, Amal, was a third-year college student. Charu got hold of him and got some reading done in the bargain, in return for which she had to oblige Amal with many favours. She had to finance his eating out and indulge his tastes in English literature. At times, Amal would call his friends over for a meal. The responsibility for organising this would fall on Charulata, who would acquit herself of this obligation in the spirit of a homage paid to her mentor. Bhupati had no demands to make on Charulata, but his cousin, Amal, would exact a heavy price for his tutorship. Oftentimes, Charu would feign anger and rebellion against his authority, but to put up with the particular chore of a particular person and his fond tumult had become somewhat obligatory for her.

Amal said, "*Bouthan*, a royal son-in-law in our college wears shoes made of carpet material hand-woven by the women of the inner quarter and I can't stand it—I need a pair of carpet-grade shoes, or I won't be able to maintain my status among my peers."

To which Charu said, "Yes, of course, now I am to slave away stitching shoes for you. Take some money and buy a pair from the market."

Amal replied, "That won't do."

Charu didn't know the art of stitching shoes, nor was she willing to admit her inability in front of Amal. But nobody asked her for anything, excepting Amal—and she couldn't possibly turn down a request from the sole supplicant to her door. So, she began teaching herself the art of stitching carpet-grade shoes when Amal was away at college. One day, when Amal himself had completely forgotten about his prayer for shoes, Charu invited him to come see her in the evening.

It was summer, and a meal had been laid out for Amal on the terrace. A brass lid had been placed on his plate to keep it from dust. Amal washed his face and hands, changed into a fresh set of clothes, and made his appearance on the terrace.

Amal sat down and took off the lid and saw a pair of brand-new woollen shoes neatly placed on the plate. Charulata erupted in laughter.

Shoes done, Amal's demands grew more and more importunate. He wanted a jacket, a silk handkerchief with a flower-patterned border sewn on, and an embroidered cloth to ward off oil stains on the armchair in the living room.

Each time, Charulata would begin by protesting noisily; and each time, she would end up satisfying Amal's expensive tastes with a lot of care and affection. Often, Amal would ask, "*Bouthan*, how is it coming along?"

"Nothing done yet," Charulata would lie, or would say, "I had completely forgotten."

But Amal was not one to let go easily. He would give daily reminders and grow impatient. After whetting the tenacious Amal's impetuous appetite by feigning indifference and unwillingness, she would, with amusement and hilarity, oversee the delivery of a cherished object.

Wealth meant that Charu did not have to do anything for anybody; only Amal insisted on making her work. All these trifles kept her heart fulfilled and satisfied.

A little plot of land lay within the Bhupati household's inner quarter. It would be an exaggeration to call it a garden, its principal vegetation being an English hog-plum tree.

A committee formed of Charu and Amal pondered over the development of this plot of land. Both got together and for a few days drew pictures, laid out plans, and, with great enthusiasm, imagined an elaborate garden on the spot.

Amal said, "*Bouthan*, you must water these plants yourself as princesses of yore did."

Charu responded, "And we'll build an enclosure in the western corner to keep some deer calves."

Amal added, "We must also have a humble little lake, for the ducks to swim in."

Charu was enthusiastic about the proposal and said, "And we'll have blue lotuses, I've always so wanted blue lotuses."

Amal said, "We'll erect a small bridge on the lake and keep a small dinghy on the shore."

Charu said, "The shore will have a landing, all in marble, of course."

Amal took up a pencil and paper, drew rules on it, and, compass in hand, drew up a map of the lake.

As the days went by, they made changes and corrections to their imaginary plans and drew another twenty-five maps.

Once the map had been decided upon, they started drawing up an estimate of the expenses involved. At first, they resolved that the garden would be set up out of Charu's monthly allowance. Bhupati wouldn't so much as glance at what was happening in his own house; he was to be given a surprise and invited there once the garden was complete; he would think that an Aladdin's lamp had been used, and an entire garden had been imported from Japan.

However, no matter how low the estimate, Charu's means would still fall short. Amal began modifying the map again. He said, "Okay *bouthan*, let's leave the lake out of it."

Charu said, "No, no! Leaving out the lake will not do at all, it will have my blue lotuses."

Amal said, "Let's do without a tiled roof for your deer enclosure. An ordinary new roof will do."

Charu said angrily, "In that case, let's just drop the idea—let it be."

It had been proposed that clover seeds would be procured from Marishol, sandalwood from the Karnatic, and cinnamon from the Sinhala country. But Amal instead proposed procuring ordinary local and English plants from Manicktala, and Charu's face grew sombre and tense. She said, "Well, let's not have a garden."

This way of reducing the estimate was not customary. It was not possible for Charu to let her imagination be stunted by an estimate, and no matter what Amal thought, in his heart of hearts, he agreed, outwardly, with her.

Amal said, "In that case, *bouthan*, you will have to bring up the matter with my cousin. He will surely consent to giving us the money.

Charu replied, "That would spoil all the fun. We will lay the garden on our own, the two of us. He can formally request the British for a Garden of Eden—what will happen to our plan?"

Seated under the English hog-plum tree, Charu and Amal gave free rein to their unrealistic fantasies. Charu's sister-in-law, Manda, called out from the first floor, "What are you two up to in the garden at this hour?"

Charu said, "Looking for ripe hog-plums."

Greedy Manda said, "Get me some too if you find any."

Charu laughed, Amal laughed. The entire happiness and pride derived from their resolution lay in their complicit togetherness. No matter what other qualities Manda might have, imagination was not one of them; how could she savour the pleasure of such projects? She was completely excluded from all committees formed by the two.

The estimate for this impossible garden would not reduce, nor would the imagination beat a retreat. Therefore, the hog-plum committee continued thus for a few days. Amal marked out the sites for the lake, the deer enclosure, the stone embankment.

Amal was marking out the spots all around the

hog-plum tree, when Charu, sitting in the shade said, "Amal, it would be great if you could write."

"Why would it be great?" asked Amal.

Charu said, "I would have you write a story describing our garden. That lake, that deer enclosure, that hog-plum tree—all that would be there. No one but us would understand; that would be so much fun. Amal, why don't you try your hand at writing and see? I am sure you can do it."

"If I write, what will you give me?" said Amal.

"What do you want?" asked Charu.

"I will draw," said Amal, "a creeper on my mosquito net, and you will have to sew it all up in silk."

Charu said, "Isn't that taking it a bit too far? A design on a mosquito net! What an idea!"

Amal waxed eloquent on making an ugly prison out of a mosquito net. "It's proof that ninety-five per cent of humanity has no sense of beauty, and is hardly bothered by ugliness."

Charu immediately accepted the truth of what Amal said in her heart, and she was happy at the thought that, 'Our secret committee of two does not fall under that ninety-five per cent.'

Charu said, "All right, I'll do the mosquito net; you write."

Amal said, mysteriously, "You think I cannot write?"

Charu, anxious, said, "That means you have written

something! Show it to me!"

"Not today, *bouthan*," responded Amal.

"No!" demanded Charu, "you have to show it today itself—go fetch your piece immediately."

It was his overeagerness to show Charu his writing that had held Amal back thus far. There was also the fear that Charu wouldn't understand or wouldn't like it; he couldn't get rid of his inhibition.

Today, Amal fetched his notebook and, a little red in the face, a little cough in the throat, began reading. Charu leaned against the tree, spread her legs out on the grass, and listened.

The subject of the essay was "My notebook". Amal had written, "O my pristine notebook, my imagination is yet to touch you. You are like the innocent and mysterious blank forehead of a child before Destiny enters the labour room. Where is the day when I will inscribe the conclusion on the last line of the first page? Your innocent childish letters cannot even imagine the ever ink-smeared end of the tale, etc." He had written extensively on the subject.

Charu, sitting in the shade of the tree, was listening in rapt attention. At the end of the reading and after a brief pause, she said, "Can't you write something else?"

That day, under the tree, Amal first tasted the heady wine of literature. The one who was serving the wine was new, and so was the tongue that was tasting it, and mysterious was its coming in the lengthening shadows of the afternoon light.

Charu said, "Amal, you'll have to pluck a few hog-plums. Otherwise, what will I tell Manda?"

They saw no point in talking to dull Manda about the reading and their discussions, so they had to pluck a few hog-plums.

## II

Amal and Charu did not even notice when their resolution about the garden got lost in the limitless expanse of their imagination.

Now, their principal topic of discussion and consultation was Amal's writing. Amal came and said, "*Bouthan*, a marvelous idea has just struck me."

Charu was excited. She replied, "Let's go to the south verandah. Manda will turn up here at any moment with her betel leaves."

Charu took her seat on a cane armchair on the Kashmiri verandah, while Amal sat down on the raised portion of the railing and spread his legs.

Very often, there was no specific topic for Amal to write on; there was no clarity. What he meant to say in his confusion was impossible for anyone to say. Amal himself would repeat again and again, "*Bouthan*, I am unable to explain myself properly."

Charu would respond, "No, I have understood a fair deal; write this down without delay."

Understanding a little, not understanding a little, imagining a lot, and relying a lot on Amal's way of expressing his emotions, she would, in her excitement, erect something in her heart, and in it she would find happiness and grow impatiently eager.

Charu would ask in the evening, "How is it coming along?"

Amal would say, "Is it possible to write in the middle of all this?"

The next morning, Charu would ask, importunately, "Haven't you written anything?"

Amal would say, "Patience, let me think some more."

Charu would be cross at this: "There you go again!"

In the evening, after having let her seethe in frustration all day, when she was on the point of ceasing all communication, Amal would, on the pretext of taking out his handkerchief, show her a bit of paper.

This would immediately break the spell of Charu's silence, and she would exclaim, "There is your writing! You cheat! Show me!"

Amal would say, "It's not yet finished. I'll read it to you in a while."

Charu would say, "No, read it to me now!"

Amal would in fact be eager to read his writing to her straightaway. But he liked to keep Charu on tenterhooks about his writing. Then, Amal would sit down and arrange his papers for a while, making a few corrections here and there with a pencil, and Charu, delighted and curious, would lean across like a moisture-laden cloud and inspect the papers.

Amal would have to read straight away the few paragraphs he had written, and the unwritten remainder would be churned out between discussion and imagination.

Thus far, they got by by picking at pies in the sky, harvesting the flowers of poesy every now and then, oblivious to everything else.

Returning from college one afternoon, Amal's pocket appeared to have weighed down a bit more than usual. When Amal entered the house, Charu noticed through the bay window of the inner quarter the fullness of his pocket.

On other days, Amal would not tarry in coming inside the house after returning from college. Today, with the load in his pocket, he went into the living room where he lingered for a while.

Charu clapped from the outer limits of the inner quarters to draw Amal's attention, but no one responded. Angry, Charu picked up a book by Manmatha Dutta and tried reading in her verandah.

Manmatha Dutta was a new name in the literary world. His writing was similar to that of Amal, which was why Amal never praised him. Sometimes he would read from his works, pronouncing the words grotesquely in order to ridicule the author. Charu would snatch the book away from Amal and throw it away disdainfully.

Today, as she heard Amal's footsteps, she held the same Manmatha Dutta's book, *Sweet Melodies*, close to her eyes, as if she was totally absorbed in its reading.

Amal entered the verandah; Charu hardly took notice. Amal asked, "So, *bouthan*, what's that you're reading?"

Seeing Charu silent, he came around behind her chair and saw what she was reading and began intoning, in a voice dripping with sarcasm, "I am a shoot, a small shoot, brother Ashoka, while you are dressed in the royal incarnadine clothes; I am only a shoot. I have neither flowers, nor shade. I cannot lift my head up to the sky. The cuckoo does not seek shelter in me in spring, does not rouse the world with its call perched on my branches. Nevertheless, Brother Ashoka, do not look down upon me from the height of your flower-laden branches. I am lain at your feet as a trifling shoot, yet do not disdain me."

Amal read this from the book and then, inventing a parody, went on, "I am a cluster of bananas; I am a cluster of unripe bananas, Brother Pumpkin, to you who frolic on the roof of the kitchen, I am only a bunch of raw bananas."

Charu, impelled by curiosity, could not contain herself anymore and burst out laughing. Throwing away the book, she said, "Jealous man, you don't appreciate anything but your own writing."

Amal said, "And you are so generous; you want to swallow the shoot that you have."

Charu said, “Okay, mister. Enough with your mirth and merriment. Now show me what you’ve got in your pocket.”

Amal said, “Guess…”

After having kept Charu guessing for a while, he finally took out a copy of the well-known monthly magazine, *Shororuho*.

Charu saw that Amal’s article on his notebook had appeared in its pages.

She saw and remained silent. Amal had thought that his *bouthan* would be very happy. But seeing no signs of happiness on her face, he added, “It’s not just anyone who gets published in *Shororuho*.”

Amal was exaggerating. The editor would grab any tolerable piece of writing of any kind. But Amal would have Charu understand that the editor was a very fussy man who would select one out of a hundred submissions.

Upon learning this, Charu made an effort to be happy, but failed. She made an effort to understand what had hurt her so much. She could find no reasonable explanation for this.

Amal’s article was the joint property of Charu and Amal. Amal was the writer, and Charu the reader. The fun was in the secrecy of it all. That essay would now be read by all and sundry and praised by not a few; there was nothing to be hurt about it. Charu couldn’t quite understand.

A writer’s aspirations cannot long be met by just one reader. Amal’s writings began appearing in print quite often. They had started to be appreciated, too.

At times, fans would write in. Amal would show these letters to his *bouthan*. Charu felt both happy about it and aggrieved. Amal was not dependent solely on her encouragement and excitement as far as his writing went. At times, Amal would also get letters of admiration from anonymous women. Charu would tease him about them, but she derived no satisfaction out of it. What had been the closed doors of their exclusive committee had suddenly burst open, letting in readers from all corners of Bengal, who now stood between them.

One day, Bhupati said in a leisurely way, “Really, Charu, I just didn’t know our Amal was such a good writer.”

Bhupati’s praise delighted Charu. Amal had been given shelter under Bhupati’s wings; Charu was proud that Amal was different from Bhupati’s other dependents. Her sentiments seemed to declare, “You have all finally began to understand why I feel such affection for Amal. I have known of Amal’s talent for long; I knew that he was not to be neglected.

Charu asked, “Have you read anything by him?”

Bhupati said, “Yes, I mean no, I haven’t found the time to. But it was our Nishikanta, who had read him and was praising him a lot. Nishikanta understands Bengali literature.”

Charu had only wanted that Amal should occupy a place of esteem in Bhupati’s mind.

## III

Umapati was giving Bhupati to understand that the latter should think about offering a range of things along with his newspaper, whereas Bhupati couldn't understand how such things could mitigate his losses.

Charu had seen Umapati entering the living room, and she left immediately. Having loitered a while outside she came back into the room and saw that the two were arguing over accounts.

Charu asked, "You are not done yet? How can you spend day and night with your blessed newspaper, I don't understand."

Bhupati set his account books to one side and laughed. He said to himself, 'It is true, I find no time to pay any attention to Charu, it's not fair. The poor thing has nothing with which to occupy herself.'

Bhupati said affectionately, "You are not reading anything today? Has your tutor run away or something? In your school, everything is upside down—the student is ready with her books, while the teacher is on the run. These days I don't see Amal giving you lessons as before."

Charu replied, "Should Amal waste time teaching me? You seem to think that Amal is an ordinary private tutor."

Bhupati caught Charu by her waist and drew her close. "Is this some ordinary private tutorship? If only I could tutor a *bouthan* like you."

Charu said, "But no! Don't say a word more! As if it isn't enough to be married to you."

Bhupati, slightly offended, said, "Okay, from tomorrow I will certainly give you lessons. Bring your books; let's see what you have been reading."

Charu said, "Big deal! You don't have to give me lessons. For now, keep looking at the account books of your newspaper. Will you be able to pay attention to anything else for the time being?"

Bhupati said, "Undoubtedly, I can. You can turn my mind in any direction you want."

Charu said, "OK, just see how wonderful this piece by Amal is. The editor says that after reading this, Naragopal *babu* had exclaimed Amal is to be Bengal's Ruskin."

A little uneasy, Bhupati took the paper in his hands. He opened it, and saw Amal's essay was titled 'The Moon in June.' For the last two months, Bhupati had been engrossed in calculations relating to the Government of India's budget, and those sums were crawling about in the crevices of his brain like centipedes—at such a time he was least prepared to read a piece of writing in Bengali called 'The Moon in June'. The essay was not of a humble length either.

The essay began somewhat like this—'Why does the moon hide thus among the clouds of June, as if it has stolen something from the heavens and can't find a place to hide its stolen property? When in the month of March, the sky is bereft of even a fistful of clouds, then before the eyes of the world it had shamelessly shown itself—and today its expansive humour like the dream of a child, like the memory of a dear one, like the tresses of Sachi akin to a string of pearls…'

Bhupati scratched his head and said, "Well written, indeed. But why me? Do I understand poetry?"

Discomfited, Charu snatched the paper from Bhupati's hands and said, "What *do* you understand?"

Bhupati said, "I am a man of the world; I understand men."

Charu said, "Oh! So, literature doesn't talk about men, does it?"

Bhupati said, "Not properly. Because when a man is physically present before you, why would anyone need to find him in contrivance?"

Touching Charu's chin gently, Bhupati added, "Just like I understand you without having read the *The Slaying of Meghnad*, or '*Chandi Jewel among Poets*'.

Bhupati took pride in not understanding poetry. However, without having thoroughly read Amal's essay, he nevertheless had respect for him in his heart. Bhupati thought, having nothing to say, but effortlessly stringing word after invented word? I wouldn't be able to do it, even if I died chopping my brain into fine pieces. Who knew Amal had such capability?

Bhupati had no illusions about being a man of refined

taste, but he was not ungenerous towards literature. He would pay the publication expenses when poverty-stricken writers urged him to. He would only say, "Don't dedicate the work to me." He would buy books, Bengali weeklies, of all types, famous and infamous, readable or unreadable. He would say, "As it is, I don't read anything; but if I don't buy, it is a sin without repentance." Because he didn't read, he was non-judgemental about bad books, though his Bengali library was well-stocked.

Amal would help Bhupati out with his English galley proofs; he entered the room with a sheaf of papers with the intention of showing some copy with illegible handwriting.

Bhupati laughed and said, "Amal, write as much as you want about 'The Moon in June' or 'Palm Wine in January', I don't object. I don't want to interfere with other people's freedoms; why interfere with mine? She insists on my reading it, I mean your oppressive *bouthan*."

Amal laughed and said, "That's right *bouthan*, if I had known you would oppress my cousin with my writing, I wouldn't have written anything at all."

Amal was angry that Charu had forced his intensely personal writing on a man impervious to the charms of literature as Bhupati, and Charu, immediately understanding Amal's vexation, felt hurt. In an attempt to change the subject, she said to Bhupati, "Get your brother married off to somebody, then you won't have to put up with his writing."

Bhupati said, "Young people nowadays are not fooled so easily. They might write poetry, but they are wordly wise when it comes to practical matters. Could you get your brother-in-law's consent to this?"

After Charu had left, Bhupati said to Amal, "Running a newspaper is a hell of a business, and Charu is left to her own devices. She has nothing to do. She takes a peek at my study and goes away. What can I do? You, Amal, if you could keep her busy with some reading, it would be just fine. If you could translate some English verse for her occasionally, she might develop an ear for it, and that would be a good thing. Charu has a taste for good writing."

Amal said, "*That* she does. If *bouthan* does a little bit more of reading, I believe she herself can become a very good writer."

Bhupati laughed and said, "I am not going that far, but Charu understands good writing in Bengali, a great deal more than me."

Amal said, "She has a good imagination, very rare among women."

Bhupati said, "Rare among men too, proof yours truly. OK, if you can nurture your *bouthan*'s talent then you can expect to be rewarded by me."

Amal said, "What will you give me?"

Bhupati said, "I will find someone to rival your *bouthan*."

Amal said, "And I'll have to keep after her. Will I be

nurturing talent all my life?"

The brothers were both men of their times, and were candid with each other.

## IV

Having established himself in the community of readers, Amal could hold his head high. Before, he was like a schoolboy; and now he carried himself as one of the notables of his society. Often, he would be called upon to read his essays before a gathering—editors and their messengers would crowd his room, and they would invite him out for a meal, and ask him to join or preside over a meeting, and the servants and relatives of Bhupati's household held him in higher esteem than many others.

Mandakini thus far had not treated him as a somebody. She would cut her betel and consider Amal and Charu's mirth-filled discussions as a sign of childishness, and she would busy herself with household chores. She considered her station to be above theirs and more necessary in the worldly scheme of things.

Amal was a great consumer of *paan*. The making of *paan* was Manda's responsibility, and she would frown on wasteful habits regarding this. Amal and Charu found it amusing to plot the depletion of Manda's stock of *paan*. Manda, on the other hand, looked askance at the delight that these two refined thieves took in stealing.

To tell the truth, one of the sheltered did not look favourably at the other. Manda was indeed offended by the extra housework she had to do for Amal. Charu was on Amal's side, and Manda could not utter a word, but she would continuously try to ignore Amal. Given the opportunity, she would not hesitate to poke fun at Amal before the servants, who would feel encouraged to do the same themselves.

But when Amal's fortunes began to rise, Manda was a little taken aback. The Amal she knew no longer existed. Now his awkward humility had entirely disappeared. It was now he who had the right to ignore everybody else. The one who is established in the world is able to promote himself without doubt or bashfulness; someone who has acquired a definite right over something, that powerful man can attract the gaze of women. When Manda saw that Amal was being respected by all, she too lifted her gaze up at Amal's exalted visage. Amal's youthful face, illuminated by the pride of a novel exploit, filled Manda's eyes with temptation. It was as if she saw Amal in a new light.

Now, he no longer needed to steal *paan*. Amal's fame dealt a fresh blow to Charu; the amusing conspiracy that had held them together was undone; *paan* would be served to Amal in unlimited quantities without his having to ask for it.

Besides, the satisfaction the two of them would derive by ganging up together and keeping Mandakini out of their joint mischief, even that satisfaction was now gone. It was difficult to keep Manda away. Manda did not like the idea that Amal considered Charu to be his friend and confidante. She was out to be compensated with interest for her previous neglect. Thus, the moment Amal and Charu found themselves together, Manda would find a way to interpose herself between them, casting a shadow, causing an eclipse. It became difficult for Charu to find even a moment in which to mock this transformation of Manda.

Needless to say, Manda's abrupt appearance on the scene bothered Amal much less than it did Charu. Amal was pleased, that the face, hitherto turned away, was turning towards him.

But when Charu, spying Manda from afar, would exclaim in mock gentleness, "There she comes," Amal would say, "So she does! What a nuisance." Expressing intolerance for the company of all the others in the world was a custom with them. Amal would say something to get it over with. Finally, when Mandakini approached, Amal would welcome her in a forced manner by saying, "So Manda *bouthan*, has your *paan* case been robbed again?"

Manda would say, "When you only have to ask for it, why steal?"

Amal would say, "It's more satisfying to steal than to ask for it."

Manda would retort, "What were you two reading? Why don't you go on? Don't stop. I like hearing."

Previous to this, no one had noticed any eagerness on the part of Manda for being read to. Charu absolutely did not want Amal to read anything for someone Charu considered unsophisticated, but Amal wanted Manda to listen to what he had written.

Charu would say, "Amal, has written a critique of *Kamalakanta's Office*, will that—"

Manda would say, "Maybe I am ignorant, but won't I understand anything if I listen a bit?"

Then Amal remembered another event on another occasion. Charu and Manda were playing rummy, when he entered with his notebook in hand, impatient to read it out to Charu; he was apprehensive that the game would not stop for him. Finally, he had to say, "Play on *bouthan;* I'll go and read it to Akhil *babu*."

Charu had immediately grabbed Amal by his shawl and said, "No, sit down, where are you off to?" And then she lost the game in a hurry and brought it to an end.

Manda said, "I suppose you're going to start reading. Time for me to go."

Charu said, out of courtesy, "Why don't you listen too?"

Manda said, "No, I won't understand your airy-fairy stories, they make me sleepy." And then she went off, offended by the abrupt ending of their sport by the two of them.

That same Manda was today eager to listen to a critique of *Kamalakanta's Office*. Amal said, "Fine, Manda *bouthan*, if you want to listen, the pleasure is all mine." He flipped the page back and started reading from the beginning. In the beginning of his piece, he had used a lot of rhetorical flourishes, and he did not want to deprive Manda of the pleasure of listening to them.

Charu quickly said, "*Thakurpo*, you had said you would get me some back issues from the Jahnavi library."

Amal said, "Not today."

Charu said, "Today, today, oh all right! You've forgotten, haven't you?"

Amal replied, "Why should I forget? You said—"

Charu said, "Okay, okay, don't. You read, the two of you. I have to go tell Paresh to go to the library." And then she got up to leave.

Amal saw trouble brewing. Manda understood the matter, and her heart was poisoned against Charu. After Charu's departure, while Amal was deliberating within himself whether to get up or not, Manda laughed and said, "Go assuage her feelings; Charu is angry. You'll get into trouble if you now read to me alone."

After this, it became very difficult for Amal to leave. Amal said, somewhat cross with Charu, "Where is the difficulty?" And he began reading elaborately from what he had written.

Manda covered his papers with her hands and said, "It's of no use. Don't read."

And as if wiping away a tear, she went away.

## V

Charu had gone out on a social visit. Manda was in her room plaiting her hair. Amal entered the room and said, "*Bouthan.*" Manda knew for sure that Amal was not unaware that Charu had an invitation to keep. She smiled and said, "Amal *babu*! Who were you looking for, and whom have you found?" Amal said, "The paddy hay on the right is as good as the paddy hay on the left; the idiot will make do with either." And he sat down.

Amal said, "Manda *bouthan*, tell me a story about your native place. I want to hear."

In order to collect material for his writing, Amal would listen, with rapt attention, to people recounting their experiences. This was why he no longer dismissed Manda as before. Manda's psychology and Manda's history, all excited his curiosity. The place she was born in, the description of her village, how she had spent her childhood, when had she gotten married, etc., were all topics on which he would question her minutely. No one had ever shown such interest in Manda's petty existence before. Manda, overcome with happiness, would chat away furiously about herself. Sometimes, she would pause to ask, "Am I making sense?"

Amal would say, encouraging her, "Sounds fine to me; do go on." Manda's father had a one-eyed rent collector who occasionally quarrelled with his second wife, and would go on a fast out of wounded pride. But wracked by hunger, he would secretly end up at Manda's father's house for a meal. Manda was telling Amal how his wife caught him red-handed one day, when Charu suddenly entered the room.

The thread of the story was lost. That she had dispersed an animated gathering was not lost on Charu.

Amal asked, "Why did you come back so early, *bouthan*?"

Charu said, "That's what I see; I have come back a bit too early." And she made to leave.

Amal said, "You did well; it's a relief for me. I was wondering when you'll be back. I had got Manmatha Dutta's new book, *The Evening Bird*, to read to you."

Charu said, "Not now. I've things to attend to."

Amal said, "Your obedient servant awaits your orders."

Charu knew that Amal would buy a book to read to her that day. Charu would praise Manmatha to the skies, to excite Amal's jealousy, and Amal would distort his reading to pour scorn on it. It was in anticipation of this that, brushing aside the importunate pleas of her hosts, she had made haste to come back on the pretext of being indisposed. Now she told herself, I was having a good time there; I might as well have stayed back. So unfair on my part.

Manda was no less brazen. She was sitting alone with Amal in a room and laughing away merrily. What will people say? But Charu could not berate Manda on this score, Manda could say as much herself about Charu. But what was sauce for the goose, was not sauce for the gander. She encouraged Amal in his composition and discussed literature with him, whereas with Manda, the question did not arise. Manda was surely laying an elaborate trap for the gullible young man. It was her duty alone to rescue poor Amal from such a perilous eventuality. How to make Amal understand the intentions of this temptress? Suppose, instead of renouncing such a temptation Amal should fall prey to it? Then?

Poor Umapati. He was working himself to death for her husband's newspaper, and here was his wife Manda sitting in a corner making schemes to distract Amal. Umapati was without a care in this regard. He trusted Manda enormously. Having seen all this with her own eyes, how could Charu restrain herself? Very unfair.

But Amal was all right before. Ever since he had made a name for himself through his writing, everything had gone awry. Charu was the source of all his writing. It was an evil hour when she had encouraged Amal to write. Could she hold the same sway over Amal any longer? Now, Amal had tasted the admiration of others, he could easily forego the admiration of one individual.

Charu saw clearly, that having slipped out of her hands and having been tangled up in other hands, Amal was in great danger. Amal no longer considered Charu to be his equal. He had overtaken Charu. Now, he was the writer, and Charu the reader. Something had to be done.

O foolish Amal, the temptress Manda, and poor Umapati!

## VI

The day was cloudy with the new clouds of June. Since it was dark inside the room, Charu had positioned herself near an open window, and was absorbed all by herself in writing something. She did not notice Amal as he silently came and stood behind her. In the cool, fresh light of a cloudy day, she kept on writing and Amal kept on reading. Next to her lay open a few of Amal's published work, for Charu, they alone merited emulation.

"So why do you say you cannot write?"

Upon hearing Amal's voice all of a sudden, Charu started, she quickly hid her notebook and said, "This is not fair."

Amal said "What is not fair?"

Charu said, "Why were you spying on me just now?"

Amal said, "Because I don't get to see this openly."

Charu made as if to tear up and throw away her notebook. Amal preempted her quickly and snatched it out of her hands. Charu said, "If you read it, I won't speak to you ever again."

Amal said, "If you order me not to read it, I won't

speak to you ever again."

Charu said, "Swear, *thakurpo*, that you won't read."

In the end, Charu had to admit defeat. Why? Because she was desperate to show Amal her writing, although she had no idea that she would feel so ashamed about it in front of Amal. When, after several entreaties, Amal started reading, Charu went numb all over with shame. She said, "I'll go fetch some *paan*." And she went to the next room ostensibly to prepare some *paan*.

Amal took the piece Charu had written, and went and told her, "It's wonderful!"

Charu forgot to add the catechu and said, "Go away! You don't have to make fun of me. Give my notebook back."

Amal said, "You won't get it back right now. I'll first copy out the piece, and then send it to the magazine."

Charu said, "No, you won't!"

Charu raised up a storm. Amal was equally adamant. When he insisted again and again, "It's worth publishing," Charu seemed on the point of despair and said, "I can't get the better of you. Once you've latched on to something you never let go." Amal said, "I'll have to show it to cousin Bhupati."

Upon hearing this, Charu stopped preparing the *paan* and got up quickly; trying to snatch her notebook, she said, "No! You shan't read it aloud to him. If you tell him about this, then I promise I won't write a single word ever again."

Amal said, "*Bouthan*, you are making a serious mistake.

Never mind what he might say or not, he will be mighty pleased about this."

Charu said, "Maybe. But I don't care two hoots for his pleasure."

Charu had resolved that she would write—she would surprise Amal; she would not stop short of proving that an enormous gulf separated her from Manda. These last few days she had written and torn up a lot of stuff. Whatever she wrote it ended up sounding like Amal; when she compared, she found that certain passages read as if they had been lifted verbatim from Amal's writing. Those were the good ones, the rest was trash. If Amal saw them, he would certainly laugh; having imagined this to herself she tore up those writings into little pieces and threw them into the pond, for fear that something might find its way into Amal's hands.

At first, she had written, 'The Clouds of August'. She had thought, 'Here is something new and tear soaked.' Then, she would be jolted out of her reverie and would see it was a carbon copy of Amal's 'The Moon in June.'. Amal had written, 'Brother Moon, why are you roaming around hidden like a thief behind clouds? Charu had written, 'Friend Kadambini, from where have you come all of a sudden, hiding the moon under the blue sky and fleeing like a fugitive, etc.'

Unable to find a way out of this space circumscribed by Amal's writings, Charu finally changed the topic of the composition. Moon clouds, the flowers of the *shefali* tree, old wives' tales—leaving all this behind, she wrote a piece called, 'Under the Aegis of Kali.' There was, in their village, fronting the shade-obscured pond, a Kali temple; that temple was the focus of all the imagined fears and eager joys of her childhood, and the strange memories attached to that place, the stories that had circulated since time immemorial about the presence and the greatness of the deity—she wrote a piece putting all these elements together. In the beginning, there was the shadow cast by Amal's splendid display of poetry, but as one progressed, one was overwhelmed by the simple, straight atmosphere, poise, and language of rural Bengal.

It was this composition that Amal had snatched and read. It seemed to him that the beginning was quite interesting, but the poetry had faltered in the end. Nevertheless, as a first effort, it was most laudable.

Charu said, "*Thakurpo*, how about bringing out a monthly magazine of our own?"

To which Amal replied, "Unless you have many wheels of silver, on what will it travel?"

Charu said, "We won't need any money. Because we won't print it. It will be written out by hand. It will only carry pieces by you and me, and circulation will be restricted to two copies. One for you, the other for me."

A few days previously, Amal would have been overjoyed at the prospect, but he had lost the taste for secrecy. Now he took no pleasure in writing except when addressing a readership. Nevertheless, he said more in homage to the past, "That would be great fun."

Charu said, "Promise that you will not publish anything except in our little magazine."

Amal said, "The editors will kill me."

Charu said, "As if I don't have weapons in my possession."

So that was that. The two editors, writers, and readers made up a committee. Amal said, "Let the magazine be called *Charupath*—a beautiful reading experience." Charu said, "No, we'll call it *Amala*."

This new enterprise had the effect of effacing Charu's distress and annoyance over the last few days. Manda could not possibly enter the space occupied by their monthly magazine, nor could people from outside.

## VII

One day Bhupati came and said, "Charu, you have become a writer, who could have imagined?"

Charu was startled, she turned red and said, "Who, me? Writer? Who said so? Never."

Bhupati said, "Caught red-handed! I have the proof in my hands." And Bhupati brought out an issue of *Shororuh*. Charu saw that all the writing that had been destined for their handwritten monthly magazine, their secret project, had appeared under their name in *Shororuh*.

Somebody had released the much-cherished parakeet from its cage into the wide-open world, or so it seemed to her. She forgot about her shame on being discovered by Bhupati, and all her ire was focused instead on the treacherous Amal, who had betrayed her thus.

"And just look at this." Bhupati opened the pages of *Vishwabandhu.* In it had appeared an essay called 'Trends in modern Bengali writing.'

Charu shoved the paper aside with her hands and said, "What am I to make of all this?" In her wounded pride, she could not bring herself to focus on anything else. Bhupati entreated her, "Why don't you read it once?"

Compelled thus, Charu ran her eyes over the article in question. In it, the critic had taken to task in harsh terms, the pompous prose of certain litterateurs. Amal and Manmatha Dutta had been singled out in withering sarcasm, and their writing had been contrasted with the artless simplicity, effortless attraction, and skilful imagery of a new voice that had emerged, that of Charubala, upon whom had been heaped fulsome praise. Furthermore, the critic had written that Amal and company would do well to emulate this style of writing, or else they would certainly and completely fail.

Bhupati laughed and said, "This is what is known as beating them at their own game."

Even as Charu savoured this praise of her writing, she could not help feeling pained at the same time. Her heart seemed to take no delight in this. No sooner would she bring the nectar of praise to her lips than she would push it away.

She understood that by getting her writing published, Amal had resolved to give her a surprise. Moreover, after the publication, he had probably wanted it to be praised so he could placate and encourage her by showing both. So why hadn't he rushed to show her the laudatory article as soon as it appeared? Surely, Amal had been hurt by the criticism and, not wanting to show it to Charu, had secreted the papers away. The little literary nest that Charu had been working on in utmost secrecy for her own comfort was in danger of being irreparably damaged by a hailstorm of praise. Charu didn't like this at all.

After Bhupati had left, Charu sat silently in her bedroom. In front of her lay the open pages of *Shororuh* and *Vishwabandhu*. Notebook in hand, Amal entered the room quietly from behind in order to surprise Charu. Drawing closer, he saw the open pages of *Vishwabanbdhu* and Charu immersed in thought.

Amal silently made his exit. 'Charu is knocked unconscious by the fact that I have been trashed, and she has been praised.' In a flash, his whole being was pervaded with bitterness. Charu had read this idiot's criticism and thought herself bigger than her guru, Amal had certainly concluded to this effect and was angry. Charu should have torn the paper into little pieces and consigned them to the flames.

Angry with Charu, Amal went up to the door to Manda's room and very loudly called, "Manda *bouthan*."

"Come in," said Manda. "Bless my stars, I am seeing you without having done anything to deserve it."

Amal said, "I have written something new. Should I read it out to you?"

Manda said, "You've been promising me to read something out for ages, but you never do. It's no use—don't know who's going to be offended and you'll get into trouble—not my lookout, is it?'

Amal responded fiercely, "Who'll get angry? Why should anyone feel angry? Okay, we'll see about that later; now you listen to me."

Manda hurriedly and eagerly composed herself and sat down. Amal grandly began reading in an appropriate tone.

Amal's writing was completely foreign to Manda; she could not make head or tail out of it. That's why she put on a smile of happiness and pretended to listen with rapt attention... Amal's voice, with this encouragement, grew louder and louder.

He read—As Abhimanyu had learnt, while in his mother's womb, how to penetrate the *Chakravyuh*, but not how to come out of it, similarly the river that flowed out of the stony womb of the mountain cave learnt to flow forward, always forward, never to turn back. Alas, the course of the river, alas youth, alas time, alas the world, it can only go forward—on the road where gilded memory scatters its pebbles and never returns by the road it has once taken. It is only the heart of man that looks behind at this world, which never so much as glances behind.

At this moment, a shadow fell across Manda's door. and Manda saw that shadow. But she pretended not to have seen it and, with an unblinking stare, gazed upon Amal's face and was all ears, listening to Amal as he read out his piece.

The shadow disappeared instantly.

Charu had waited for Amal to turn up to trash *Vishwabandhu* and to berate Amal for breaking their oath and getting their writing published in a magazine.

The time for Amal's visit had elapsed, and he hadn't shown up. Charu had prepared a piece that she wanted to read aloud to Amal. That too lay unread.

And then she heard Amal's voice coming as if from Manda's room. Pierced as by an arrow, she got up. Without making a noise, she came and stood at the door. The piece that Amal was reading out to Manda was new to Charu. Amal was saying, "It is only the heart of man that looks back; this world without end doesn't so much as glance behind."

Charu could not go back as silently as she had come. That day she had sustained one injury after the other, and she was at the end of her tether. She wanted to scream out that Manda understood not a word of what she was hearing and that Amal, like a fool, was deriving satisfaction from reading out his piece to her. But being unable to do so, her angry steps resounded on the floor. Reaching her room, she slammed the door shut behind her.

Amal stopped reading for a moment. Manda laughed and hinted that Charu had been here. Amal told himself, 'Why should *bouthan* be so oppressive? Has she decided that I am her slave? I cannot read out my stuff to anyone but her. This is terribly tyrannical of her.' He continued to read to Manda in an even louder voice.

Having finished reading, he made his way out, crossing Charu's door in the process, without pausing even once. He saw that Charu's door was shut.

Charu understood from the footsteps that Amal had gone past her room, and had not stopped even for a moment. She was so angry, so cross, that she couldn't cry. She took out the notebook with her new piece and sat down to tear every page of it into little pieces, which made a small pile. Alas, what an inauspicious moment it must have been when all this writing began.

## VIII

In the evening, the pleasant fragrance of *jui* flowers was coming from one of the pots in the verandah. The stars in a refreshing sky were peeping out from behind scattered clouds. Charu had not done her hair, had not changed into a fresh set of clothes. She sat in the dark, near the window, her hair blowing to the slow rhythm of a gentle breeze, and she herself could not understand why the tears would not stop flowing from her eyes.

At that very moment, Bhupati came into the room. His face was despondent, his heart heavy. It was unusual for Bhupati to show up at this hour. He was often late because he had to write something for the paper and look at the proofs. That day he had come as if in search of some consolation.

There was no lamp lit in the room. In the dim light of the window, Bhupati could barely make out Charu sitting next to the ventilator; he slowly came and stood behind her. Charu, despite having heard his footsteps, did not turn to look at him—she sat still and stiff like a statue.

Bhupati, a little surprised, said, "Charu."

Hearing Bhupati, Charu made haste to get up. She didn't know when Bhupati had come into the room. Bhupati ran his fingers gently through Charu's hair and asked, in a most tender voice, "Why are you sitting like this all alone in the dark? Where is Manda?"

The whole day had passed as if nothing had gone according to her expectations. She had certainly expected Amal to come and beg forgiveness—she had prepared herself for such an eventuality. and was waiting for it to happen. Upon hearing, contrary to expectation, Bhupati's voice, her last defences crumbled, and she broke down.

Bhupati, overwhelmed and anxious, started saying, "Charu, what's wrong, Charu?"

It was difficult to say what was wrong with Charu. What, after all, was the matter? Nothing really untoward had happened. Instead of reading out his new composition to Charu first, he had read it out to Manda. How could she complain about this to Bhupati? Bhupati would just laugh it off. It was beyond Charu to say where the gravity of her complaint lay hidden, hidden within such a trifling matter. The fact that she could not understand completely why she was suffering beyond reason seemed to increase her pain even more.

Bhupati said, "Tell me, Charu, what's the matter with you? Have I done something wrong? You know well how frightfully occupied I am with the complicated business of running a paper. If I have hurt you in any way, I did not do so deliberately."

Not a single one of Bhupati's questions had any answer, and that was why Charu was beside herself with anxiety. She just wanted Bhupati to release her from the grip of his interrogation and go away. She would be relieved.

Not having elicited a response for the second time in a row, Bhupati spoke to her with tender affection, "I cannot always come to you, Charu, for that I feel guilty, but it won't happen again. From now on, I promise not to worry my head off day and night over the paper. You'll get as much of my time as you want."

Charu said impatiently, "It's not that."

Bhupati asked, "Then what is it?" And he sat down on the bed. Charu could no longer hide her irritation and said, "Let it be for now. I'll talk to you later tonight."

Bhupati was silent for a while, and then said, "Okay, let's leave it for now." He got up slowly and left the room. He had come to say something. It remained unsaid.

Charu knew she had rebuffed Bhupati. She thought, 'I'll call him back.' But what would she tell him? She was seized with pangs of remorse, but could find nothing with which to allay them.

Night fell. Charu had taken special care to serve Bhupati dinner and had planned to fan him herself.

At that moment, she heard Manda call out, "Braja! Braja!" When Braja the servant responded to the call, she asked, "Has Amal babu had his dinner?" "He has," replied Braja. Manda said, "He's had his dinner, and you haven't taken him his *paan* yet!" Manda started scolding Braja with utmost severity.

At this point, Bhupati came into the inner quarter, and sat down for dinner. Charu fanned him.

Charu had resolved to be cheerful and pleasant and engage Bhupati in a free-wheeling chat. She had thought of a few topics and was prepared. But Manda's voice had made a mess of her elaborate plans; she could not address a single word to Bhupati during the entire meal. Bhupati, absent-minded and distracted, picked at his food. Charu once asked him, "Why aren't you eating?"

"But I have!" protested Bhupati.

When they were together in the bedroom, Bhupati said, "You said you had something to tell me tonight."

Charu said, "Listen, for the last few days Manda's behaviour has been highly improper. I don't feel secure about having her around anymore."

Bhupati said, "Why? Has something happened?"

Charu said, "The way she carries on with Amal, it's downright shameful."

Bhupati laughed and got up and said, "Ha! Are you out of your mind? Amal is just a boy. He was one till the other day—"

Charu said, "You know nothing of what's going on around here; you are only bothered about gathering news about the world. You don't even bother to enquire; no sooner does the lime fall off from Amal's *paan* than she starts scolding the servants."

Bhupati said, "You women are a bit too suspicious, I have to say."

Angry, Charu said, "Okay, so we are suspicious, but I won't have any loose conduct in this house; let me make that clear."

Bhupati had a quiet laugh over Charu's baseless apprehensions, but he felt happy about them. He found pleasant and grand the gaze full of suspicion, the extra care that sweet womanhood employed to keep conjugal life free of the slightest trace of even approximate, imaginary scandals so that purity could be preserved in the household.

Bhupati, overcome with respect and fondness, placed a kiss on Charu's forehead and said, "You won't have to bother yourself with all this anymore. Umapati is going to set up a practice in Mymensingh, and will take Manda with him."

Finally, in order to dispel all his foreboding and the unpleasantness of the discussion, Bhupati picked up a notebook from the table and said, "Why don't you read me something by you, Charu?"

Charu snatched the notebook out of his hands and said, "You won't like it; you'll only make fun of it."

Bhupati was hurt but didn't show it. He said, "Okay, I won't make fun of it; I'll sit so still that you'll be deluded into thinking I've gone off to sleep."

But Bhupati could gain no traction—the notebook disappeared from before his eye into domestic creases and folds.

## IX

Bhupati couldn't tell Charu everything. Umapati was the administrator of Bhupati's paper. Raising subscriptions, running the printing press, repaying loans, paying the employees, all of this fell under the purview of Umapati.

While all this was going on, Bhupati suddenly received

a legal notice from the distributors saying Rs. 2700 was due to them. Bhupati was shocked. He called Umpati and said, "What's going on? I thought I had given this money to you. The paper's dues shouldn't be more than four or five hundred rupees."

Umapati said, "These people have surely made a mistake."

But the news couldn't be suppressed any more. For quite some time Umapati had been embezzling money. Not only with sums related to the newspaper, but he had also been raising money in Bhupati's name from the market. He had been building a brick and cement house in the village and had procured the construction materials in Bhupati's name, and had paid off the supplies with funds earmarked for the newspaper.

When finally caught out, he had said, gruffly, "I'll work it off gradually. If I owe you even a penny, my name is not Umapati."

The tarnishing of his reputation afforded Bhupati no consolation. Bhupati was upset not so much over the financial losses incurred, but that the betrayal had flung him away from his house and into the void.

That day, he had gone into the inner quarter in an untimely manner because he knew that that was one place he could trust with eyes blindfolded.

It was at that precise moment that Charu, lights put out, was sitting near the window, in the dark, in grief.

Umapati was ready to depart for Mymensingh the next day. He wanted to slip away before his creditors got the news. In his disgust, Bhupati had refused to talk to him—Umapati, on the other hand, was relieved at Bhupati's silence. Amal came and said, "Manda *bouthan*, what's up? You are packing all your stuff? But why?"

Manda said, "Alas, my good man, one has to leave. Can't stay forever."

Amal said, "Where are you off to?"

Manda said, "Back home."

Amal said, "But why? What was the problem here?"

Manda said, "The problem was not mine; truth be told, I was happy with all of you here. But some people had problems with that—" Saying which, she glanced towards Charu's room.

Amal grew sombre, but remained silent. Manda said, "Disgusting! What a shame! I don't know what the master of the house thinks of all this."

Amal chose not to delve into the matter any further. He understood this much that Charu had said something to Bhupati about Manda and himself that could not be repeated.

Amal went out and wandered in the streets. He did not feel like returning to this house anymore. If indeed Bhupati, his cousin, had given credence to what *bouthan* had told him, and had held him guilty of, then he would do what Manda was doing right now. Bidding Manda goodbye in a way presaged his own eviction—only it had not been made explicit to him. After this, his course of action was clear to him—he would not stay here a moment longer. But it was inconceivable that Bhupati would unjustly nurse a grievance against him. How could he make his brother understand that the unconditional trust upon which he had taken Amal under his wing had not been violated in any way?

Bhupati, at that point, was holding his head in his hands over the ingratitude of his relatives and the fact that he was being hounded by creditors, the sorry state of the account books, and his empty treasury. There was nobody to hold his hand in his moment of grief—Bhupati was preparing himself to fight both pain and debt all by himself.

In the middle of all this, Amal swept into his room like a storm. Bhupati, immersed deep in his sorrow, was startled. "What's the news, Amal?" he said. Intuitively, he felt that Amal had come to him with another piece of serious bad news.

Amal said, "Do you have any reason to suspect me?"

Bhupati, taken aback, said, "Suspect you!" He thought to himself, 'the way the world is going, the day may not be far when I might suspect Amal too.'

Amal said, "Has *bouthan* accused me regarding my character to you?"

Bhupati thought to himself, 'Oh, I see what the matter is! What a relief! Pride wounded out of affection.'

He had thought that another catastrophe had occurred on top of the one that had already taken place. But during a serious crisis, one has to listen even to such trifles. In this world they shake the bridge from one end, and from the other make importunate demands to transport a sackful of spinach across it.

At another time, Bhupati would have joked with Amal, but that day he was not in the mood for humour. He said, "Are you crazy?"

Amal repeated himself, "*Bouthan* hasn't said anything?"

Bhupati said, "If she has said something out of affection for you, I don't see any reason to be angry."

Amal said, seriously, "I must go elsewhere in search of employment."

Bhupati rebuked him sharply, "You don't know how puerile you sound. Concentrate on your studies. There is plenty of time to think about working."

Amal went away, crestfallen.

Bhupati started balancing his books between the price paid by his paper's subscribers, and the expenses accumulated over the last three years.

## X

Amal had made up his mind to have it out with Charu; he must see this to the end, he told himself. He began to rehearse all the tough speeches he would make in front of *bouthan*.

Charu had decided that once Manda had left, she would summon Amal and placate him. But she would have to think of a topic to write about before she did that. She had schemed out an essay in imitation of Amal, called the 'Light of the Moonless Night'. Charu had understood this much, that Amal didn't like her independent style of writing.

The full moon illuminates with all its intensity, and Charu, in her latest composition, had so berated the full moon and shamed it. She wrote, 'Even in the bottomless darkness of a moonless night, the light of all the sixteen digits of the moon is contained within several levels; not a single ray is lost. Thus, compared to the brightness of the full moon, the darkness of a moonless night—etc.' Amal makes all his writing public to everyone; Charu does not—was the comparison between a full moon night and a moonless one an expression of this situation?

Elsewhere, the third person in this drama, Bhupati, had gone to see his friend Motilal to seek a way out of the clutches of debt yet to come.

Bhupati had loaned a few thousand rupees to Motilal when the latter had been in trouble—he had gone to recover some of that debt in an extremely confused state of mind. Motilal was fanning himself after a bath, and was inscribing in very small letters on a piece of paper posed on top of a wooden box, the thousand names of

Goddess Durga. On seeing Bhupati, he greeted him with heartfelt warmth—"Come, come—one hardly gets to see you these days."

On hearing of the loaned money, Motilal was plunged into deep thought and asked, "Which money are you talking about? Have I borrowed some from you of late?"

Upon Bhupati mentioning the year and the date, he said, "Oh, I see, but that had lapsed quite a while ago."

In Bhupati's eyes, it seemed as if all the faces around him had undergone a transformation. Seeing the part of the world that had dropped its mask, Bhupati, terrified, felt his body being pricked by a thousand thorns. Just as one confronting a sudden flood seeks the highest ground possible, Bhupati, riven by apprehensions, sought refuge from the outside world, and made a rapid entry into his inner quarter, saying to himself, 'No matter what, Charu won't neglect me.'

At the time, Charu was sitting with a pillow on her lap and a notebook poised on top, over which she was bent, engrossed in writing something. When Bhupati came and stood very close to her, she became aware of his presence, and she quickly placed the notebook under her feet and sat up straight.

When there is pain in the heart, even a small blow hurts a lot. Seeing Charu hide her writing with such unnecessary alacrity Bhupati's heart rang out.

Slowly, Bhupati sat down next to Charu on the bed.

Charu, interrupted in the flow of her composition in an unexpected fashion and having had to conceal her notebook from Bhupati, was caught unawares and could not find anything to say to him.

That day, Bhupati had nothing to give or say of himself. He had come empty-handed as a supplicant to Charu's door. Any old question from Charu out of her anxious love, maybe a tender caress, anything would have acted as a salve upon his wounds. But, O Lakshmi, O wretched me! Charu couldn't find anywhere the key to her treasure of affections, even to satisfy a momentary need. Each to their own difficult speechlessness, and the silence in the room grew dense with tension.

After a spell, Bhupati let out a sigh, got up from the bed, and slowly left the room.

Elsewhere, Amal, carrying a heavy load of difficult words in his heart, was directing his steps, in some haste, towards Charu's room, when he came across Bhupati, who had such a withered, pale look on his face that Amal came to a halt and, worried, asked him, "Cousin, are you ill?"

No sooner did Bhupati hear Amal's pleasant voice, his entire heart with its burden of tears swelled like a wave inside him. He was unable to speak for a while. He forced himself to control himself and said, gently, "Nothing, Amal. Can we expect to see a piece by you in the magazine again?"

Amal could no longer find the difficult words he had

saved up for Charu. He quickly went up to Charu's room and asked, "*Bouthan*, what's the matter with my cousin?"

Charu said, "Why? I didn't notice anything. Maybe some rival paper has trashed his paper or something."

Amal shook his head.

That Amal had come without being called and had reopened a conversation in the most natural way brought comfort to Charu. She at once broached the topic of writing and said, "Today I was writing an essay on 'The Light of the Moonless Night' and he almost saw it!"

Charu had probably thought that Amal would be very eager to see her new composition. With that in mind, she turned a few pages in her notebook this way and that. But Amal fixed her once with an intense look on his face—who knows what he understood, what he knew. Startled, he got up. A traveller on a mountain path, suddenly sees, as soon as the cloud of fog lifts, the deep abyss into which he was about to hurl himself. Without uttering a single word, Amal hurried out of the room.

Charu could make neither head nor tail of Amal's unexpected behaviour.

## XI

The next day Bhupati again paid an untimely visit to the bedroom and called for Charu. He announced, "Charu, I have received a very good proposal for Amal."

Charu was absent-minded. She asked, "A good what?"

Bhupati said, "A marriage proposal."

Charu said, "Why? Isn't one pleased with me?"

Bhupati laughed out loud and then said, "Whether he is pleased with you or not, I haven't put the question to Amal. Even if he is, I shall have a small say in the matter that I won't give up in a hurry."

Charu said, "O Lord, you don't know what you are saying. You said you had a good marriage proposal for yourself—"

Charu turned red.

Bhupati said, "In that event, would I have rushed to you like this? It's not as if you would have given me a *baksheesh*."

Charu said, "It's a proposal for Amal? Good, why delay matters?"

Bhupati said, "Raghunath *babu*, a lawyer from Burdwan, wants to give his daughter in marriage and send Amal off to England."

Charu, intrigued, echoed, "England?"

Bhupati said, "Yes, England."

Charu said, "Will Amal go to England? Sounds fun. Very good, very good indeed. Speak to him about it."

Bhupati said, "Instead of my speaking about it, mightn't it be better for you to have a word with him on the subject?"

Charu said, "I've done so three thousand times already. He doesn't pay any attention. I can't tell him."

Bhupati said, "What do you think, he won't give his consent?"

Charu said, "He has been spoken to several times before, but he wouldn't hear of it."

Bhupati said, "But it won't be proper on his part to turn down this proposal. My debts have piled up, I can't afford to keep Amal under my wings anymore."

Bhupati sent for Amal. When the latter arrived, Bhupati said, "There is a marriage proposal for you on behalf of the daughter of Raghunath *babu*, a lawyer from Burdwan. His wish is to send you to England after marriage. What do you say?"

Amal said, "If I have your approval, I won't say no."

Bhupati and Charu were surprised on hearing these words. Nobody had expected him to agree so readily.

Charu teased him, "If his cousin approves, he will give his consent. Such an obedient little fellow! Where was your faith in your cousin till yesterday, *thakurpo*?"

Amal tried to laugh it off without offering a reply.

Seeing Amal silent, Charu tried to provoke him with redoubled sarcasm and said, "Why don't you just say you don't have an opinion of your own? What was the need for putting on a show of indifference all this time? Hunger in the belly, but the tongue is coy."

Bhupati, savouring the humour, added, "It was for you that Amal had suppressed his appetite all these days, lest you become jealous of your prospective sister-in-law."

Charu blushed at this. She began to say a bit loudly, "Jealous! Oh really? I am never jealous. It's not fair on your part to say so."

Bhupati said, "Now wait a minute. Can't I make fun of my own wife?"

Charu said, "No, I don't like this kind of fun."

Bhupati said, "Okay, okay, it's a serious mistake, I admit. Pardon me, madam. But the marriage proposal goes through? Yes?"

Amal said, "Yes."

Charu said, "Won't you even bother to go and see if the girl is to your liking or not? There was not even a hint that your plight was such."

Bhupati said, "Amal, if you want to see the girl, I can arrange for it. Reports are she is beautiful."

Amal said, "I don't see the need for all that."

Charu said, "Why do you listen to him? Is that done? Can one marry without seeing the girl? Okay, he doesn't want to. What about us?"

Amal said, "No, cousin, I don't see why we should waste our time over such things."

Charu said, "No use daddy, any delay and he'll burst. Why don't you go out dressed as the groom straight away? Who knows, somebody else might snatch this precious gem away from under your nose."

Amal remained impassive. Charu's barbs had missed their mark.

Charu said, "You must be frantic about running away to England. Why? Were we beating you up over here? Young fellows these days think they can't make it without dressing up in a coat and a hat. *Thakurpo*, will you deign to recognise blackies like us after you come back from England?"

Amal said, "Why else would anyone want to go to England for?"

Bhupati laughed and said, "Why cross the seven seas unless you want to forget all these black faces? No fear, Charu, we are there to see to it that blacks have their faithful."

Happy, Bhupati dashed off a letter to Burdwan straightaway. The date for the marriage was fixed.

## XII

Meanwhile, the paper shut down. Bhupati could no longer meet the expense. The enormous and heartless thing called public opinion, at whose altar Bhupati had worshipped day and night, for so long, and with such devotion, he had to give it up in an instant. The habitual path through which, for the past twelve years, he had concentrated his efforts, and which had sustained itself ceaselessly, came to a sudden halt as if in the middle of the ocean. For this Bhupati was entirely unprepared. In which direction would he turn his focus to after such a lengthy endeavour that had met with a sudden obstacle? Like a hungry orphan, the world around Bhupati stared at him, who took to the compassionate, healer in his inner quarter.

And what was the woman thinking? She was wondering, 'What a surprise that Amal is to marry; it's a good thing. But after such a long time he will leave us to marry into another family and go to England; but this doesn't arouse any sense of hesitation in him even if for a moment. All these days spent here, and the first occasion he gets to escape, he seizes it promptly, as if he has been waiting for the opportunity. And his words as sweet as love. You just can't tell with people. Who knew that a man who writes so well doesn't have a heart after all?

Charu, comparing her own fullheartedness with the void in Amal's heart, tried very hard to be indifferent to the latter, but she couldn't. Inside her, a sensation of acute pain impaled her pride like a burning stake. 'Amal will leave one of these days, and he hasn't come to me yet. Not even to clear up the bad blood between us.' Charu expected Amal to turn up at any moment now—their little games with each other could not come to such a sorry end, but Amal never turned up. At last, when the date for departure drew closer, Charu herself sent for Amal.

Amal said, "I'll go a little later."

Charu went and sat on the chair in the verandah. The clouds had piled up since morning, and it was hot and humid—Charu had tied up her hair in a loose knot and was fanning her tired body languidly.

It grew very late. Her hand fan stopped moving. Charu felt the anger, sorrow, and impatience rend her bosom. She told herself, 'So what if he does not turn up?' Yet no sooner did she hear footsteps, than her heart ran towards the door.

The clock struck eleven at a church far away. Bhupati, after a bath, would soon come for his dinner. An half an hour still remained for Amal to come. No matter what, their silent quarrel of the past few days had to be cleared up—one couldn't see Amal off in this state. The sweet relationship between these two people of the same age—with all its friendly, miffed silences, cruel affection, confidential discussions, all tangled up in an ever shade-giving bower of creepers—would Amal today bring the whole structure down and go far, far away for many, many days? Would he feel no compunction? Wouldn't he, for a last time, water the roots—no tears shed over their relationship of such long standing?

Half an hour went by. Loosening her unruly bun, Charu's fingers were impatiently undoing and redoing her tresses. No use concealing her tears anymore. The servant came and said, "*Maa thakrun*, a coconut has to be served to the master." Charu undid the keys of the storehouse tied to the loose end of her *sari* and, with a clanging noise, threw them at the feet of the servant—who, surprised, picked up the keys and went away.

Something was making its way from Charu's breast up to her throat.

Bhupati, smiling broadly, sat down for his meal at the usual time. Fan in hand, Charu saw Amal had also come with Bhupati. Charu didn't look at him. Amal asked, "*Bouthan*, you had sent for me?" Charu said, "No, there is no need now."

Amal said, "Then I'll be off. I have a lot of packing to do."

For once, Charu looked, her eyes flaming, at Amal's face and said, "Go."

Amal looked at Charu and then went away.

At the end of the meal, Bhupati was in the habit of spending some time with Charu. Today, Bhupati had been busy with his creditors and his accounts, so he was upset about not being able to spend much time in the inner quarters. He said, "I can't stay for long today—I am up to my ears in it."

Charu said, "Then go."

Bhupati thought Charu's pride had been hurt. He said, "That doesn't mean I have to be off immediately; I have some time to kill." And he sat down. He saw that Charu was despondent. Bhupati, remorse-stricken, sat for a while but couldn't get a conversation going. After trying hard to chit chat with his wife, he finally said, "Amal is going away tomorrow; you will feel lonely for a few days." Charu made no reply and suddenly got up as if to fetch something from the other room. Bhupati waited for a while and then left.

Charu had noticed, looking at Amal's face, that he had lost a lot of weight in these last few days—his face was bereft of the sprightliness of youth. Charu was both content and pained by the thought. She had little doubt that Amal was afflicted at the thought of their imminent separation. Even so, why should Amal behave thus? Why was he behaving like a fugitive? Why was he deliberately turning the moment of farewell into a moment of bitter conflict?

Thinking about this lying on the bed, she suddenly woke up with a start. She suddenly remembered Manda. Could it be possible that Amal was in love with Manda? Was it because Manda had gone away that Amal was thus—fie on it! Could Amal's heart be made of such stuff? So petty? So polluted? Would his heart go out towards a married woman? She tried to reason her way out of suspicion, but the suspicion had buried its fangs deep into her.

And so arrived the moment of departure. The clouds hadn't cleared up. Amal came and said with a tremor in his voice, "*Bouthan*, the time has come for me to go. Look after cousin Bhupati from now on. He is in serious trouble—he has no means of consoling himself but you."

Amal had found out about Bhupati's troubles through the latter's stricken, colour-drained face. Amal fell silent at the thought that Bhupati had shielded his close relatives from the catastrophe that had overtaken him, and had silently and alone fought against the blows of misfortune without help, without comfort. Then he thought about Charu and about himself; this made him blush to the root of his ears, and he said, impetuously, "To hell with 'The Moon in June' and the 'Light of the Moonless Night'. If I can become a barrister and come back to help cousin Bhupati, I'll consider myself a man."

Throughout the night before, Charu had rehearsed what she would tell Amal at the moment of parting—those words had been polished into a radiant and sharp state in gay but wounded pride and cheerful indifference. But at the moment of leavetaking, she could not utter a word. She could only say, "You will write to us, won't you Amal?"

Amal bent down and touched her feet. Charu ran towards the bedroom and shut the door behind her.

## XIII

Bhupati returned home after marrying Amal off in Burdwan and seeing him off at the docks.

Having received injuries from various sides, the trusting Bhupati had become detached and indifferent in his attitude towards the outside world. Committees and conferences, ordinary socialising, gave him no pleasure. He thought to himself, 'Being involved with all this all these days, I was only running away from myself—the best years of my life are gone—consigned to the dungheap.'

Bhupati said to himself, 'The paper's gone, good

riddance! I am a free man now!' Just as birds return to the nest as night begins to fall, so Bhupati abandoned his preoccupation of yore, and went to Charu in the inner quarter. He had made up his mind, 'Enough! I am not going anywhere else; this is my place. The paper boat I used to play with the whole day, that boat has sunk, let's go ashore now.'

One understands that Bhupati was subject to a common belief—nobody has to acquire a right over one's own wife; a wife, like the North Star, shines a light on her own—it doesn't go out in the wind, doesn't need oil. When things began to be smashed about outside it hadn't occurred to Bhupati even once to go see if the vault in his inner quarter had also developed a crack.

Bhupati returned home from Burdwan one evening. He washed himself quickly the next morning and had his breakfast. Thinking that Charu was waiting eagerly to hear everything about Amal's marriage and his departure for England, Bhupati did not tarry. Bhupati went to the bedroom, lay down on the bed, and started puffing away at his hookah. Charu was, as yet, absent; it was understood she was busy with household chores. Having burnt a bit of tobacco, Bhupati began drifting off to sleep. From time to time, he would wake up with a start and think, 'Why isn't Charu coming?' Unable to contain himself, at last, he called for Charu. Bhupati asked, "Why so late today, Charu?"

Charu made no attempt to answer Bhupati, and said, “Yes, I am a bit late today.”

Bhupati waited for Charu’s eager questions; but Charu asked no questions. This upset Bhupati. Did that mean Charu did not love Amal? As long as Amal was present, Charu was absorbed in distractions and affections, but no sooner does Amal go away than Charu becomes indifferent towards him. This seemed a little odd to Bhupati, and he asked himself, ‘Was there no depth to Charu’s feelings? Did that mean she could only seek diversion and entertainment without love? It is not good for a woman to be so detached from things.’

Bhupati took pleasure in Charu and Amal’s camaradarie. Their childish friendship and tiffs, their little games and intrigues, were like sweet curiosities to him; the care and attention that Charu lavished on Amal was proof of Charu’s heartfelt tenderness, and Bhupati delighted in it. Today, he was astonished and thought, ‘Was all that just floating in the air, without foundation, without feeling? If Charu was heartless, then where would he, Bhupati, find solace?’

To test these propositions, Bhupati asked a series of questions. “Charu, have you been feeling all right? You haven’t been sick, have you?”

Charu’s response was curt, “I am fine.”

Bhupati said, “Amal is now married.”

And Bhupati kept mum. Charu tried very hard to

find something pertinent and to the point to say, but no words came to her; she sat stiff and rigid. It was natural of Bhupati to notice nothing, but since he was himself slightly mournful about Amal leaving them, he was hurt by Charu's indifference. His desire was to unburden himself a little by sharing the pain in his heart with Charu.

Bhupati said, "The girl is quite good-looking—are you sleeping, Charu?"

Charu said, "No."

Bhupati said, "Poor Amal, he had to go away all by himself. When I saw him off, he started crying like a baby, and seeing this, this old fellow could not restrain his tears anymore. There were two white men in the carriage; they were having fun seeing grown-ups cry."

The lamp extinguished in the bedroom; Charu turned over in the darkness and then suddenly hurried out of the bed and went away. Bhupati, stunned, asked, "Charu, are you sick?"

Having received no reply, he got up too. He heard someone crying on the verandah next door and, alarmed, went and saw Charu on the floor, lying flat on her stomach, trying to keep herself from crying.

Bhupati was amazed at this display of unbounded grief. He thought to himself, 'Had I misunderstood Charu? Charu was so reserved that she can't express the pain she feels even to me?' Those who are such, their love is profound, and so is much greater than the pain they feel. Charu's love, unlike that of ordinary women, was not visible from outside; Bhupati could understand this much within himself. Bhupati had never seen this spate of love in Charu, and today, he understood clearly that Charu's love had gone deep within, secretly. Bhupati himself was not too adroit about expressing his feelings openly. Seeing that it was in Charu's nature to have her emotions frozen deep within her, Bhupati derived some satisfaction.

Then, Bhupati sat next to Charu and, without saying a word, started to tenderly caresss her. Bhupati didn't know how to console Charu—he did not understand one thing: when someone wants to kill his or her grief by strangling it in the dark, it doesn't feel good to have witnesses around.

## XIV

When Bhupati finally took leave of his paper, he had drawn up a picture of his future in his mind. He had resolved not to venture into anything based on false hopes and ill-directed efforts; he would spend his days with Charu, reading, involving himself in the day-to-day trifles of the household, all done lovingly. He had thought all the homely pleasures easily got and not any less pleasurable for that, always worth dabbling in, and yet pure and healthy, through this readily available happiness he would light the evening lamp in his corner of the world and, having done so, establish a tranquil shelter filled with laughter, stories, jokes, and modest arrangements for mutual entertainment, and all this would require no great effort and yet would bring this great happiness.

However, he saw that in practice, simple happiness was not all that simple. The thing that one doesn't buy, if it is not found close at hand, then there is no way to find it anywhere else.

Bhupati somehow never managed to hit it off with Charu in spite of trying very hard. In this, he blamed himself. He thought this: 'Having spent 12 years writing for the paper, I've forgotten the art of conversing with women.' No sooner was the evening lamp lit than Bhupati would go eagerly to his room—he would say one or two things, Charu would respond with one or two things, after which Bhupati could not think of anything to say. He was ashamed of his awkwardness with his wife. He had thought that it would be easy to talk to his wife, and yet, for a dullard, it was so difficult. It was easier to deliver speeches before an audience. The evening that Bhupati had imagined would be filled with laughter, curiosity, romance, and tenderness, spending these evenings together now proved to be burdensome. After a few moments of silent effort, Bhupati felt like getting up—but he could not, what would his wife think? He would say, "Charu, let's play at cards." Charu, not finding anything else to do, would answer, "Okay," and would reluctantly go fetch the deck and would carelessly lose—there was no joy in the game.

After giving it a good deal of thought, Bhupati asked Charu one day, "Charu, why don't we call Manda back? You are so lonely."

Charu was inflamed at the mere mention of Manda. She said, "No, I don't need Manda."

Bhupati laughed. Inside, he was happy. Female ascetics, it is said, grow impatient at the slightest infringement of womanly duty and sacrifice.

Having managed the first onset of envy, Charu thought, 'With Manda around, she would probably have kept Bhupati in a good mood.' She was unable to provide Bhupati with the contentment of heart and mind that he desired of her, and realising this, Charu was troubled. Bhupati, having left the whole world, was trying to situate all the joy and attraction of his life in Charu alone, and Charu, noticing this single-minded effort, realised the poverty of her soul, and was rendered fearful. How could things go on like this, and for how long? Why doesn't Bhupati take up something else? Up to now, Charu hadn't needed to make it a habit of diverting Bhupati's mind; Bhupati had never asked her for any favour, and not sought any happiness with her; he had never moulded Charu in her totality, according to his needs. Today, all of a sudden, he asks Charu to fulfil all the needs of his life, and he finds nothing anywhere. What Bhupati wants and what would satisfy him, Charu doesn't understand well, or even if she did, she would not know how to go about giving it.

If Bhupati had proceeded slowly, perhaps that would have made things easier for Charu. But having been declared bankrupt overnight, he had sat down with a beggar's empty bowl and had confounded her.

Charu said, "Let's see, if you call Manda, then you would be better looked after."

Bhupati laughed and said, "Me? Looked after? No way!"

Bhupati thought, with some bitterness, 'I am such a boring man; I am utterly unable to keep Charu happy.'

Then he turned to literature, when friends called at home, they were surprised to find Bhupati absorbed in Tennyson, Byron, and Bankim Chatterji. Seeing Bhupati develop such tastes late in life, they would tease and mock him. Bhupati would laugh and say, "Even the bamboo puts out flowers, but no one can say when."

One evening, having lit the big lamp in the bedroom, he hesitated a bit, for he was abashed. Then he said, "Should I read out something?"

Charu said, "Do."

Bhupati said, "What should I read out?"

Charu said, "Whatever you like."

Bhupati, seeing Charu not too eager, felt cowed down. Even so, he picked up some courage and said, "Let me read out a translation from Tennyson."

Charu said, "Go on."

It all went badly. Diffident and discouraged, Bhupati's

reading lacked finesse; he couldn't find the correct Bengali equivalents. From Charu's vacant stare, he understood that her mind was unreceptive. That little room, lit by a lamp, that little occasion in the evening did not fulfil its promise.

Bhupati tried one or two lines more, but he had to abandon his effort to discuss literature with his wife.

## XV

As when the nerves go dead after a significant assault on the body and at first, no pain is felt, even so at the beginning of their separation, Charu did not miss Amal so much.

Finally, as the days went by, the void in her world caused by Amal's absence went on increasing. Charu was stunned at this discovery. Stepping out of a lush tropical garden, she found herself in a desert—as one day went past another, the desert seemed to grow bigger and bigger. She knew nothing about this desert.

She would wake up in a startle only to remember Amal wasn't there. In the morning, when she would sit down to prepare her *paan,* she could not help thinking that Amal would no longer creep up from behind. At times, thoroughly distracted, she would make so many *paan* and then remember with a start that there was nobody to share so many *paan* with her. When she entered the kitchen storeroom, she remembered she wouldn't have to serve Amal drinks and snacks. Her impatient heart would remind her as she reached the boundary of the inner quarter that Amal would not be back from college anymore. There was nothing to look forward to; no new book, new pieces of writing, or information, some new source of fun; there was no one for whom to sew something, write something, or buy something expensive.

Charu herself was astonished by her own suffering and restlessness. This relentless pain frightened her, and she would continually question herself. 'Why? Why am I suffering so much? Who is Amal to me that I should put up with so much pain over him? What has happened to me that I should suffer even after so many days, what is this? Maids, servants, loaders by the wayside are roaming carefree, going about their business, but why am I like this? O God! Why have you placed me in such peril?'

She could only question and be surprised, but she could not alleviate the pain. The memory of Amal had so suffused her soul, inside out, she could find no escape from it.

Bhupati, that separation-afflicted affectionate fool, instead of protecting her from the assaults of Amal's memory, would only keep reminding her of Amal.

Finally, Charu gave up completely. She ceased to wage war against herself. She accepted defeat, and accepted her condition without conflict. She carefully installed Amal's memory in her heart.

Over time, it so happened her single-minded meditation on Amal became a secret source of pride for her—as if that memory was her life's only prize.

She set aside time for that memory after her household duties were over. During that time, she would be all alone, the doors to her room shut and she would systematically think about each incident of her life spent with Amal. Lying flat on her stomach, her face on the pillow, she would repeatedly say to herself, 'Amal, Amal, Amal'. And a voice would seem to float across the seas, "*Bouthan*, what is it *bouthan*?" Charu would close her afflicted eyes and say, "Amal why did you go away with so much anger in your heart? I did you no harm. If you had taken leave in good spirits, then maybe I wouldn't have suffered so awfully." Charu would utter these words as if Amal were present before her, "Amal, I haven't forgotten you for even a day. Not a day, not a bit. All that was worthy in me, it is you who had brought it out. I will give the best of myself and worship you every day."

Thus, underneath the substratum of her domesticity, her household duties, Charu dug a tunnel, and in that desert-silent darkness, she built a secret shrine to her grief, decorated with her tears. In this, her husband or any other man in the world had no right of entry. Of utmost secrecy as the place was, so was it the deepest and the most precious. At its gate, she would discard all earthly disguises, and she would enter unconcealed, true to herself, and emerging from there, she would put on her mask and participate again in the merry drama of the worldly theatre.

## XVI

Thus, Charu, having abandoned all conflict and contention in her mind, found in the midst of her great sorrow, a sort of peace, and with single-minded determination, served her husband with devotion and care. When Bhupati slept, Charu would slowly place her head near his feet and take the dust off it into her parting. Where service, well-being and household chores were concerned, there was no trace of incompleteness in satisfying her husband's most trifling wishes. As for those who were sheltered and looked after by Bhupati, knowing her husband would be hurt if they were not taken care of properly, Charu would not make the slightest error in extending her hospitality. Having fulfilled her duties, she would partake of Bhupati's leftovers as a divine offering and retire for the night.

As a result of this service and care, lord and master Bhupati seemed rejuvenated. It would seem as if he had not been married before but was so now. Maturing in beauty, laughter, and mockery, Bhupati shoved aside all the misapprehensions concerning his world. The appetite increases after recovering from an illness, the body's capacity for material enjoyment develops and can be experienced consciously. Bhupati felt, after a long time, similarly, and a strong and unprecedented feeling of excitement coursed through his veins. Unknown to his friends and, for that matter, to Charu, he devoured books of poetry. He said to himself, 'My paper is gone, and I have been through untold sorrow, but after so many years, I have been able to discover my wife.'

Bhupati said to Charu, "Why have you given up on your writing?"

Charu said, "Fat lot of good it was."

Bhupati said, "I am serious; I don't see any other writer these days who can produce the kind of writing you do. I completely agree with what *Vishwabandhu* had said about you."

Charu said, "Stop it!"

Bhupati exclaimed, "But it's true!" And he brought out a volume of *Shororuh* and started comparing Charu's and Amal's writing. Charu, red in the face, snatched the copy out of Bhupati's hands and tucked it away in the folds of her sari.

Bhupati thought to himself, If there is no companion, nothing gets written. Wait, let me practice writing a bit, then over time Charu too, will find her enthusiasm to write again.

It was top secret, but Bhupati sat down with a notebook and started practicing writing. He consulted the dictionary and rewrote frequently, copied out again and again, and the days of Bhupati's leisure were spent thus. He was writing with so much difficulty, so much effort, that he grew fond and faithful towards the fruits of his toil.

Finally, he had one of his writings copied out in fair, and gave it to his wife.

He said, "One of my friends is trying his hand at writing. Since I don't understand much of these things, I suggest you take a look at it. Let's see what you make of it?"

Handing the notebook to Charu, Bhupati went out. This ruse by Bhupati, the simpleton, did not remain undetected by Charu.

She read, she laughed at the style and the subject of the writing. Alas! Charu was making so many arrangements for her husband with devotion; why did he have to scatter around the sacred offerings in this childish manner to elicit praise from Charu? Had he done nothing, had he never striven to attract Charu's attention, it would have been simpler for Charu to worship him. Charu's only wish was that Bhupati is not diminished in her eyes in any respect compared to her own self.

Charu folded the notebook, leaned back on the pillow, peered into the distance, and thought for quite a while. Amal too would bring his writing to have it read by her.

In the evening, Bhupati began inspecting the flowerpots in the verandah adjacent to the bedroom, not daring to ask the question.

Charu took the initiative and said, "Is this your friend's first attempt at writing something?"

Bhupati said, "Yes."

Charu said, "It's wonderful—doesn't read like

something from a beginner at all."

Bhupati, extremely pleased, began thinking how to substitute his own name for the fictitious author to whom he had attributed his piece.

Bhupati began filling the pages of his notebook at a furious pace. There was no delay either in making known the real author's name.

## XVII

Charu kept track of the arrival of letters from England. First, there was a letter for Bhupati from Aden, in which Amal had sent respectful greetings to *bouthan*; another letter followed from Suez, and *bouthan* was respectfully mentioned in that too. There was a letter from Malta too, and, again, *bouthan* was duly and respectfully greeted.

Charu did not receive a single letter from Amal. She asked Bhupati for the letters, and turning them this way and that, read and reread them—apart from the respects paid, there was no trace of her in the letters.

The few days Charu had spent under the shady canopy of her tranquil sorrow were rent asunder by Amal's indifference. It seemed as though, inside of her, her heart was again being torn apart. Her stable world of domestic duties was shaken by another earthquake.

Now, Bhupati would often get up in the middle of the night to find that Charu was not beside him. One day, he searched and searched and at last found Charu sitting beside a window in the room to the south. Seeing him, Charu got up hurriedly and said, "It was so hot in the bedroom, so I came to take a little breeze here."

Anxious, Bhupati made arrangements to have a fan installed over the bed, and anticipating a breakdown in Charu's health, he kept a steady eye on her. Charu would say, laughing, "I am fine, really; don't bother yourself so much." She had to mobilise all her strength to produce that laughter.

Amal reached England. Charu had concluded that by not getting sufficient opportunity to write independently, Amal would write back at length once he reached England. But that long letter never came.

Every time it was a question of the mail arriving, Charu would fidget nervously through her duties and her conversation. Lest Bhupati say, "There is no letter for you," she could not pick up the courage to put the question to him directly.

With her in this state, one day when the mail was supposed to arrive, Bhupati slowly ambled along with a smile and said, "Want to see something?"

Charu, in a fluster, started up and said, "Show."

Bhupati mischievously did not show it to her.

Beside herself with impatience, Charu got up and tried to snatch the forbidden substance from beneath Bhupati's shawl. She thought, 'Since morning I have had this feeling that today there will be a letter for me— I can't always be wrong.'

It encouraged Bhupati in his prank. He started circling the bed in an effort to elude Charu's grasp.

Irritated beyond all measure, Charu sat down on the bed, and her eyes welled up with tears.

Happy at seeing Charu so eager, Bhupati quickly brought out of the folds of his shawl his notebook full of his compositions and dropped it into Charu's lap, saying, "Don't be angry. Here it is!"

## XVIII

Even though Amal had informed Bhupati that his studies would not allow him the time to write home frequently, nevertheless not having received any letters for one or two months, Charu's world became a bed of thorns.

In the evening, among other subjects of conversation, Charu would slip in, in a casual and calm manner, "How about sending a telegraph to find out how Amal is doing?"

Bhupati said, "We got a letter two weeks ago, he's busy studying."

Charu said, "Oh, it's all right then. I thought being abroad if he fell sick or something, one can't really count on anyone."

Bhupati said, "No, if he really hadn't been well, we would've known. Telegraphs are expensive you know."

Charu said, "Is that so? I thought it might cost one or two rupees."

Bhupati said, "What are you saying? It's at least a hundred rupees."

Charu said, "Then I suppose the question doesn't arise."

Two or three days later, Charu said to Bhupati, "My sister is in Chinsurah, we have to go visit her."

Bhupati said, "Why? Is she ill?

Charu said, "No, she isn't ill. You know how happy she will be to see you."

Upon Charu's request, Bhupati called a carriage and set out for Howrah Station. On the way, a convoy of bullock carts came and blocked his way.

At this point a runner for the telegraph, spotting Bhupati, handed him a telegram. Seeing it was a telegram from England, he took fright. He thought, Maybe Amal has fallen ill. Fearfully he opened the telegram and read: I am fine.

What did this mean? Scrutinising it, he realised that it was a reply to a prepaid telegram.

He couldn't go to Howrah. He returned home and handed the telegram over to his wife. Charu's face blanched with fear when she saw the telegram in Bhupati's hand.

Bhupati said, "I can't make head or tail out of it." On probing a little, Bhupati understood. Charu had pawned some jewellery and borrowed money to send the telegraph.

Bhupati thought, 'So much expense wasn't really

required. If she had really wanted to, she could have requested me, and I would've telegraphed him. Sending a servant secretly to the market with her jewellery—this is not right.'

The thought occurred again and again to Bhupati, 'Why did Charu go to such lengths?' A vague suspicion began nettling him. That suspicion Bhupati didn't want to look at consciously, he tried to forget about it. But the pain wouldn't leave him alone.

## XIX

Amal is fine and well, yet doesn't write home. How did this tremendous situation arise? The desire was to come face-to-face and get an answer to the question, but there was the ocean in between—and no means to cross it. Cruel separation, insurmountable separation, separation beyond all question, beyond all remedy.

Charu could no longer keep herself straight. Work was neglected; she would fall into error on all matters, the servants stole, people noticed her condition and whispered among themselves; it was as if she were unconscious. It came to a point where she would start up all of a sudden; she had to break off in the middle of a conversation to go cry; her face would lose colour at the mere mention of Amal's name.

Finally, Bhupati saw everything. And thought that

which he hadn't thought, even for a moment—his world had grown old, gone dry, and had withered away.

The few days for which he had been blinded in a blooming of joy now made him ashamed. The inexperienced monkey who doesn't recognise a jewel when he sees it should be fobbed off with a fake.

The words Bhupati had forgotten, words uttered in devotion and care, he now remembered them, and they would cry out, 'Fool fool, fool,' and cane him on the back.

Finally, it arose in his mind, the compositions he had so laboured, so toiled over, and he asked the world to break asunder into two. Goaded, he rapidly strode up to Charu and said, "Where are my compositions?"

Charu said, "They are with me."

Bhupati said, "Give them to me."

Charu was, at that point, frying egg fritters for Bhupati. She said, "Do you want them now?"

Bhupati said, "I want them now."

Charu took the wok off the fire, and went and brought out of the almirah the notebooks and papers that Bhupati had asked for.

Bhupati impatiently snatched everything out of her hands, and threw them all into the belly of the stove.

Charu threw herself into rescuing them from the fire and said, "What have you done?"

Bhupati caught her hand in a vice-like grip and roared, "NO!"

Charu stood there astonished.

All the notebooks and paper were burnt to ashes.

Charu understood. A deep sigh escaped her lips. She left the fritters as they were, and slowly went away elsewhere.

It was not Bhupati's resolve to burn his writing. But the fire was burning right in front of him, seeing which, there was a sudden rush of blood. Not being able to control himself, like an innocent victim, he threw all his effort into the fire in front of the one who had cheated him.

When everything had turned to ashes, Bhupati's sudden access of recklessness was satisfied , and then Charu, carrying the weight of her own guilt, her manner that of one who had gone away in deep sorrow, silent head bowed, that manner presented itself to Bhupati's mind—he saw in front of him that she had been preparing the food that Bhupati was especially fond of, with her own hands.

Bhupati stood supporting himself on the railing of the verandah. He thought to himself, 'All this untiring effort on the part of Charu, all her desperate deceit, what could be more pathetic in this world? All this cheating, it is not simply the accumulated cheating of a cheat, for this deceit, a wounded heart had multiplied its pain fourfold, such that the miserable wretch had to squeeze blood out of her heart every moment of everyday. O weakness! O misery! I didn't need this; I needed nothing of all this. All this while, without love, I didn't even know I wasn't loved; all this while I had spent my time checking proofs and writing for the paper, there was no need to do so much for me.'

Reviewing his life faraway from Charu's—as a doctor looks at a seriously ill patient, so Bhupati, like a man without human ties, looked at Charu from a distance. That feeble woman's heart had been assailed from all sides by the world. There was no one to whom she could confide; there was no word that could be uttered; there was no place where she could have revealed her heart, all of it, and raised a cry of despair—yet, that heart carried this unexpressed, unavoidable, unremediable, ever-accumulating weight of sorrow, and with an easy personality, and like her other healthy neighbours, she had to carry out her daily household chores.

Bhupati went to his bedroom and saw Charu holding the bars of the window, tearless, unblinking, staring out at the world. Bhupati slowly came and stood next to her—without saying a word, he placed his hand on her head.

## XX

Friends asked Bhupati frankly, "What's up? Why this sudden bustle?"

Bhupati said, "The newspaper—"

Friends said, "The newspaper again? Are you going to wrap all your assets in a newspaper and throw it into the Ganges?"

Bhupati said, “No, not my newspaper this time round.”

Friends said, “Then?”

Bhupati said, “There is this paper coming out in Mysore; they want me to edit it.”

Friends said, “You’ll leave everything here and go away to Mysore? Are you taking Charu along?”

Bhupati said, “No, maternal uncles are going to come here.”

Friends said, “You couldn’t get over the high of being editor after all.”

Bhupati said, “Men need a fix of something to get by.”

At the time of departure, Charu asked, “When will I see you again?”

Bhupati said, “If you feel lonely, write to me. I’ll come.”

Having bid goodbye, Bhupati had reached the door when, all of a sudden, Charu ran up to him and grasped his hand and said, “Take me along. Don’t leave me behind like this.”

Bhupati stopped short and looked at Charu. Charu’s grip loosened, and her hand slipped from its position. Bhupati moved away from Charu, and came and stood in the verandah.

Bhupati realised that the memory of Amal’s separation that surrounded the house, was burning and Charu, like a deer caught in a forest fire, was trying to flee the house.

‘But she didn’t think of me even once? Where will I run to? The woman who consecrates her heart to another, will she find the time to forget him in another land? Even in a desert, friendless and exiled, will I have to give her company always? After the toil of a working day, when I return home in the evening, how terrible that evening must be to spend with a silent woman in mourning. The one who bears death in her soul, how shall I embrace such a woman, how long will I be able to carry on like that? How many more years will I have to live like that? The nest that has been shattered to pieces, I will not be able to leave its debris behind, but will have to go around carrying it on my shoulders."

Bhupati came up to Charu again and said, "No, I can't."

In an instant, the colour drained from Charu's face, she became white as a sheet of paper, and grabbed a bedpost with her clenched fists.

On the spur of the moment, Bhupati added, "Okay, Charu, come with me."

"No," said Charu. "Let it be."

*Baisakh–Agrahayan,* 1901

# The Ending

Apurbokrishno, having passed his B. A., was coming back from Calcutta to his native place.

The river was small. At the end of the rains, it almost dried up. Now, at the end of July, it has swollen up and is kissing the limits of the village, the feet of the bamboo grove.

After many days of torrential downpour, today the skies are clear of clouds, and the sun is shining forth all bright.

If one could look into the mind of Apurbokrishno, the passenger of a country boat, one would see a picture of a youth, the river of whose consciousness was in spate from shore to shore due to fresh rainfall, shimmering in light and rippling under the effect of a breeze.

The boat came ashore at the *ghat*. From the banks of the river, through the trees, one can see the concrete roof of Apurbo's house. No one in his family knew of Apurbo's coming, and so nobody from his house had come to receive him at the *ghat*. The boatman showed willingness to take

Apurbo's bag, but Apurbo stopped him and picking up his own bag with some gusto, quickly got off the boat.

The shore was slippery, and no sooner had Apurbo alighted than he and his bag fell down in the mud. And no sooner had he fallen than a shrill stream of laughter burst forth, startling the birds in the fig trees.

Apurbo, deeply embarrassed, quickly got a hold over himself and looked around. He saw that a fresh pile of bricks from the money lender's boat had been stacked high on the bank, and on this very pile sat a girl convulsed in laughter as if she would burst into a thousand fragments.

Apurbo recognized her as the daughter of their new neighbours, Mrinmoyee. Their house used to be far away, on the shore of the big river, and, the river having changed its course, they had had to abandon everything and come to this village, two or three years ago.

This girl was notorious. The men of the village called her "crazy" out of affection, but the ladies were fearful, worried, and, indeed, terrorised by her wild spirit. She would play only with the boys of the village; she had no time for peers of her own sex. In the kingdom of childhood, this girl was some sort of a troublesome raider.

Being the apple of her father's eye, she had grown up to be a domineering spirit. In this matter, Mrinmoyee's mother would never fail to accuse her husband in front of her friends; even so, her father loved her, and when he was at home, Mrinmoyee's tears would sound the depths of his heart. Because of this, remembering her absent father, Mrinmoyee's mother could never make her daughter cry.

Mrinmoyee was dark-complexioned. Her hair fell on her back in tiny curls. The expression on her face was that of a boy. In her large black eyes there was no shame, no fear, no trace of the play of gestures or the deportment typical of a girl. She was tall, her body firm and healthy, strong but no one would ask whether she was older or younger than she looked; had the question arisen, people might have blamed her parents for her as yet unmarried status. The day some non-local landlord's boat would park itself at the *ghat*, the people of the village made themselves busy out of deference; the curtain would fall on the theatre of the women's faces up to their noses, but, from somewhere, with a naked infant clasped to her waist, her curly hair swaying upon her back, Mrinmoyee would run and present herself at the *ghat*. Like deer calves in a country without hunters, without danger, she would stand and stare in frank curiosity, and then return to the other boys in her gang and describe at length, the nature and behaviour of this new creature who had just arrived.

Meanwhile, our Apurbo, who had come home on a vacation, had seen this wanton girl on two or three occasions and had, at leisure or otherwise, thought about her. In the world, one comes across many faces, but some faces embed themselves in the mind for no apparent reason. And that has nothing to do with beauty; there is some other quality in them. That quality is, I think, artlessness. In most faces, human nature cannot express itself in a manifestly obvious way. The face whose innermost, mysterious persona comes out without obstacles, that face is noticed among a thousand, and in a flash, impresses itself in our hearts. In this girl's demeanour there was a fierce, independent, and untamed womanhood, like a swift wild deer, visible and playful, which is why this face, full of the restlessness of life, once seen was never easily forgotten.

Needless to add, dear reader, the stinging tonality of Mrinmoyee's laughter, be it as sweet as it may, had caused the unfortunate Apurbo some pain. He quickly handed his bag over to the boatman and, red-faced, made his way homewards.

The décor was exceedingly beautiful: on the banks of a river, the shade of a tree, the song of a bird, the rays of dawn, and Apurbo was twenty years old. Of course, the pile of bricks was not so remarkable, but the person who was sitting on it had bestowed upon this hard, silent seat, a fetching grace. Alas, what else could it be but the cruelty of fate that the first step in this scene had robbed it of its poetry and turned it into a farce?

## II

Listening to the laughter flowing out from the top of the pile of bricks, his shawl and bag smeared with mud, hugging the trees, Apurbo finally made it home.

His widowed mother was delighted by his sudden arrival, and immediately people went out in search of cream, curd and fish, and even people in the neighbourhood stirred to life.

After a meal, his mother brought up the question of Apurbo's marriage. Apurbo was prepared for this. The question was not a recent one, but the son, in deference to the latest doctrines, had stubbornly refused to entertain it before successfully clearing his BA exams. It was for this that his mother had waited so long; hence, there was no longer any occasion for lame pretexts. Apurbo said, "First let me look at some prospective brides, then a decision will be taken." His mother said, "We have already found a suitable match; don't bother yourself over it." Apurbo prepared himself to bother about it and said, "I won't marry without having seen the girl." His mother thought such an oddball had not been heard of anywhere up till now. But she agreed.

That night, when Apurbo blew out the lamp and lay down to sleep, from beyond all the sound and silence of a rainy night, in his lonely, sleepless bed, there began to play in his ears, rising to a crescendo, the overflowing, utterly sweet-throated sound of laughter. The mind tormented itself with the thought of the misstep of that morning and how it could, by some means, be rectified. The girl could not know that, "I, Apurbokrishno, have acquired a lot of knowledge and have lived in Calcutta for a number of years, such that even if I accidentally slip and fall in the mud, I am not some country hick, the butt of ridicule and mockery."

The next day, Apurbo was to go see the girl. The house was not very far; it was in fact, part of the neighbourhood. He took care to dress up properly. Discarding the dhoti and the shawl, he put on a long silk tunic, and on his head a round turban, and a pair of well-polished shoes on his feet. Thus dressed, a silk umbrella in hand, he stepped out early in the morning.

No sooner had he stepped into his prospective in-laws' house than it was plunged into collective ceremoniality and ritual.

At last, at the opportune moment, with a trembling heart, the girl, scrubbed and cleaned, painted, tinsel in her bun, wrapped in a light, colourful fabric, was presented to the prospective groom. Silent, her head almost touching her knees, she sat in a corner with an aged servant stationed behind her. to give her courage. The would-be bride's brother, no more than a boy, began intensely inspecting the turban, the chain of the pocketwatch, and the newly sprouted beard of this unlawful entrant. Apurbo, after twirling his moustache for a while, finally asked, with suitable gravity, "What do you read?" The one weighed down by her clothes and jewellery, a heap of coyness to boot, made no reply. The question having been put to her twice or thrice, and several pokes of encouragement delivered to her back by the trusted servant, the girl, in a sweet voice and without pausing for breath, said, at top speed, "*Charupath* part 2, grammar part 1, geography, arithmetic, and Indian history." At this point, the sound of agitated steps was heard outside, and in an instant, Mrinmoyee entered the room running and panting, her hair bouncing on her back. Without looking at Apurbokrishno, she seized the hand of the girl's brother, Rakhal, and began dragging him away. Rakhal was engrossed in his own inspection; he would not leave. The servant, taking care to preserve a semblance of genteeleness in her voice, began berating Mrinmoyee. Apurbokrishno gathered together all his gravity and dignity, his turbaned head lofty, and remained seated. He began fiddling with the chain of his watch that dangled near his torso. Eventually, unable to agitate her friend, Mrinmoyee gave a resounding slap on his back, and quickly pulling the veil off the girl's head, she stormed out of the room. The servant thundered after her, while Rakhal, having witnessed the sudden unveiling of his sister, burst out laughing. He did not think that the slap on his back was undeserved, for such exchanges were not unusual between them. In fact, previously, when Mrinmoyee's hair dropped beyond her shoulders to her back, it was Rakhal who had silently crept up on her and had snipped it off with a pair of scissors. Furious, Mrinmoyee had snatched the scissors and, with unfeeling cruelty, had cut off the remaining hair on her back, her locks of curly hair falling like bunches of black grapes from the vine to the ground. This form of punishment was common between the two.

Thereafter, this silent examination could not proceed further for long. The lump of a girl somehow regained her elongated form and went away into her inner quarters with her servant. Apurbo, with utmost solemnity, twirling his thin moustache, got up to leave the room. Once at the door, he noticed that his well-polished pair of shoes was not in its place, nor was it possible, after an extensive search, to locate it.

The people in the house were greatly confused. And a lot of abuse and vilification was showered on the culprit. After searching high and low, Apurbo had to settle finally for the old, battered, ill-fitting slippers of the master of the house and the pantaloons, tunic and turban intact, made his way carefully across the muddy tracks of the village.

Alongside the pond, along the deserted paths, came again that shrill, noisy laughter. As if some forest deity, fond of amusement, peeking through the tree-cover, noticing the contrast between Apurbo's slippers and the rest of his attire, could no longer contain her laughter.

Caught unawares, and brought to an abrupt halt, Apurbo hesitatingly inspected his surroundings, when from behind the dense foliage, emerged the brazen culprit who placed his new shoes in front of him and made to flee. Apurbo quickly put forth his arms and made her a prisoner.

Mrinmoyee wriggled this way and that, trying to escape, in vain. The rays of the sun pierced through the branches of the trees and fell on her mischievous, robust face, covered by her curly hair. Just as a curious traveller gazes engrossed at the bottom of a clear, sunlit, restless river, Apurbo looked, his eyes serious and profound on Mrinmoyee's upturned face, and into her fluid lightning eyes, and very slowly, relaxing his grip as if leaving some duty unfulfilled, released his captive. Had Apurbo beaten Mrinmoyee in anger, there would have been nothing surprising in it, but on this deserted path, he would not have been able to make sense out of this incomparable tranquil peace.

Like the jingling of the bells in the anklet of a dancing nature, restless peals of laughter resounded in the sky, and, deep in thought, Apurbokrishno, walking at an extremely leisurely gait, reached his house.

## III

On one pretext or another, Apurbo avoided going to the inner quarter to meet his mother. He had an invitation outside; he attended it. It was difficult to understand why a learned, serious, thoughtful person should want to reclaim his lost pride, give complete notice of his inner excellence to an illiterate girl, and be so anxious about it. A country waif thinks him to be an ordinary person. So what? Even if, for a moment, she shows alacrity in making fun of him and, forgetful of his existence, makes play with an unlettered boy called Rakhal, where is the harm in that? Why was it necessary to prove that he reviewed books for a magazine called *Vishwadeep,* that in his steel trunk were stored perfume, shoes, Rubini's camphor, coloured writing paper, and a book called *Learning to Play the Harmonium*, as well as a well-filled notebook that, like dawn in the womb of night, was awaiting a publisher? But it is difficult to convince the heart, and Mr Apurbuokrishno Ray, B.A., was not ready to admit defeat before a country girl.

Entering the inner quarter in the evening, his mother asked him, "How did it go, Apu? How did you find the girl? You liked her, didn't you?"

Apurbo, caught slightly unawares, said, "I have seen them, *Maa*, and one of them I liked."

The mother, taken aback, said, "How many girls did you see?"

Finally, after much hesitation, it was established that her son had liked their neighbour Sharada's daughter, Mrinoyee. After so much education, this was his choice?

At first, there had been a good deal of shame on Apurbo's part, but when his mother began remonstrating with her son, he shook off all shame. Out of sheer cussedness, he declared, "I will marry none other than Mrinmoyee." The more he thought about the other puppet-like woman, the more he felt disgusted at the whole idea of marriage.

After a few days of refusing food and sleep on both sides, it was Apurbo who won. His mother reconciled herself to the inevitable by saying that Mrinmoyee was a child, and her mother had not educated her well and that after marriage she would take charge of things and Mrinmoyee's character would change. And gradually came around to the view that Mrinmoyee was good-looking. But soon her short, unruly hair would rear its head on the road of her imagination, and fill her heart once again with despair. Nevertheless, she hoped that, by binding her hair and applying oil generously, over time, even this defect could be set aright.

People in the neighbourhood named Apurbo's choice a choice without precedent, an excellent choice. Many loved the crazy Mrinmoyee, but that did not mean they considered her worthy of marrying their sons.

Mrinmoyee's father, Ishan Mazumdar, was duly informed. He was deputed as a clerk with a steamer company at an obscure riverine station and, in a shed covered with a tin roof, was in charge of loading and unloading as well as selling tickets.

Upon hearing of the marriage proposal for his daughter Mrinmoyee, he wept unabashedly. It was difficult to assign an exact figure to the quantum of happiness and sorrow he felt at this news.

Ishan applied to his bosses for leave to attend his

daughter's wedding. The higher-ups, considering the matter to be a trifle, turned down his request.

Ishan wrote home to say that he might be entitled to a week off during the *pujas*, and to postpone the marriage till that time. But Apurbo's mother said, "There is a good date this month; I cannot put it off any further."

Being refused at both ends, Ishan, with pain in his heart, raised no further objections and returned to weighing goods and selling tickets as previously.

Thereafter, Mrinmoyee's mother and the elders of the community, together, began day in and day out advising Mrinmoyee on her future responsibilities.

Athletic ability, a rapid gait, shrill laughter, talking to boys, eating whenever she had an appetite were all taboo, such that they were all successful in turning the marriage into a real ordeal. Full of anxiety and apprehension, Mrinmoyee thought she was to be imprisoned for life and eventually to be hanged.

Like a naughty pony, she shook her head, stepped back, and said, "I will not marry."

## IV

But marry she had to, nevertheless. And then her education began. Within the span of a night, Mrinmoyee's world came to be confined to the inner quarter of Apurbo's house.

The mother-in-law embarked upon her programme of

reform. Putting on a stern visage, she said, "Look here, child, you are no longer a young girl; such lack of manners will not do in our house."

Mrinmoyee didn't take this in the spirit in which it was said. She thought, if it won't do in this house, then maybe I should be elsewhere. In the afternoon, she wasn't to be seen. Where had she gone? The house was agog. In the end, the traitor Rakhal had her discovered in her secret hideout. She had taken refuge in Radhakanta's abandoned broken chariot under the banyan tree.

The readers can well imagine in what terms Mrinmoyee was humiliated by her mother-in-law and the notables of the locality.

At night, it rained heavily, the clouds were dense and the noise of rain falling was loud. Apurbokrishno slowly sidled up to Mrinmoyee and whispered gently into her ear, "Mrinmoyee, don't you love me?"

Mrinmoyee spiritedly spoke up and said, "No. I will never love you." All her rage and all her punishment were concentrated in those words; it was as if a bolt of lightning had struck Apurbo on the head.

Apuirbo, offended, asked, "Why, what wrong have I done you?"

Mrinmoyee said, "Why did you marry me?"

It is difficult to explain such a crime. But Apurbo said to himself, 'No matter how, I have to tame this untamed spirit.'

The next day, the mother-in-law, perceiving all the signs of rebellion in Mrinmoyee, shut her in a room and went away. The latter, at first, like a newly caged bird, began pacing up and down the room in a flurry. Finally, finding no means to escape, in frustrated anger, tore up the bed cover with her teeth into little shreds, and then, lying prone on the floor, began crying, calling her father silently.

Meanwhile, someone slowly came and sat beside her. Affectionately, this person tried to lift her dust-laden hair above her forehead. Mrinmoyee shook off his hand from her head. Apurbo bent his head to her ear and said, gently, "Nobody saw me open the door. Come, let us run away to the *khirki* garden." Mrinmoyee rapidly shook her head and said, tearfully, "No." Apurbo tried to hold her by the chin and lift her face up and said, "At least, see who has come." Rakhal, astounded, gazed at Mrinmoyee lying on the floor. Without looking up, Mrinmoyee pushed Apurbo's hand away. Apurbo said, "Rakhal has come to play with you; let's go and play." With a voice full of irritation, she said, "No." Rakhal understood that things were not going too well and, heaving a sigh of relief, ran away. Apurbo sat in total silence. Mrinmoyee cried herself to sleep, and Apurbo tip-toed out of the room and, having bolted the door shut, went away.

The following day, Mrinmoyee received a letter from her father. He regretted not having been able to attend the wedding of his dearest daughter and blessed the couple from his heart.

Mrinmoyee went and told her mother-in-law, “I want to go to my father’s place.” At this sudden and impossible request, the mother-in-law berated her, “She doesn’t even know where her father lives, and she says, ‘I want to go to my father’s place.’ Of all things!” She went away without giving an answer. Mrinmoyee went to her assigned room, shut the door, and, just as a desperate man prays to the gods, began saying, “Baba, please take me away. I have no one here. If I have to live here, I will die.”

In the middle of the night, while her husband was in deep slumber, Mrinmoyee, slowly opening the door, left the room. Even though there were passing clouds; on a moonlit night there was enough light for her to see where she was going. Mrinmoyee had no idea which road to take in order to get to her father. She had always been under the impression that if one took the route taken by the ‘runners’ of the post, one could reach any address in the world. Mrinmoyee began walking along the path taken by the runners. She walked until she was weary, and the night drew to a close. In the woods, when a few birds called out, occasionally, on an uncertain note, even though unable to determine the time in a sure manner and, therefore, hesitant, Mrinmoyee, at the end of the path, came upon what looked like a great *bazaar* on the banks of a river. She was thinking which direction to take when she heard a familiar sound of bells. Carrying sacks of letters on his shoulder, the runner of the post came breathless up to the market. Mrinmoyee quickly went up to him and, in a timid, tired voice, said, "I want to go to Kushiganj to my father, can I come along with you?" The runner replied, "I don't know where Kushiganj is." And having woken up the oarsman of the postal department boat, off he went. He didn't have the time to take pity on Mrinmoyee, or ask questions.

In a while, the market gradually came to life. Mrinmoyee got down to the embankment and asked a boatman, "Boatman! Will you take me to Kushiganj?" Before the boatman could reply, someone from another boat called out, "Look who's that! Mimi dear, how have you landed up here?" Mrinmoyee burst forth with eagerness, "Banamali, I am going to my father at Kushiganj, take me in your boat." Banamali was a boatman from their village; and he knew this unruly girl only too well. He said, "Want to go to your father? That's fine. Come, I'll take you there." Mrinmoyee embarked straightaway.

The boatman set out on his boat. It started raining in torrents. The river grew more and more full, as it does in July or August; it rocked the boat, Mrinmoyee's body was overtaken by sleep; she lay down on the loose end of her *sari*, and this uncontrollable girl, rocked by the river, Nature's favourite child, slept a sleep free of care, a picture of docility.

She woke up to find herself on the bed of her in-laws'

place. Seeing her awake, the maidservant started scolding her. Hearing the maidservant's voice, the mother-in-law came and reprimanded her harshly. Mrinmoyee, her eyes exorbitant, stared at her in silence. Finally, when the mother-in-law started criticising Mrinmoyee's father for her faulty upbringing, then Mrinmoyee quickly went to the next room and locked the door from the inside.

Apurbo, feeling thoroughly ashamed, came and said, "What's the harm in sending my wife to her father's place for a couple of days?"

Apurbo's mother gave no quarter in remonstrating with her son and complained bitterly that there being so many girls in the country, why had he brought home this bone-crunching rogue of a girl.

## V

That day, the thundershowers prevailed throughout, and within the house, too foul weather held sway.

The following night, Apurbo slowly woke up Mrinmoyee and said, "Mrinmoyee, do you want to go to your father?"

Mrinmoyee quickly grasped Apurbo's hand and said, "Yes."

Apurbo said quickly, "Then come, let the two of us run away. I have booked a boat at the *ghat*."

Mrinmoyee looked at her husband with gratitude.

And then she quickly got up, discarded her clothes, and got ready to go outside. Apurbo left a letter behind to relieve his mother of all worries.

That dark night, on the deserted, silent village road, Mrinmoyee, for the first time, of her own will, held her husband's hand in complete trust; the upsurge of emotion and of joy in her heart communicated itself through her soft touch to her husband's nervous system.

The boat left that very night. In spite of her restless excitement and happiness, Mrinmoyee fell asleep very soon. The next day, what freedom, what joy! On both sides lay villages, markets, fields, and forests, and there was the to and fro of boats.

Mrinmoyee peppered her husband with questions on every trifling subject, such as–what was the name of the place, what was there in that boat, where was it coming from, questions to which Apurbo could not find answers in his college-educated mind, and for which his experience in Calcutta did not suffice. Friends, on learning that Apurbo had replied to each of these questions and that his answers had fallen well short of the truth, would have been embarrassed. Thus, he had identified a sesame boat as a linseed boat, mistook Panchbere for Rajnagar, and a lower civil court to be a landlord's tribunal without the slightest hesitation. Despite this low deception, not the slightest injury was caused to the trusting heart of the questioner.

The following evening, the boat reached Kushiganj. In

a tin shed, by the light of a lantern with rectangular shades and an oil wick, a huge leather-bound register on a small desk, stripped to the waist, Ishan Chandra sat on a stool, working on his accounts. The newly wed couple entered the room. Mrinmoyee called out, "*Baba*!" In that room, such a voice had never been heard before.

Ishan's eyes overflowed with tears. He couldn't think of what to say or do. His daughter and his son-in-law were like the heirs-apparent to an empire. Where to find a throne to seat these distinguished personages among the sacks of jute, his bewildered mind could not devise a means.

And then there was the question of food—another source of worry. The poor clerk was in the habit of cooking lentils and rice for himself—what would he do? What would he feed his guests on this joyous occasion? Mrinmoyee relieved him of his worries, "*Baba*, today we will all cook together." Apurbo accepted this proposal with enthusiasm.

In the house, there was a lack of space, lack of people, and a lack of food, but as a fountain erupts more forcefully through a small hole, so from poverty's mean mouth, happiness flowed in full measure.

Three days went by thus. Twice a day, the steamer would put in regularly, so many people, so much bustle; in the evening the banks of the river would be deserted, and what freedom without constraint there would be! And the three of them, together, would procure a variety of supplies and would, by mistake, cook up one thing while aiming to cook another. And then Mrinmoyee's affectionate hands, with their tinkling bangles, would serve the father and the son-in-law alike, making ample display of a thousand mistakes in both cooking and in housewifery, causing amused laughter with which the young girl would stir up a messy quarrel and express verbally her wounded pride. Finally, Apurbo let it be known that it would not do to prolong their stay any further. Mrinmoyee, filled with sadness, requested that they spend a few more days. Ishan said, "Won't do."

On the day of their departure, Ishan drew his daughter to his bosom, placed a hand on her head, and in a voice trembling and tearful, said, "Dearest child, may you be the glory of your in-laws' household. Let no one blame my Minu for anything."

Mrinmoyee, in tears, took leave with her husband. And Ishan returned to his twice-blighted narrow confines and day after day, month after month, resumed weighing goods.

## VI

When the guilty couple returned home, the mother-in-law had on a grave demeanour, and did not say a word. She did not accuse anyone of their behaviour such that it would necessitate an explanation on her part. This silent accusation, this tranquil pride, lay on all the womenfolk as a heavy iron ball.

At last, finding it unbearable, Apurbo came and said, "*Maa*, college has reopened. I have to go and study law."

His mother replied with indifference, "And your wife?"

Apurbo said, "My wife shall remain here."

Mother said, "No, son, that won't do. Take her along with you." On occasion, his mother was in the habit of addressing Apurbo with the familiar "thou".

Apurbo, offended, replied, "Okay."

The shift to Calcutta had to be organised. The night before his departure, Apurbo, before going to bed, saw Mrinmoyee crying.

Suddenly, he felt as if a blow had struck at his heart. He said, morosely, "Mrinmoyee, don't you don't want to come with me to Calcutta?"

Mrinmoyee said, "No."

Apurbo asked, "Why? Don't you love me?" He got no answer to that question. Often the answer to such a question is easy, but at other times, there are such psychological complexities connected to it that one cannot expect an answer from the girl.

Apurbo asked, "Do you feel bad about leaving Rakhal behind?"

Mrinmoyee replied, most naturally, "Yes."

This learned graduate saw dawning upon himself, vis-a-vis the boy named Rakhal, a very subtle, and yet very sharp feeling of jealousy. He said, "I won't be able to come back in a long while." To this piece of news, Mrinmoyee had no comment to offer.

"Perhaps two years or even more."

Mrinmoyee gave an order: "When you come back, get a picture of a three-headed swan for Rakhal."

Apurbo, who was reclining, got up a little and said, "So you will stay here then?"

Mrinmoyee said, "Yes, I will stay close to *maa*."

Apurbo exhaled and said, "Okay, so be it. As long as you don't write to me asking me to come, I won't. Very happy, I take it?"

Mrinmoyee, considering a reply to this question to be futile, fell asleep. But Apurbo couldn't sleep; he propped himself up on a couple of pillows and remained thus.

In the night, suddenly, the moon rose, and its light fell on the bed. In that light, Apurbo looked at Mrinmoyee. Looking at her, it seemed to Apurbo that somebody had waved a silver wand over a princess and had rendered her unconscious. If only he could get hold of a golden wand, he would wake up this sleeping soul, and exchange marriage vows with her. The silver wand was laughter; the golden wand was tears.

At dawn, Apurbo woke up Mrinmoyee. He said, "Mrinmoyee, it's time for me to go. Come, I'll drop you off at your mother's place."

When Mrinmoyee got up from bed, Apurbo grabbed

her hands and said, "Now I have one request to make. I have helped you on numerous occasions in various ways; will you reward me when I am going away?"

Mrinmoyee, surprised, said, "What?"

Apurbo said, "Out of your own will, out of love, give me a kiss."

Upon hearing this strange request uttered so solemnly, Mrinmoyee laughed. Controlling her laughter, she raised her mouth for a kiss, but as she drew closer, she could not hold back. She broke out in peals of laughter. She made two more attempts, and then gave up, hid her mouth with her sari, and laughed at Apurbo and, in mock severity, pulled her ear.

Apurbo was a man of tough resolve. For him, to assume the character of a bandit and to snatch and loot was equivalent to betraying his soul. Like a god, he wished to remain sovereign, and to receive a gift voluntarily given, he would not, of his own, take something into his hands.

Mrinmoyee laughed no more. In the light of dawn, through deserted paths, Apurbo escorted her to her mother's place, and returning home, said to his mother, "I've thought it over; taking my wife with me to Calcutta would interfere with my studies, and she too, would have felt lonely there. You don't want to keep her here, so I have gone and left her at her mother's place."

In solemn pride, the mother and the son parted ways.

## VII

Coming to her mother's place, Mrinmoyee found that her heart could not dwell on anything. It was as if the house had changed from top to bottom. Time would not pass. She couldn't decide what to do, where to go, whom to meet.

It seemed to Mrinmoyee that nobody was left in her house or in her village. Like a solar eclipse at noon, she just couldn't understand why she felt like going away to Calcutta so much. Where was this feeling the previous night? Then, she didn't know that that part of her life, the abandonment of which caused so much agitation in her heart, that entire temperament had undergone a sea change. Like a leaf ripe on a tree, today she willingly hurled herself away from her entire previous existence, as if nipping it from the stalk.

One hears stories that there are makers of weapons so skilled who can make swords so subtle that when used to slice a man into two, one remains unaware of the result until shaken, and then the two halves fall away from each other. The sword of God is of this make. Mrinmoyee did not realize when that sword had sundered her childhood from her youth. In pain and in surprise, Mrinmoyee saw that with a shake, the child had fallen away from the young girl.

In her mother's house, she no longer felt her old

bedroom to be her own; the person who inhabited it was no longer there. Now, all her heartfelt memories began humming around another house, another room, another bed.

Mrinmoyee could see no one outside. The sound of her laughter was heard no more. Rakhal took fright every time he saw her. The thought of playing together would no longer cross his mind.

Mrinmoyee said to her mother, "*Maa*, take me to my in-laws."

Elsewhere, Apurbo's mother was heartbroken when she remembered her son's sorrowful face at the time of parting. That he had, in anger, left his wife at her mother's place struck her as contrary to custom, and she took this to heart.

Days went by, and one day, Mrinmoyee, her head covered, sad faced, fell at her mother-in-law's feet. The mother-in-law, tears glistening in her eyes, clasped Mrinmoyee to her bosom. In a flash, the two were united. The mother-in-law was astonished when she gazed at her daughter-in-law. The Mrinmoyee she knew was gone. Such a drastic transformation was rarely seen. Big changes required a big force.

The mother-in-law had thought that she would correct Mrinmoyee's faults one after the other, but now, it seemed that a providential corrector, using a secret and abridged method, had given birth to Mrinmoyee anew.

Now, Mrinmoyee understood her mother-in-law who in turn could recognize her; the way the branches hang from a tree, so all the qualities of a housewife were gathered in Mrinmoyee, in one fell swoop.

Here, a profound, refreshing, huge feminine character that was Mrinmoyee's waxed, line after line, upon Mrinmoyee's entire body and entire soul, and this somehow began to torment her. Like the first dark cloud of June, in her heart, there stirred a tearful, all-pervasive, wounded pride. That wounded pride threw over her long, shadowy, eyelids another deeper shadow. She said to herself, "I could not understand myself, but why couldn't you understand me? Why didn't you punish me? Why didn't you shape me according to your wishes? Demon-me! When I didn't want to go to Calcutta with you, why didn't you forcibly drag me there? Why did you listen to me, accede to my request, tolerate my rebelliousness?"

And then, in the morning, on the deserted banks of the pond, when after capturing her, Apurbo had wordlessly looked at her face, when she thought of that path, that tree, the light of that morning, and the heartfulness of that deep gaze, she understood completely the meaning of that gaze. And then, on the day of his departure, the kiss she had tried to plant on Apurbo, but had eventually moved her face away from, the incomplete kiss, like a thirsty bird on its way towards a mirage, she now continually chased that lost opportunity, but never was her thirst slaked.

Now, with increasing frequency, would arise in her heart, the words, "If only I had done this, or said that, at that time, if only it had happened thus."

Apurbo was angry that Mrinmoyee had not known who he was completely. Mrinmoyee, too, sat and thought, "What did he take me for, what did he understand of me?" He only knew her as an uncontrollable, fickle, unthinking, uncomprehending girl, not as a complete woman capable of satisfying the thirst of love with the flowing nectar of the heart, and this tormented her; she, said fie upon her, with regret and shame. And she began to acquit herself of the debt of a kiss on Apurbo's pillow. Some days passed thus.

Apurbo had said, "If you don't write to me saying so, I won't return home." Remembering this one day, she closed the door to her room, and sat down to write to him. She took out the coloured paper with a golden border, and sat down and thought. Very carefully, the lines, bending, ink on her fingers, and in letters at times big and at other times small, with no formal greeting on top, she wrote, "Why don't you write to me? How are you, and come home." She couldn't think of anything else to say. She had said all she wanted to say, but in our society of men, it is necessary to be a bit more elaborate in expressing what is in the mind. Mrinmoyee too, understood that, which is why she took some more time to think and added a few more new things to say—"Now you write to me; write to me how you are and come home. *Maa* is well, Bishu and Putu are also well; yesterday our black cow had a calf." And she finished her letter on that note. She inserted the paper in an envelope, and placing a dot above every letter, with love in her heart, she addressed her letter to, 'The Honourable Sir Apurbokrishno Ray'. Howsoever much may have been the love, the lines were not straight, the letters were ill-proportioned, and the spellings erratic.

Mrinmoyee did not know that one had to add something after the name. Embarrassed at the thought of the letter falling into the hands of her mother-in-law, or someone else in the family, she arranged to have the letter posted by a trusted servant.

Needless to add, this letter bore no fruit. Apurbo did not come home.

## VIII

The mother-in-law saw that it was vacation time, and Apurbo hadn't come home. She thought Apurbo was still angry with her.

Mrinmoyee had concluded that Apurbo was irritated with her, and then remembering her letter, she nearly died of shame. That letter was so trivial; it said nothing of consequence and did not contain the slightest expression of what she felt. Apurbo must surely have considered her a child having read Mrinmoyee's letter, breeding more contempt in his heart for her. Whenever Mrinmoyee would think of all of this, she would grow fidgety and desperate, as if pierced by an arrow. She would call the servant and ask her, again and again, "Have you dropped that letter off at the post office?" The servant would reassure her, a hundred times over, "Yes, of course, I dropped it in the box myself. *Babu* has surely received it by now."

At last, Apurbo's mother called Mrinmoyee to her side and said, "It's been a while since Apu came home. I am thinking, how about going to Calcutta and visiting him over there? Will you come?" Mrinmoyee, with a nod of her head, signifying willingness came back to her room, shut the door behind her, fell on the bed, clasped the pillow to her bosom, laughed, fidgeted about, and liberated the feelings within her. After which, she grew pensive, sad, was seized with anxiety, and sat down to cry.

Without telling Apurbo anything, these two penitent women set off for Calcutta to beg for Apurbo's pleasure. Apurbo's mother went and put up at her son-in-law's place.

That same evening, disappointed at not receiving any letter from Mrinmoyee, Apurbo went back on his pledge and sat down to write to her. Nothing he could say pleased him. He was looking for a greeting in which there would be love but hurt pride as well; not finding one, his lack of respect for his mother tongue grew more firm. Then, he got a letter from his brother-in-law: "Mother has come.

Come quickly and have dinner with us. All is well." Despite this last assurance, Apurbo could not shake off the feeling of dread and remained unconsoled. Going to meet his mother without delay, he asked, "*Maa*, is everything okay?" His mother said, "Everything is okay. Why didn't you come home for the holidays? I have come to take you back with me."

Apurbo said, "Where was the need to bother yourself like this? I was preparing for my exams." Etc.

At mealtime, his sister asked, "*Dada*, why didn't you bring your wife with you this time?"

The brother, in a serious tone, began saying, "I am studying law, etc."

His brother-in-law laughed and said, "All that is a lame excuse. You are scared of bringing her over."

His sister said, "A frightening character indeed. Seeing a boy, she might suddenly take fright."

And so they went, the pleasantries back and forth, but Apurbo remained disconsolate. He took no pleasure in the conversation. He felt since his mother had come to Calcutta, Mrinmoyee, too, had his mother so wished, could easily have accompanied her. Perhaps his mother had even tried to bring her along, but she was not willing. Feeling inhibited, he refrained from questioning his mother on the subject—man's life and the spectacle of the world seemed to him full of delusions.

After the meal, a furious wind started to blow,

and it began to rain.

The sister said, "*Dada*, stay the night over."

The brother said, "No, I have to go back. I have some work."

Apurbo's brother-in-law said, "What kind of work is it that you do at night? If you stay over, you are not answerable to anyone; why worry?"

After a lot of cajoling and coaxing, and in spite of his dogged disinclination, Apurbo at last, consented to staying the night over.

His sister said, "*Dada*, you look tired; don't tarry any longer; come, go to bed."

Apurbo felt likewise. Tired of arguments and counterarguments, he was relieved to be able to at last be alone in a bed in the darkness.

Coming to the bedroom, he saw the place was dark. His sister said, "I see the lamp has been extinguished by the wind. Should I fetch another, *dada*?"

Apurbo said, "No, I'll manage, I don't keep the lamp on at night."

His sister having left, Apurbo groped his way in the darkness towards the bed.

As he was preparing to go to bed, he suddenly heard the jingling noise of bangles, and a tender arm embraced him tightly, and a pair of lips, soft as the petals of a flower, locked onto his mouth with a bandit force in a kiss that was dense, moistened with tears, leaving

Apurbo no time for even surprise. Apurbo was, at first, taken aback, and then he understood that a long-since incomplete and laughter-bound attempted kiss had been brought to an end today in a flood of tears.

*Ashwin,* 1893

# A Suitable Boy and a Suitable Girl

Hitherto, the Creator had never graced my forehead, but once he had inhabited the lotus of my mind. I was sixteen. And then, just as a light sleep, once disturbed, is followed by durable sleeplessness, so was my condition. Some of my friends, in the matter of taking a wife, were promoted twice, even thrice; while I had to content myself among bachelorhood's last benches, counting the joists of my empty household.

I had passed the entrance exam at the age of fourteen. At that time, no one took age into account either for the entrance, or for marriage. I had never swallowed a textbook in my life and thus never had to suffer from mental or physical indigestion. Just as a rat tears to bits anything it can set its teeth on, whether edible or not, so, as a child, I would read any book I could lay my hands on; such was my nature. In the world, there are more unread books than read; thus, in the solar system of my world, the earth of my schoolbooks was a million times smaller than the sun of my non-school books. Yet, despite the dire predictions of my Sanskrit teacher, I passed my exams.

My father was a deputy magistrate, and we were living in Satkhira, or in Jehanabad, or in some such place. It's better to say at the very outset, that any clear mention of time, place, and characters in my story would be a clear lie; and those whose curiosity outstrips their taste will be cheated. *Baba* had gone out for an investigation. *Maa* was keeping one of her ceremonial vows; she required a Brahmin, both for the ritual and for the preparation of the feast. For such spiritual needs, our family priest was *Maa's* principal resource. Because of this, *Maa* was especially grateful to him; even though *Baba* entertained the exact opposite sentiment regarding the person.

In the matter of gifts and fees, at the end of the feast, I too figured on the list of beneficiaries. In essence, the discussion that had taken place on the subject was that—it was time for me to go to college in Calcutta. It was therefore necessary to find a means to avoid the pain of being separated from one's son. If a child bride played in my mother's lap, she could spend her days in educating and nurturing her. Kashishwari, the priest's daughter, was suitable for this—for she was a child, well-behaved, and the sums of her horoscope matched mine, sum for sum. Besides, there was the attraction of the spiritual fruit involved in relieving a Brahmin of the burden of having to support a daughter.

*Maa* was agitated. The moment she let it be known that it was her duty to take a look at the girl, the priest jumped in and said that his 'homemaker' had arrived with the girl just the night before. *Maa* didn't lose any time in taking a liking for the girl; for when taste and spiritual merit were weighed together, the choice proved to be well-balanced. *Maa* said, "the girl has all the favourable signs—that is, even though she was not exactly good-looking, there was quite some room for consolation."

I heard the word through the grapevine. The very priest, whose material form I had gone in fear of up to that point, had come with a marriage proposal on behalf of his own daughter—this incongruity was what at first attracted me. Like a fairy tale, suddenly, the chapter on case endings, having shed all nasal and spirant accents, the girl was transformed into a princess.

One evening, *maa* called me to her room and said, "My dear son, there are sweets and mangoes from the pundit's house; have some."

*Maa* knew that if she fed me twenty-five mangoes, another twenty-five would complete the line of the verse, and then, only then, would I be able to find the rhyme. Which is why she had chosen the juicy, gustatory means of the tongue to summon me. Kashishwari sat in her lap. My memory is no longer as sharp, but I remember—she was olive-complexioned. Her eyebrows were thick, and her eyes were those of a domesticated animal, gazing without inhibition. I don't remember the rest of her face—I think that it awaited finishing in God's factory; only the rough cast had been done. Whatever else she may have been, she looked like a nice person.

It made my bosom swell. I said to myself, 'This tinsel and jacket-wrapped commodity was entirely mine—I am her lord; I am her god. For other rare commodities, one had to strive and strain after them, but not for this unique object. I just had to wag my little finger, and God would grow importunate in his desire to grant me this boon.' I had seen my mother, and therefore, knew what the word 'wife' was supposed to mean. I had seen that *Baba* was always cross about all other vows, but as far as the *Savitri* vow of chastity and devotion to the husband was concerned, no matter what he openly said, in his heart of hearts he would delight in it. I knew *Maa* loved him. But *Baba's* sense of being a man would be most satisfied, most contented to know that *Maa* feared the things that would make him angry and irritate him. The gods are probably indifferent to the practice of worship, because that is their legitimate due. But for men, it is illegitimate, which is why it destabilises them. The attraction exercised by the looks and the qualities of that girl did not affect me, but that I was worthy of worship, stirred the fourteen-year-old man in me. That day, I ate the mangoes with a great deal of pride, even setting aside three to show off, something that has never occurred before in my life; as a result of which the entire afternoon was passed in regret.

That day, Kashishwari was not informed in what category fell her relationship with me—but she undoubtedly learned of it no sooner than she had reached home. Thereafter, whenever we met, she would hurry up and look for a place to hide. I liked her distress upon seeing me. That my appearance would cause, in some place, in some form, the communication of a profound influence; this biochemical fact would please me no end. That someone should take fright or feel ashamed or do something upon seeing me would inform me by running away that she was, in this world, especially, completely and mysteriously, mine.

Having been suddenly elevated to this place of honour after long years of insignificance, my blood started ringing in my ears. The way *Baba* had made *Maa* anxious about not committing an error while carrying out her household chores, cooking up a meal, or making arrangements for this and that, I too, began tracing an outline of the same picture. The way *Maa* would use, very carefully, diverse and pleasing skills to secure a goal that *Baba* disapproved of, I saw Kashishwari, in my imagination, resorting to the same means with regard to me. At times, in my mind, I would see myself giving, fearlessly and suddenly, anything from a fat wad of banknotes up to diamond jewellery to her. On certain days, I would see her, in my mind's eye, sitting down to eat but unable to partake of food, sitting by the window and wiping her tears with the loose end of her sari, and I cannot say that I found this lamentable. *Baba* was very strict about developing qualities of self-reliance in his son, keeping one's room neat and tidy, one's clothes properly folded and stacked. I had to do everything on my own. The images of the householder's condition that emerged in my consciousness, I am describing one of them below. Needless to add, in the history of my parents, just such an incident had previously occurred; there is no originality in my imagination in this respect. The image was—around noon, on a Sunday, after lunch, I would be lying propped up on a pillow in a somnolent posture, legs spread out, reading the newspaper, the nozzle of the hookah in my hand. The nozzle would fall from my hand. In the verandah, Kashishwari would be dealing with the laundry with the laundryman, and I would call her. She would run towards me and restore the nozzle to my hand. I would tell her, "See, in the living room, on the third shelf of the the almirah to the left, there is a thick book in English with a blue cover; bring it to me." Kashi would bring me a blue book. I would say, "No, not this one! The one I'm asking for is thicker, and on its spine its name is inscribed in gold." This time she would bring me a green book—which I would let drop with a thud on the floor and get up angrily. Kashi's face would seem to shrink, and her eyes would well up. I would go and see that the book is not on the third shelf, but on the fifth. Carrying the book in my hand, I would come to my room and, without a word, lie down on my bed. I would not utter a word about my mistake to Kashi. Head bowed, sorrowful, she would resume her dealings with the laundryman, and would not forget to hold herself culpable of having disturbed through lack of intelligence, her husband's repose.

Baba was investigating an incident of banditry, and my days were passing thus. And here, in relation to me, the pundit's behaviour changed in a moment from the active voice to the impersonal voice and this was, exceedingly, a friendly voice.

And then the banditry probe was over, and *Baba* came home. And I knew that *Maa*, slowly, taking her time, through many convolutions, would be serving *Baba* his favourite vegetable dish, and at the same time, gradually making it a bit more bearable, would be ready to broach the topic. *Baba* despised the pundit as a mercenary. *Maa* must have firstly, mildly criticised the pundit, and yet, praised to the skies the man's wife and daughter by way of laying the foundation for the word to come. But unfortunately, due to the pundit's overjoyed, garrulous reaction, the news had spread in all directions. He had let everyone know that the marriage had been arranged, and talks were in progress to fix the date. He had even gone so far as to discuss at the appropriate place, and how many days he would need the head clerk's room during the marriage festivities. Everybody had agreed to help him bring off this happy occasion successfully. The lawyers in Baba's court had agreed to defray the expenses incurred for the wedding by way of a donation drive. The third son of the secretary of the local entrance school, who was in the third grade, had already written, in the *tripadi* meter, a poem based on the moon and the white lotus. And the secretary had recited that poem to whomever he could get hold of in the street or elsewhere. The people of the village nursed fond hopes for the boy.

Therefore, upon returning, *Baba* was given the good news even before entering the house. After that, *Maa's* tears and refusal to touch food, everyone dazed with fear, the arbitrary fining of the servants, the bench dismissing the matter with expedition and decreeing summary punishment, the sacking of the pundit, and his disappearance along with Kashishwari and her tinsel-wrapped plaits—and before the holidays were over, the separation from *Maa* and my forcible exile to Calcutta, all followed in due course. My heart collapsed like a punctured football—its jumping about in the air from sky to sky stopped completely.

## II

Beginning with this obstacle at the very beginning in the way of my marriage, the Creator's malign favour was shown to me again and again. I don't feel like giving an elaborate description of this—I'll just leave one or two brief notes on the subject of my failure. At the age of twenty I had cleared, at a lively pace, my M.A. examination, put on a pair of spectacles, and had grown a moustache long enough to be twirled. *Baba* was in Rampurhat, or in Noakhali, or in Barasat or in some such place. This time I had churned an ocean of words and secured a gem of a degree, now it was time to churn an ocean of money. *Baba*, in trying to contact his high-placed patrons, saw that his biggest, most important contact had departed this world; the next in line was in pensioned retirement in Ol' Blighty, and the next had been transferred to the Punjab, and the one remaining in Bengal gave hope to every candidate in the introduction, only to let them down in the conclusion. When my ancestor was deputy magistrate, my guardian's market was not so constricted; whence the sequence from salary to pension and from pension to salary ran in the same family, it was like crossing on a ferry. The times have changed, and things are no longer so easy, which is why my father was thinking with a lot of anxiety whether his descendant should descend from the high cage of government employment to the lower rungs of a mercantile ladder when the only daughter of a rich brahmin came to his notice. The brahmin was a contractor, and the way he made money was known to be more due to the depths of the netherworld, than to the manifest face of the earth. At this time, he was busy distributing oranges and other gifts in suitable vessels on the occasion of Christmas when I made a sudden appearance in his locality. *Baba's* house was right in front of his; a road ran between the two houses. Needless to say, the postgraduate son of the deputy magistrate was a 'worthy fruit' for the one who would give away his daughter. Which is why the contractor was arms outstretched where I was concerned. His arms were pendulous with the weight of half-crowns, which I have already mentioned—at the very least those arms reached the deputy magistrate's heart effortlessly. But my heart aimed higher still.

My age was then touching twenty; I was greedy for a precious woman; no other precious thing could satisfy me. Not only that, the glow of sensitivity was also still alive in my heart. In other words, the meaning I attached to the word 'wife' was different from that prevalent in the market. In our time, in our country, a household was under constraint on all sides; when it came to thinking and contemplation, the mind was generously afforded the space for knowledge and thought, but when it came to conduct, that same world was reduced to slender means and petty dimensions. This I could not tolerate in my mind and heart. The woman whom I wanted as a companion on my journey towards the ideal, I was not willing to accept that that woman would be a mere housewife, living behind bars, who would place shackles on my feet and at every turn, and hold me back with a tinkling sound. No, such an ill-boding star I could not accept. Truth be told, in our country's farcical world, those who are mocked as modern, I had emerged fresh from college as just such a dense modern person. In our time, we moderns were more numerous than those found these days. What was surprising was that we really believed that conforming to social norms was to plunge straight into hell, and to resist was progress.

There I am, Mr Sanat Kumar, washed up against the wide-open mouth of a bag of money proffered by a powerful giver away of daughters. *Baba* said, "*Subhasya sheeghram*, it's best to hurry up." I held my tongue and thought to myself, 'Let's play this carefully.' I kept my eyes and ears open—I saw some in good measure; I heard much more. The girl was as small as a doll and pretty—the rules of character that had prepared her for this did not show on her face—it was as if somebody had parted every strand of hair on her head, down to her eyebrows; she had been built brick-by-brick. She could recite praise texts on the Ganges in Sanskrit. Her mother, it seems, would cook only on fires kindled by coal washed in the water of the Ganges; the world that was the abode of creatures held many, many castes, and thus she was careful of all contact with the world; most of her dealings were with water because fish were not Muslims, and onions did not grow on water. The supreme task of her life was to purify and refine her body, her house, her clothes, her pots and pans, her beds, and her crockery. The completion of all these tasks would keep her busy till 2:30 in the afternoon. She had with her own hand, and in full measure, so purified her daughter that the latter had no opinion to call her own. In any situation, no matter how difficult, one can all the more easily conform to rules if valid reasons for the same are not explained. She didn't wear good clothes while eating lest they be soiled; she had learnt to judge even shadows. Just as she would bathe while remaining inside her palanquin, so she could move around in the world surrounded by the eighteen *Puranas*. Even my mother, who had enough reverence for customary wisdom and laws, couldn't tolerate the fact that someone else had more respect than her, and that that person would secretly take pride in that respect. That is why when I told her, "*Maa*, I am not a worthy prospect for this girl," she laughed and said, "No, it's not easy to find someone for her in the *Kali* age."

I said, "Then I can leave?"

*Maa* said, "Why, Sunu? Didn't you like her? She's so good-looking."

I said, "A wife is not meant just to be stared at; she must also be intelligent."

*Maa* said, "Just listen to him! What proof of lack of intelligence have you found in the meantime?" I said, "An intelligent person would be unable to live with these meaningless, worthless things day and night. He would die asphyxiated."

*Maa's* face shrank. She knew that my father had almost committed to this marriage with the other party. She also knew that *Baba* frequently forgot that the other person may have something called a wish of his own. In brief, if *Baba* hadn't displayed such anger and tried to force things upon me, I might, in course of time, have settled for that puranic doll and, one day, showing steely resolve in the mumbling of daily prayers and the taking of baths and keeping of vows, have achieved final beatitude on the ghats of the Ganges. In other words, if arranging this marriage had been up to *Maa*, then she would have taken her time, proceeded with utmost caution, occasionally uttering a few meaningful words into the ear, occasionally shedding a few tears, and she would have accomplished her purpose. When *Baba*, furious, began to roar and thunder—and only to roar and thunder—I said, rather desperately, "From childhood, you have taught me to be self-reliant in all my doings; then does it mean that in the sole matter of marriage self-reliance will not do?" Save while passing the paper on logic in college, I have never seen anyone succeeding on the sole basis of the law. Close reasoning has never doused the flames of a bad argument; on the contrary, it's like pouring oil on it. In *Baba's* mind, he had given his word to the other party, and there could be no greater proof of the justness of this marriage. If I had reminded him that *Maa* too had, once, given her word to the pundit, and yet not only did that marriage not take place, but the pundit's livelihood also had died with it—then, on this occasion, it might have set up a criminal case. That, compared to intelligence and taste, sacred formulas and rituals are a great deal better; its poetry is profound and beautiful, its integrity is much greater, its fruit excellent, that symbolism is idealism. These were the matters that *Baba* had me hear at times, both appropriate and inappropriate, and had discussed with me. I held my tongue, but I could hardly silence my mind. The thought that would come to the tip of my tongue and be turned away was, "If you accept all this, then, while breeding, why do you breed chickens?" Another thing would come to my mind: it was *Baba* who, at times, upon suffering inconvenience or loss due to the fixing of auspicious dates, the celebration of festivals, the laying down of what is done or not done, and the giving of alms and gifts, had harshly dealt with *Maa* over the futility of these things. *Maa*, accepting her wretchedness, implying that women, being the feebler sex, were naturally lacking in judgment, and lowering her head had warded off the first blow of irritation, immersed herself in the elaborate task of feeding brahmins. But the Maker had not made creatures by pouring them into the solid mould of logic. Therefore, you cannot win over somebody by pointing out that they are not consistent in their saying or doing, but maybe you can make them angry. If one swears by the law, injustice increases correspondingly—those who are politically minded or respectful towards domestic agitation, they too should keep this matter in mind. When a horse thinks the carriage behind him is unjust and uses a stick to beat it with, then not only does the injustice remain intact, but he also hurts and wounds his own leg. Carried away by youth and arguing a bit, my condition was similar to the horse above. Thus, I saved myself from having to marry that mythomaniac girl, but I also had to lose the protection of my father's modern treasury. *Baba* said, "Go and be self-reliant."

I touched his feet and said, "Your wish is my command."

*Maa* came and sat weeping.

*Baba* had shown a lack of interest, but, with *Maa* coming in the way, the money order peon would be seen from time to time. The cloud had stopped raining, but clandestinely, the anointment by the dew of pleasant nights continued. I started a business on the strength of that anointment. The foundation was laid with exactly seventy-nine rupees. Today, the capital of that business, though much less than an envy-driven rumour would have it, is not less than two million rupees.

The Creator's factotums began swirling around me. The gates that were shut before had henceforth their bolts drawn. I remember, under the spell of an irresistible ambition, my heart had gone out towards a sixteen-year-old girl (I have made the age a bit more bearable, keeping in mind the sensibilities of readers today); but I was informed that the girl's mother was aiming for a well-placed civilian—she would not settle for anything less than a barrister. I was below the zero point. But later, in the same house, on another day, I stayed not only for tea, but for lunch the next day as well, and played whist with the girls at night after dinner and heard from their mouths an English spoken only by the elite of the country. My difficulty was that my English had been honed on Russel's *Deserted Village* and Addison and Steele, I was not up to keeping up with these girls. Exclamations such as 'O my, O dear, O dear,' would not slip off my tongue in the correct intonation. Given my knowledge of the language, I could at most use it to buy and sell things in the market, but at the thought of carrying on an amorous conversation in twentieth century English, it is my love that ran away. On the other hand, given their extreme scarcity of Bengali, carrying on a genteel conversation in the fashion of Bankim Chatterjee would lead to fraud and cheating. Just wages would be denied. Be that as it may, these hoity-toity girls were once easily available to me. But the wondrous world I had peeped at through closed doors vanished entirely, when the door was opened. Then I had the feeling that our vow-keeping girls, those who were caught up in the constant repetition of meaningless rituals, and who satisfied their stunted minds with it, were not much inferior to those girls who, with the same stunted intelligence, circumambulated the most trifling symbols of English ways and manners day after day, year after year, spending their days in these pursuits, effortlessly and indefatigably. Just as the first would, at the slightest infringement of touch and hygiene go into paroxysms protesting disrespect, so the latter would, at a failure of accent, or in the manipulation of cutlery, grow suspicious of the person's humanity. One is a native doll, the other is an English doll. They are not moved by the heart; they are wound up by habit and, thus, are moved. As a result, little by little, I came to despise the female species itself; I decided that since they were so lacking in intelligence, how could they survive the great non-actions of bathing, mouth-washing and fasting. I had read in a book that there is a species of microbe that constantly goes around in circles. But man doesn't; so, man walks straight ahead. Has God ordained that men should marry an enlarged version of that microbe?

Meanwhile, as I grew older, my hesitation regarding marriage grew apace. There is an age in man's life when he can marry without thinking. To marry beyond that age requires a bit of courage. I am not a part of that reckless gang. What I could never understand is why any normal woman would marry without any reason and, in one breath, a man such as I? I had heard that love is blind, but, here, there was no burden on this blind one. There are eyes other than the two eyes of worldly wisdom—when those eyes look upon me without intoxication, what do they see, I wonder? I probably have good qualities, but those are not quickly detected; they are not understood at a glance. I know that the shortness of my nose is compensated by the development of my intelligence, but it is the nose that is explicit, and God has decreed that intelligence remain amorphous. Be that as it may, when I see that a nubile young woman has not the slightest objection to marrying me at the shortest of notices, then my respect for women goes down further. If I were a girl, then with a big sigh emitted by Mr Sanat Kumar's short nose, her hope and her honour would be pulverised.

In this way, the weightless boat of marriage at times would come ashore without reaching the port. The other elements of a womanless household went on increasing with the success of my business. I had forgotten one thing—I was growing older. And all of a sudden, an incident reminded me of it.

I had gone to inspect a mica mine in a Chotanagpur town, where I saw that my old Sanskrit pundit had built a house in the shade of *sal* trees, by the banks of a small river. His son worked there. My tent was pitched in that *sal* forest. I was famous, throughout the country, for my wealth. The pundit said that he knew that over time I would become someone out of the ordinary. Maybe, but he had kept it a secret, well-hidden to a surprising degree.

Besides, I can't say how he had this foreknowledge. Perhaps people out of the ordinary know nothing about nothing as students. Kashishwari was at her in-laws, which is why there was no hindrance to my becoming a part of the pundit's house. His wife had died a few years ago—but he was surrounded by granddaughters. All of them were not his own; two of them belonged to his late brother. The old man had adorned, through them, the twilight of his life in varied colours. The flow of Amaru's hundred stanzas of *Arya Saptasati*, of *Hamsadoot*, of *Padankadoot*, of the shlokas of all these works, with the force of pebbles scattered in all four directions by the leaping foam of a mountain stream, swirling around these girls, produced a sound as of laughter.

He said, "In your English treatises, it is said that Saturn wears a garland of moons—this is my garland of moons."

What I saw at this poor man's house reminded me, in an instant, of my own loneliness. I understood that I had grown weary of my own burden. The pundit didn't know that he had grown old, but I knew I had. To grow old is to understand that one has lived through everything, that things are slackened on all sides, and there are gaping holes left behind. Those holes cannot be covered with money or fame. I was getting no fun out of life; I was just accumulating objects, the futility of which it is possible to forget through habit. But when I saw the pundit's house, I understood that my days were dry and my nights a void. The pundit is surely convinced that I am the more fortunate man—and at this thought, I laughed. Surrounding this world of things, there is a world of joy. If we are not suspended in the void like Trishanku, that was the difference between us. Placing my legs on the arms of the easy chair, pulling on my cigarette, I began thinking that of the four stages in a man's life, each has its own guardian deity. In childhood, the mother; in youth, the wife; as an adult, his daughter, daughter-in-law; and in old age, granddaughters, or granddaughters-in-law. Thus, it was through women that men made themselves whole. In the rustling *sal* forest, this fact overwhelmed me. Before me, I kept my prospective old age and saw its end—seeing its extreme sterility produced in my heart a howl of despair. On that desert trail, carrying the weight of profit, I would have to stagger and fall, face down, and die. It won't do to delay matters any further. I had just crossed forty—and fifty sat by the road to rob me of my last pouch of youth, I could see the point of its stick already. It was time to stop talking of the pocket and start thinking of life. But one can't go back to that part of life that was held in abeyance. Yet, it was not time to put a lock on what had been rent asunder.

From here, I had to go to a city in the west on work. There resided Biswapati *babu*, a wealthy Bengali banker. I had to discuss some work-related matters with him. The man was shrewd, and therefore arriving at a settlement with him proved to be a time-consuming matter. One day, as I thought with annoyance, "Can't get my work done through this fellow," and I had even instructed my servant to pack my things, when Biswapati *babu* came in the evening and said, "You are probably in touch with a wide variety of people, so with a little bit of care you can save the life of a widow."

The story goes thus—

Nandakishore had first come to Bareilly as headmaster of an English-medium school catering to the local Bengali community. He had done a good job. Everybody had been surprised—how could such a competent, educated man have left his home to come so far to work for such a meagre salary? It wasn't as if he was known only for getting pupils to pass exams; he had lent a hand in every good cause. It somehow came out that his wife was beautiful, but not of very reputed family. She was of lowly origins, and it was said that her touch rendered potable water unfit for consumption and other mysterious ritual purities could be polluted. When everyone one cornered him on the subject, he said, "Yes, she is low caste, but still, she is my wife." Then the question arose of how such a marriage could be considered legitimate. To the person who had put the question to him, Nandakishore *babu* said, "You have married twice with the *shalgram* as witness, and have given many proofs that a word given to two parties cannot be kept. I can't vouch for the *shalgram*, but God knows that my marriage is more legitimate than yours, legitimate at every moment, every day—I don't wish to discuss the matter with you beyond this."

The person to whom Nandakishore had addressed these words was not happy. Besides, this person's capacity for harming people was considerable. In the upshot, Nandakishore left Bareilly and had begun a legal practice in this present town. The man was very fastidious—he would rather go hungry than fight on the wrong side. Initially, he had to face some difficulties but eventually fortune smiled on him. Because the judges trusted him completely. No sooner had he built himself a house and was settling down for good than an epidemic broke out. The land was devastated. When he told the magistrate that some of those who had been entrusted with the distribution of relief materials were cheating, the magistrate said, "Where do I get trustworthy people?"

He said, "If you trust me, I am willing to shoulder a part of the responsibility."

He was given the responsibility, and it was while discharging his responsibility that one day at noon, under a tree, he died. The doctor who inspected him said that he had died of a heart failure.

I had already known the story up to that point.

In a curiously superior way, I had spoken of this at our club. "People like Nandakishore," I had said, "who had failed and withered away in life—left neither name nor money behind—they are God's assistants and take the world to a higher—"

Having said this much, like a boat in full sail running aground on a sandbar, my words remained incomplete. Because, amongst us was one very wealthy person of great repute, who was reading the newspaper—he looked at me over his spectacles and said, "Hear hear!"

Let that be. We heard that Nandakishore's widow and daughter had taken up residence in that locality itself. The girl was born on the night of Diwali and, therefore, her father had named her Deepali. The widow, not finding a place in any sort of social set, had given the girl an education on her own and had raised her. The girl was over twenty-five years old. Her mother was ailing, and she was quite advanced in age—she could die at any moment, and her girl would be left to fend for herself in a hostile environment. Biswapati had specially appealed to me, "If you can find a suitable boy for this girl, it would be a meritorious act of charity."

I knew Biswapati to be a worthless, selfish dolt and didn't respect him in my heart of hearts. Still, my heart melted upon learning of his commiseration with the widow's daughter. I thought, if edible grains that had been extracted from the digestive tract of a long-dead mammoth can grow shoots, a man's humanity might not die completely even after having been buried under a heap of corpses.

I told Biswapati that I knew someone, "I know someone; there won't be a problem. Go ahead and fix a date."

"But without seeing the girl—"

"No need."

"But if he is after property, he will be disappointed. After the mother dies, he will get that house and a bit more; that's all."

"He has his own property; don't worry about that."

"His name and other details—"

"I won't disclose that now; the marriage may be jeopardised if people come to know about it."

"I'll have to tell the girl's mother something about him."

"You'll say the person is like any other, with ordinary virtues and vices. The vices are not such as to cause undue worries; the virtues are not such as to arouse greed. As far as I know, the girl's parents are particularly fond of him; what the girl herself thinks is not known."

When Biswapati *babu* expressed his gratitude, my reverence for him grew manifold. The deal over which hitherto I had been unsatisfied as to its cost, I was encouraged enough to sign a contract even though I would thereby incur a loss. He said while taking leave, "Tell the boy he won't find a more accomplished girl anywhere."

Would a woman deprived, by society, of shelter and respect, be miserly in devoting herself to a man who installs her in his heart? The woman who harbours great expectations is perennially expectant. But the lamp of this Deepali is earthen, it would not be disregarded in a corner of my own earthen house.

In the evening, I was reading an English paper by the light of a lantern when I was informed that a girl had come to see me. There are no women in my house, so I was a bit fretful. Before I could devise a decent means of dealing with the situation, the girl entered the room and touched my feet. It may not be obvious to everyone, but I am a very shy person. I neither looked at her nor addressed a word to her. She said, "I am Deepali."

Her voice was sweet. Picking up the courage, I looked at her; that face shone with intelligence and tenderness. Her head was uncovered—her sari was of plain white cotton of the local make but worn in conformity to current fashion. I was thinking of what to say to her when she said, "Don't exert yourself in trying to get me married off."

Whatever else might have been the case, I had not expected such a strong objection from Deepali. I had thought that the marriage proposal had filled her mind, body, and soul with gratitude.

I asked her, "You will not marry anyone known or unknown?"

She said, "No one."

Even though my experience was in dealing with things rather than minds—especially not the minds of women, a subject I found more difficult than Bengali spelling, even as the plain sense of the word did not strike me as being truthful. I said, "The person I have chosen for you is not worthy of being dismissed."

Deepali said, "I am not dismissing him, but I won't marry him."

I said, "That man respects you from the bottom of his heart."

"But no, don't ask him to marry me."

"Okay, I won't, but can't I put you to some work?"

"If you can procure me a job as a teacher in some girls' school and take me away from here to Calcutta, I would be most obliged."

I said, "There is work. I can get you a job."

This was not the complete truth. What was I supposed to know about girls' schools? But there was no harm in establishing one.

Deepali said, "You must come to our house and discuss this matter with my mother."

I said, "I'll go tomorrow morning itself."

Deepali went away. I had to stop reading the newspaper. I took a trip to the roof and sat down on a chair. I asked the stars, "Are you, millions of miles away, silently weaving the relationships and work in the life of this man?"

At this point, without any notice, Biswapati's middle son Sripati presented himself on the roof. Here is the gist of the discussion I had with him—

Sripati was so eager to marry Deepali that he was willing to forsake society for her. His father had threatened to disinherit him if he took such a misstep. Deepali says, she is not worth accepting so much pain, dishonor, and sacrifice for. Besides, Sripati had been brought up in the lap of luxury. He would not, unlike Deepali, be able to put up with the fall from social grace and shelterlessness that is the lot of the poor. The argument was going on, and there seemed no solution at hand. By setting up another marriage proposal in the middle of this crisis, I had increased manifold the complexity of the problem. It is for this reason that Sripati was requesting me to exit the play, like the counterfoil of a proofsheet.

I said, "Since I have come in, I am not getting out. And if I exit, I'll cut the knot and exit."

The day of the marriage wasn't changed. Only the groom was changed. I had respected Biswapati's appeal, but he wasn't happy about it. I hadn't respected Deepali's request, but I understood she was satisfied. I didn't know if there was a vacancy in a girl's school, but the place of a daughter in my house was, indeed, vacant and that was filled. That a poor creature like me was not extremely useless; my wealth brought home this fact to Sripati. He set up a domicile in my house in Calcutta. I had thought that having postponed marrying for so long, I would at long last fill that void by marrying late; but I saw that if someone up there likes it, one can get a promotion even by skipping a couple of grades. Today, at the age of 55, my house is filled with granddaughters, and I have even got a grandson in the bargain. But my business dealings with Biswapati *babu* have ceased for good—he didn't like the groom.

*Poush,* 1917

# Sunday

The principal character of my story comes from an ancient line of Brahmins. As far as worldly matters go, the father understood the business of law to its core; and as far as other-worldly matters were concerned, he was pickled in the brine of the *Shakta* persuasion. He doesn't have to appear in court these days. On one side, the rituals of the faith; on the other, counselling on legal matters from within the confines of his house: He keeps these two activities satisfied parallelly, the needs of this world and the next, and he proceeds cautiously. No slip-ups on any side.

If in such a solid, ritual-bound Hindu house, through a crack, bursts forth a thorny atheist, as if by an act of God, and that foundation-and-wall-destroying mind heaves furiously against the brick and wood frame of that ancient dwelling. In the clan of this punctilious Vedic Brahmin arose a notorious iconoclast heretic, our hero.

His real name was Abhayacharan. He had rubbed off

the imprint of the clan pride in his name. He changed it to Avik Kumar. Plus, he knew that he was not your garden-variety human being. He didn't like the idea of his name being lost in a crowd, sweated out in the push and shove of the common thoroughfare.

Avik's face was surprisingly of an English mould. He was well above six feet tall, fair, with brown eyes, sharp nose, and his chin bent, as if in protest against some adversary. His fists were unfailing in their impact, and those who had had the misfortune of suffering a handshake would recommend remaining a hundred feet away from him.

His father, Ambikacharan, was not unduly bothered about his son's atheism. He had a huge precedent to go by in Prasanna Nyayaratna, his own uncle. The old Nyayaratna was a sharpshooter of argumentation; sitting in a school that taught the four Vedas, he would bombard the believers with nasals and aspirants. Hindu society would laugh and say, 'I swallowed the bombs' and there is not a dent on the solid wall of society. Hanging the cage of rituals and sacraments on the terrace, and releasing the bird of faith into the void of the sky, does not create a communal disturbance. But Avik would, on every occasion, despatch popular beliefs through a broken window in the direction of a heap of ashes. Inside the room and in all directions, the unchecked movement, in twos, of fowl always proved, through a loud clamour, the intimate attraction that the head of the family felt for them. All these impure foreign behaviours reached, from time to time, the father's ears, but the latter would remain impassive. However, those who, as friends, gave him the news were quickly shown the path to the main gate, without uproar. When the crime is not so obvious, society, in its own interest, skirts it. But eventually, Avik exceeded all limits in such a way that it became impossible to ignore his misdemeanour. Bhadrakali was the household deity; she was widely known to be very powerful. Poor Bhrigu, Avik's classmate, went in genuine fear of the goddess's displeasure. Growing intolerant and wishing to prove that his friend's devotion was, in fact, lacking in respect, Avik had committed an atrocity within the prayer room, such that his father, furious, said, 'Get out immediately; I don't want to see your face!' Such harshness, so swift in its execution, is possible only in the family of a doctrinaire Brahmin.

The son went to his mother and said, "*Maa*, I have abandoned the gods since long, and to be abandoned in such a state appears excessive. But I know that if I extend my arm through the barricades, I can get some *prasad*. There, the gods cannot do their goodness, no matter how powerful they might be."

The mother, wiping her tears, undid the knot in the loose end of her *sari* and fetched out a banknote. She said, "When I won't need this note all that much, I'll ask for it. You need a lot of force to deal with misfortune; you cannot throw a challenge to the goddess with a banknote in hand."

I must say one or two things more about Avik. In life, he had two opposite tastes: one was to repair mechanical objects, the other was painting. His father had three cars, his vehicle of choice for venturing into small towns. Avik's apprenticeship in the mechanical sciences had begun with those cars. One of his clients had a motor vehicle factory, and Avik had spent a while labouring there without pay.

Avik had gone to a government art college to learn painting. In a few days, his belief grew firm that if he continued there, his hand would become machine-like, and his head would be cast in a mould. He was an artist, something he set out to prove loudly. He organised an exhibition of his art, and the advertisement in the paper said he was India's foremost modern painter, Bengal's Titian. The louder he proclaimed, 'I am an aritst,' the more it echoed in the caves of some shallow hearts; they were overwhelmed, conquered. His circle grew large with disciples, especially female disciples. They called their opponents philistine. Or bourgeois.

Finally, fallen upon hard times, Avik discovered that the white radiance that emanated from his artist's name was, in fact, illuminated by the light reflected on it by his wealthy father's treasury, that was the reason behind the incandescent glow of his fame. He discovered another fact: being deprived of his due share of wealth had made little difference where the devotion of girls was concerned. In the ultimate analysis, the devout, eyes exorbitant, proclaimed, in a loud and gentle tone, 'Artist!' With a few exceptions, they only suspected each other of not understanding anything of art, of being, in fact, charlatans. So irritating!

In Avik's life, the aftermath is long and unclear. Wearing a dirty cap and clad in an oil-stained blue shirt and corded shorts, he worked for a while in Burn Company's factory, first as a mechanic and then as a chief mechanic. He fell in with the Muslim sailors; he lived cheaply on parathas that cost four paise each and on forbidden meat that cost even less. People said, "He's now a Muslim," he responded, "Are Muslims more important than atheists?" No sooner had he saved a little money than he returned from exile and once again took up the Bohemian life of an artist. He got a few disciples of either sex. Young girls with spectacles gathered in his studio and, in the modern, shameless way, discussed the psychology of the nude, while thick cigarette smoke hung over his disrepute. They cast sidelong glances and pointed fingers at each other, saying, "Positively vulgar."

Vibha was completely outside this group. She had met Avik right at the outset in college. Avik was eighteen; his face glowed with youth, and his leadership was recognised by all, even by his seniors.

Having been brought up within a Brahmo environment, Vibha was not inhibited in her interactions with menfolk. But, in college, there was an obstacle. Some boys had been incited to misbehave with her through laughter, glances, hints, and signals. But one day, the uncouthness of a city-bred boy expressed itself in a way she thought was overfamiliar. Coming to the notice of Avik, he dragged the boy up to Vibha and said, "Say that you're sorry." After hemming and hawing, the boy had to finally apologise. Since this event, Avik took upon himself the responsibility of protecting Vibha. And for this, he had to suffer snide remarks from many, but all this was like water off a duck's back for this broad-chested fellow. He wouldn't even acknowledge them. People gossiping made Vibha extremely uncomfortable, but at the same time, there was an adventurous joy in her heart.

Vibha's face conveyed grace rather than beauty. One could not explain logically why she was attractive. Avik had once told her, "For the uninvited, all food is sweet. But your beauty is not sweet to the ordinary person. It is meant for the artist; something that can only satisfy a Leonardo da Vinci. Inscrutable!"

Once, in a college test, Vibha had scored better than Avik; she couldn't stop her tears from flowing and could not control her rage. It was as if she had been personally insulted. She said to Avik, "Here you are, spending your days and nights making art and you fall behind in the tests; I feel ashamed of myself."

It so happened that the words were heard in the adjacent verandah and one of Vibha's friends, screwing up her eyes, made a snide remark, "I am proud in your pride, beautiful in your beauty."

Avik said to them, "Those worthies who have their wisdom by the rote don't know why I keep passing these exams devoid of prestige. You weep over my paintings, and my eyes have gone dry over your withered punditry. You will never understand because you lie blind at the feet of those who have a name, while we look down from the height of infamy."

Where art was concerned, there was keen competition between the two. That Vibha did not understand Avik's work was true. When other girls would go gaga over anything he had painted, would assemble and garland him, Vibha would be embarrassed at what she considered to be the preciosity of fools. But Avik's heart was restless with anger over the lack of appreciation on Vibha's part. His own countrymen thought his work was insane and he couldn't bear the thought that Vibha in her heart of hearts might join them. He would often imagine that one day he would go to Europe and be greeted by a chorus of triumph, and then, Vibha too, would thread a garland of victory for him.

A Sunday morning. Upon returning from the *Brahmo* temple, she found Avik sitting in her room. The brown paper used for packing books was lying in the dustbin. Avik was using a portion of it to sketch something with ink and pen.

"You here?" asked Vibha.

Avik said, "I have a valid reason, but that is of

secondary importance; the real reason might not appear valid if stated openly. Be that as it may, don't suspect me of robbery."

Vibha went and sat at her desk and said, "In such an eventuality, I shall abstain from informing the police."

Avik said, "I am always faced with the open jaws of eventualities. Seizing other people's property is often meritorious but not possible for me, lest the blame be laid at the door of pure atheism. We have to proceed more carefully than those who believe in God in order to save our god of denial from dishonour."

"You have been waiting for a while?"

"Yes, I was wrestling with an insoluble psychological problem, namely, that you are educated and appear to be intelligent, and yet you believe in God. How? I haven't found the answer to that question till now. Perhaps, coming here frequently might help me in figuring out this research problem."

"There you go making fun of my faith again."

"That's because your faith mocks me. That which separates us cuts to the bone. I cannot forgive it. You cannot marry me because the one that you believe in, I do not believe, being intelligent. But nothing stops me from marrying you, no matter the absurdities you believe in, in your uncomprehending heart. You cannot accept the race of atheists. That is the superiority of my conscience. It is you, and not any god, who is the manifest truth, and there is no god who can make me forget the truth."

Vibha sat silent. After some time, Avik explained, "Is your God like my father? Who has disinherited me?"

"Oh, just stop it!"

Avik knew what was the hard reason for Vibha not marrying. He wanted to hear it from Vibha's mouth, but Vibha stayed silent.

From her infancy, Vibha had always been her father's daughter. She had never given so much love, so much devotion, to any other man. Her father, Satish, too, had showered all his affections on his daughter. For this, her mother was jealous of her. Vibha had a pet duck, and her mother, irritated, had said, "Those creatures go on quacking all day and night." Vibha had got a sky-blue jacket made for her sari; and her mother had said, "This fabric does not suit Vibha's complexion at all." Vibha loved her maternal uncle's daughter, and wanted to attend the latter's wedding, and her mother had prevented her from going. saying, "There's malaria over there!"

Being thwarted by her mother at every step, Vibha's dependence on her father had grown deeper, more ingrained.

The mother died first. Thereafter, serving her father over a considerable period of time, was for Vibha, her only creed. The wishes of this affectionate father had become Vibha's own wishes. Satish had bequeathed all his property and possessions to his daughter, but through trustees. She was allocated a monthly allowance. The entire estate was intended for a suitable boy whom Vibha would marry. Who could this boy be in the light of her father's ideals? Vibha knew at least there was no doubt as to who would not be suitable. One day Avik brought up this matter. He had said, "The person you do not want to hurt is no more, and the one who suffers cruelly, he is alive. You are afraid of plunging the knife into the air, but you show no mercy towards this flesh and blood creature's breast."

Vibha went away weeping on hearing this. Avik understood that the argument about God could go on, but not the one about her father.

It was nearly 10 am. Vibha's niece Sushmi came and said to her, "Aunty it's late." Vibha dropped the keys into her niece's hand and said, "Take whatever you need from the pantry. I'll be with you in a moment."

The unemployed, knowing no schedules or timetables, have to toil more. Such was Vibha's household. It was because her duties towards her relatives were lightly borne that those towards non-relatives were varied and diverse. It was her habit to discharge the responsibilities of her self-constructed life by her own agency, lest servants take liberties with anyone. Avik said, "It would be unfair on your part to go away now, unfair not only to me but also to Sushmi. Why don't you give her the time for some autonomous action? Bestow dominion status on her just for today. Besides, I want to carry out an experiment on you. I have never spoken to you about work, but today I shall. It will be a new experience."

Vibha said, "Amen. Why leave it for another day?"

Avik drew a leather case out of his pocket, opened it, and showed it to her. A wristwatch.

The watch was made of platinum, the strap was of gold, the whole encrusted with diamonds. "I want to sell it to you," said Avik.

"You surprise me. Why would you want to sell it?"

"What's so surprising about it?"

Silent for a moment, Vibha finally said, "This is the watch Manisha gave you on your birthday. It seems that the pain in her heart is still beating away in there. Do you know how she suffered, put up with loose talk, and how much difficulty and expense she had to incur to give you a gift worthy of you?"

Avik said, "Yes, it is she who gave me this watch; she even saw to it that nobody knew until the last moment who had given it. But I am not an idolater who will erect an altar to it in his breast pocket and sound the gong and blow the conch shell over it day and night."

"You astound me. It's just been a few months since the typhoid—"

"Now she's beyond pleasure and pain."

"She believed till the end that you loved her."

"She was not mistaken."

"Then?"

"Then nothing. She is no more, and if her gift of love

bears fruit, is there something greater than that?"

An expression of acute pain came over Vibha's face. After a pause, she said, "Why do you have to sell it to me, of all people?"

"Because I know you won't haggle over it."

"That means I am the only one in Calcutta who is willing to be cheated?"

"That means love is happy to be cheated."

It is difficult to be angry with such a person. A loud and proud infant. He simply does not know whether there is something to be ashamed about. This is his honest folly, this way of his of leaping over the done/not done barrier with ease; this is what endears him to women. They don't find the wherewithal to reprimand him. Those who go by their sense of responsibility, women take the dust off their feet. And those who are unruly and have no time for nice distinctions between fair and unfair, women throw their arms around them.

After doing knots and crosses with a blue pencil on the desk's blotting paper, Vibha finally said, "If I have the money, I'll give it to you for nothing. But I will not buy that watch from you."

Avik, excited, exclaimed. "Alms! Had I been as rich as you, I would have taken your money as a gift and would have given a gift of an equal amount in return. It is I who am fulfilling the role of a man. Fine! Just take this watch. I'll not take a penny for it."

Vibha said, "It is in the nature of a woman to always take. There is no shame in it. But that does not mean I am taking this watch. Okay, tell me, why are you so bent on selling it?"

"So, listen. You know well that I have an extremely shameless Ford motorcar. I am fed up with its waywardness. It is only because it is me that it is not being reduced to scrap. For only eight hundred rupees, I can replace it with a Chrysler of my grandfather's generation. I can renovate it with my own skills."

"What will you do with that Chrysler?"

"I won't go and get married in it."

"And why would you even do a civilised thing like that?"

"Right! So let me ask you first—you've seen Sheila—the daughter of Kuloda Mitter?"

"I have seen her around you, everywhere, always."

"She has made a place for herself beside me by shoving another bunch out. She's so progressive. She's happy to shock a few boys from respectable backgrounds."

"Is it only that? Doesn't she want girls to feel a stab of envy in their hearts? That is not a lesser happiness."

"I have thought of that, it sounds valid coming from you. Tell me frankly, that girl's beauty is of an unjust variety, is it not? God's excesses can be called God's excesses."

"So, you do believe in God when it comes to beautiful women?"

"When one needs to criticise, then one has to set up an

adversary anyhow. Fallen on hard times, when wounded pride tugs at his sleeve, Ramprasad the mystic had set himself against the Mother Goddess and had said, "I won't call you Mother anymore." Whatever he got by calling out to the mother of gods, he may have got more by not calling out to her—meanwhile, the devotee satisfied his appetite for pungent criticism. I too have taken the name of God while criticising him."

"Criticising what?"

"I am going to tell you. I was in the car with Sheila, coming down from the football stadium, the car growling merrily along, stuffing the nostrils of pedestrians with foul smoke. At that very moment, the good dame Mrs Pakrashi—you know her, right? The one upon pronouncing whose name one chokes before highly exaggerating her status as tolerable—she was coming from somewhere in her new Fiat. She waved us to a stop and got down to exchange pleasantries with us. And from time to time, glancing furtively this way and that, took in the peeling paint on the hood and my battered footboard. Had your God been a communist, he would not have endowed women with such unequal beauty so as to cause in the street conflagrations in the hearts of persons."

"So that is why—"

"Yes, that's right; I have decided to, as quickly as possible, ride around town with Sheila on a Chrysler under the nose of the good dame Mrs Pakrashi, blowing my horn all the way. Tell me the truth; in your heart, there isn't the least—"

"Why are you dragging me into this? God hasn't really bothered about my looks. And as for my car it can hardly be said to be in a better condition than yours."

Avik quickly left his seat, sat down on the floor, at Vibha's feet, grabbed her hand and said, "Comparing who to whom! Amazing, you are amazing! I say you are amazing. I see you, and I fear that someday I will fall into the trap and start believing in your God. And then, I shall never attain salvation. I just couldn't arouse your jealousy in any way. Or at least, you did not let me know. Despite knowing—"

"Shut up. I know nothing. I only know you are an unusual fellow, you laugh at the Creator."

Avik said, "You may not open your mouth, but I am certain that you want to know the functioning of my psyche regarding Sheila. I am getting used to her at a furious pace. The way I got used to cigarettes at a young age. My head would spin, but I wouldn't let go. A bitter taste in my mouth, and pride in my heart. She knows how to intensify my craving day by day. The intoxication there is in the love of women, that is my inspiration. I am the artist, and she is the wind in my sail. Without her, my brush is stuck in a sandbar. I understand that when Sheila sits next to me, there burns a red flame in her heart; it's a red alert; its heat penetrates my nerves—'Don't blame yourself. O you who meditate, you think that is a luxury, no! No—It is a need.'"

"That's why you need the Chrysler so much!"

"Yes, I admit it. When pride is awakened in Sheila, there is a sparkle in her. That is why one has to get clothes and jewellery for women. We seek sweetness in women; they seek wealth in us. It is wealth's golden glow that is the background to their illumination. This is the trick nature plays to lift men up to greatness."

"It may be true. But the argument is over what constitutes true wealth. Those who say Chrysler is wealth, I think they are belittling men."

Avik, now agitated, exclaimed, "I know, I know, what you call wealth, you could have taken me to its ultimate summit. Your God came and stood blocking the path."

Vibha freed her hand from Avik's grasp and said, "Don't keep repeating the same thing over and over again. I have always heard the contrary. Marriage is like a noose around an artist's neck. It asphyxiates inspiration. If I could make you great, if I had that power—"

Avik shook himself out of his spell and said, "Could? But you already have! This, that this pain is mine, that is the wealth you couldn't recognise. If you had, you would have freed yourself of all religious shackles and stood next to me as a companion. You wouldn't have brooked any obstacles. The boat comes ashore, but the passenger cannot find the harbour to take him on his pilgrimage.

That is my condition. Yes, my queen bee, tell me, when will you discover me whole and complete?"

"When you will not need me any longer."

"Those are extremely hollow words. Inflated by a lot of mendacious wind. Admit it, "if you can't do without me," this utterance is recognition that your entire body and soul is anxious. Will you hide them from me?"

"Of what use is this utterance, and why should I even hide? My mind may contain anything, but I cannot live like a pauper."

"I want to, for I am a pauper. I will say; this night and day, I want, I want only you."

"And you will also say, 'I want a Chrysler.'"

"That is it, that is jealousy. The mountain, too, is levelled. May the dense fumes of jealousy rise now and then, let the embers of love be concealed within the heart's glow. Your heart is not an extinct volcano; it is the boiling Vesuvius."

Having said this, Avik stood up, lifted his hand and said, "Hurray."

"Don't be childish! Is it for this that you came so early this morning, with your plans ready?"

"Yes, for this, I admit. Otherwise, I could have found among those I have mesmerised, some to whom I could sell this watch without the pretext at an exorbitant price. But I haven't just come to you for securing a deal; I wanted to offer prayers after opening the wound of your pain at its source. I fell between two stools."

"Then do you know? Fortune doesn't always play hide and seek. But see, let me tell you something—you sometimes ask me whether the shows put on by you prick my heart or not. To tell you the truth, it does."

Avik, excited, cried out, "But that is good news."

Vibha said, "No need to get excited. This is not jealousy; this is insult. Your overfamiliar friendliness with women, this vulgar lack of inhibition; this is but an expression of your disrespect towards the feminine race. I don't like it."

"What sort of talk is this? Respect has nothing especially individual about it. Race after race, do I have to go around respecting everyone everywhere? No inspection of goods instead, wholesale respect? This is called a protection racket in business parlance, imposing an artificial tax to increase prices."

"Don't argue like a fool."

"Meaning you can argue, but I can't. That is what they say: 'The times are terrible; the women will speak, and the men will remain silent.'"

"Avi, you are just looking for an opportunity to quarrel. You know very well that maintaining a distance from women is what is civilized about men."

"Naturally maintaining a distance, or unnaturally? We are modern; we don't believe in pseudo-civilised conduct we believe in authentic nature. With Sheila, I rattle along in my old Ford; what is natural is her proximity. To keep her at arm's length would have been disrespecting what is natural."

"Avi, you all have decided on your own to attach a certain value to women and render them precious; it is out of selfishness that you do not humiliate them. If you subtract that value today, you will render your wishes cheap; you will cheat yourself. But I am lying; the modern era itself is a humiliation."

Avik replied, "I won't call it humiliating; I'll call it shameless. The Shiva of yore meditated with his eyes closed, and the *nandis* and *bhringis* of today hold a mirror and mock their own faces—what people call debunking. I was born in this age; I can't just chant '*Bom Bholanath*' and sit with an eye on my forehead; if I can make *nandi-bhringi* grimaces, I can make a name for myself today."

"Oh okay, go make grimaces all over the place to make a name for yourself. But, before that, tell me the truth on this matter: all these women who, encouraged by you, make such a big fuss over you—doesn't this blunt the sharp edge of your pleasure? What you people often call "thrill"? Don't you trample it under your foot with all your pushing and shoving?"

"Let me speak plainly then, Vi, the thing called "thrill," the thing called "ecstasy," comes before anything else; when fortune favours. But what you call pushing and shoving, that is a pawn shop, a stain here, a tear there, but it sells, cheaply. How many are wealthy enough to afford the real thing?"

"You can, Avi, certainly you can; you can afford it. But your nature is curious; you artists are fascinated by the torn things, the soiled things; you are curious about them. A thing, whole in itself, is not 'picturesque' to you. To hell with all this useless argumentation. For the time being, let's take care of the Chrysler."

Having said this, Vibha got up from the chair and went to the adjoining room. She came back and handed Avik a bundle of notes and said, "Here is your inspiration bearing the mark of John Company. Just don't ask me to take this watch of yours."

Avik continued sitting on the floor with his head leaning against the chair. Vibha quickly pulled at his hand and said, "Don't get me wrong. You need the money; I don't need it, and in such a situation—"

Avik stopped Vibha and said, "I am in need; I am tremendously in need. It is in your hands to fulfill it. What will I do with money?"

Vibha stroked Avik's hand gently and said, "What I cannot do, I will forever feel its pain. But what I can do, why deprive me of its pleasure?"

"No, no, no, never! I will take it from you and go driving around with Sheila? I had thought you would scorn such a proposal; I had hoped you would get angry."

"Why should I get angry? How long will your mischief

last? This is terrible for Sheila, not at all for you. I have seen this childishness hundreds of times, and have laughed every time. I know you cannot do without playing these games every few days. I also know that if there's any stability, you stop functioning. Maybe you want something, but you cannot bear the thought of something wanting you."

"Vi, you know me too well, which is why you remain so implacably serene. You have come to know that I love women, but it is an atheist's love; there is nothing binding about it. I won't shackle that ritual in a stone-crafted temple. I have seen scenes of florid necking with girlfriends; I am physically affected by that overwhelming effeminacy. But women are to me the goddesses of an atheist, that is, of an artist. An artist, having enjoyed, does not die; he swims, and swimming, he crosses over to the other side. I am not greedy. The woman who is jealous about me, is greedy. You are not greedy; the biggest gift of your detached heart is freedom."

Vibha laughed and said, "Stop your hosannas now. You artists are like little children; might as well take from me the toy for the new game you are planning."

"Will not happen, will not happen! Okay, let me ask a question. How did you extract this money out of your trustees' grip?"

"If I talk about it openly, you might not like it. You know I am studying mathematics with Amar *babu*."

"In everything, you want to surpass me in knowledge?"

"Don't jabber, just listen. Uncle Aditya is one of my trustees. He is himself a math medallist from the university. In his opinion, if he were to get the opportunity, he would have been the second Ramanujan. He had solved some problems and had sent them to Einstein, and I saw the answer he got. To help such an individual, one has to pay attention to his self-esteem. So, I said I wanted to study mathematics with him. He was very happy. He has put at my disposal a certain lump sum for education from the trust fund. I pay him out of that lump sum."

Hearing this, Avik's face took on a strange colour. Attempting to laugh, he said, "There are artists who, given the opportunity, might have got close to Michelangelo's beard."

"Perhaps they could have reached thus far even without the opportunity. Say now whether you will take the money from me or not?"

"The price of the toy?"

"Yes, dear, we are used to paying the price through the ages. What's wrong with that? And after that the garbage dump."

"Rest in peace, Chrysler. Let the progressive Sheila progress happily on my rattling, broken Ford. I don't feel like talking about that any further. I hear that Amar *babu* is saving money for a trip to England, where he hopes to prove that he is no ordinary man?"

Vibha said, "It is my deepest wish that that should

happen. It'll be quite the honour for the country."

Avik said loudly, "Even I have to prove the same thing, whether you wish or not. This task is easier; it's a question of logic—Art's path lies through taste; it is a private path for people of taste. It's not the Grand Trunk Road. I will not find my way in this country with its blinkered oil presses. I will go to that country where the eye is free. So that one day, your uncle is forced to admit I am not an ordinary man, your uncle and his niece—"

"Don't drag the niece into this business. She has not had to wait to find out whether you are Michelangelo's peer or not. With her, you are extraordinary without any proof. Just say whether you want to go abroad?"

"I dream of it day and night."

"So, take this money, my humble contribution at the feet of talent."

"Please, please, please, desist; I hear discord. May glory crown the efforts of the math teacher. As for me, if not this era, I will wait for the next; posterity will wait. Let me tell you—the day will come when, in the middle of the night, you will have to thrust your face into the pillow and admit, your name could have been joined to mine forever but wasn't."

"I won't have to wait till posterity, Avik, a cruel punishment has begun already."

"I don't know what punishment you are talking about, but I know that your biggest punishment is that you did not understand my art. A new age has dawned, and in the felicitation meeting you will not see me sitting in the big chair."

Avik got up and made for the door.

Vibha said, "Where are you going?"

"Have to attend a meeting."

"What meeting?"

"To organise a Durga Puja for the students during the vacations."

"You will do puja?"

"I will do puja. I don't believe in anything. In the vacuum of my non-belief, there will be no tussle for space between the 330 million gods and demons. The sky is empty so that the whimsy of all creation can be exposed."

Vibha understood that this sarcasm was directed at her God. She desisted from arguing any further, and her head held low, she sat silently in her chair.

Avik came back from the door and said, "See Vi, you are a tremendous nationalist. You dream of uniting the nation. But in a country where people murder each other over religion, it is only us atheists who have taken the sacred vow of uniting all religions. I am the saviour of India."

Vibha knows why Avik's atheism had grown so violent. She could not feel angry about this. She could not think what its outcome would be. Vibha could give whatever else she might have had, the only obstacle being her father's dying wish. That wish was not an opinion, nor a belief, nor something to argue over. It was a part of his nature. It would brook no protest. She had thought again and again of surmounting this obstacle. But at the last moment her feet would not move.

The servant came and informed her that Amar *babu* had come. Avik hastily took to the staircase. Something began twisting in Vibha's bosom. At first, she thought about telling the teacher that she wouldn't take her lesson that day. The next moment she strengthened her resolve and said, "Send him here. Ask him to take a seat. I'll be with him in a moment."

She went to the bedroom and threw herself on the bed, prone. She grabbed a pillow and cried. Having cried quite a bit, she regained her composure, splashed some water on her face and eyes, and came back to the room with a smile on her face, and said, "I'd thought of skipping my lesson today."

"You must not be feeling well?"

"No, I am fine. The truth is that the Sunday holiday is now part of my blood; sometimes its rage grows strong."

The professor said, "The holiday microbe wasn't given the opportunity of entering my bloodstream. But I'll take a holiday today. Let me explain. There is going to be an international mathematics conference in Copenhagen this year. I don't know how I came to their notice. I am the only Indian invited. I cannot possibly let go of such an opportunity."

Vibha responded with enthusiasm. "You must go."

The professor smiled a little and said, "The higher-ups who could have sent me on deputation are not willing to do so, lest I lose my wits. Therefore, their anxiety is about my well-being. If only I could find a friend who is not very bright. I am going in search of one. The collateral that I can produce for such a loan can neither be weighed on a pair of scales nor can it be tried against a touchstone. We scientists, we want solid proof before we believe anything; even the worldly ones look for proof—you cannot hoodwink a scientist."

Vibha cried out in excitement, "Don't worry, I will find a friendly soul from somewhere, maybe someone not as clever."

No solution could be found in the few words exchanged between them. They arrived at a half-baked conclusion that day.

Amar *babu* was of medium build, dark complexioned, and thin with a broad forehead, and a receding hairline. His face was pleasant to look at; one understood that he hadn't made any enemies thus far. The eyes were not absent-minded; they were what might be called fixed on unworldly pursuits—that is, when he walked on the road, it was other people's responsibility to keep him safe and secure. Friends he had only a few, but they held him in high esteem. Others who knew him turned up their nose and called him 'highbrow.' He was a man of few words, and people took that as amiability's brevity. On the whole, the public had had little to do with his life. The comforting thing about his psychology was that he had no idea of what other people thought of him.

The eight hundred rupees that Vibha had so hastily arranged for Avik, was the desperation of a blind impulse. Her uncle was firm in his belief in Vibha's character. There had never been a cause to think otherwise. Being a worldly man, he could not imagine from which direction a jolt of deviation from rules could come into a woman's life. It was upon seeing in her heart the shame and punishment for this sudden folly that Vibha, in a moment's gust of storm winds, had dedicated her offering to Avik. That gift, refused, had once again returned to the scaffolding of rules. In the present field she could not remember the audacity of her love. She could not, transgressing her rights, conceive of lending somebody money; she did not have the courage for it. That's why Vibha had planned that she would ask her mother for the jewels that would be bequeathed to her, and selling these, she would make Amar the occasion for giving back to her own country.

Those boys and girls who were being nurtured by Vibha, she helped them with their studies. Today is a Sunday. After a meal, her class had finally assembled. In the morning, she had given them a day off.

She had brought out a box, and, having spread a quilt on the floor, she was arranging her jewels one by one. She had sent for their family jewellers.

At that moment she heard Avik's footsteps on the staircase. Her first thought was to hide her jewels, but she let them be as she had arranged them. It was against her nature to hide anything from Avik for whatever reason.

Avik entered the room and regarded the spectacle for a few moments and then understood what it was all about. He said, "Money for the genius's ferry. In my case, you are Goddess Mahamaya; you lull me; with the professor you are Goddess Tara, you come to the rescue. Does the professor know that a nubile young woman with her lotus-stem-like hand is securing the means to send him ashore?"

"No, he doesn't."

"If he knew, wouldn't it hurt this scientist's male ego?"

"I only know this that a donation made by a respectful, humble person is the ungrudging right of a great man. Through this right they honour us, show us pity."

"I understand that, but a woman's jewels are meant to please us men, no matter how small we may be—not to send someone abroad no matter how big he may be. It is to our male gaze that you women have offered sacrifices right from the beginning. To match a ruby with a pearl in this necklace, I had seen this around your neck when we were little acquainted with each other. This necklace is mixed up with my first memories of you. Is that necklace only yours? It is mine too."

"Okay, let's say you take that necklace."

"A necklace taken away from your goodness would be entirely meaningless. It would be theft. My expectation is to take that whole thing along with you. Meanwhile, if you give away that necklace, you will be cheating me."

"These jewels were given to me by my mother as part of my wedding trousseau. What meaning can I ascribe to these jewels if I don't marry? In any case, don't expect to see this putative bride with ornaments on any auspicious or inauspicious date."

"I take it that a suitable boy has been found?"

"Found on the shores of the river one has to cross to reach the abode of the dead. I can do one thing. I can leave this for the girl whom you will marry."

"Should I take it that there is no road for me to take from the shores of your river?"

"Don't say that. A lot of nubile women are hanging on to you by your collar."

"I won't lie. The appeal of the collar is not altogether improbable. When catastrophe beckons, if the absence of a female companion becomes acute, it is time for the man to confront mortal danger."

"That may be so, but shortly after that, the emergence of a woman is mortal. Then that mortal danger is difficult to overcome. What people call "circumstances"."

"What one calls bondage by compulsion. The question may be hypothetical; but the possibility is so near that arguing about it would be fallacious. Which is why I say, the day you see me suddenly wearing a *lal cheli*, lucre seized from another, then—"

"Don't frighten me anymore, then I too might discover there is no dearth of others."

"Yuck, that didn't sound good from your mouth. Men call you goddesses and worship you, and when they disappear, you are willing to wither away. No one even dreams of calling a man a god. Because when they are in want, they, intelligently, go about meeting that want. They don't stand on honour. Whereas, you women, in order to save your reputation for single-mindedness, have to give your life. Let us keep the psychology aside, my proposal is—give us the responsibility for Amar *babu*'s immortality. Do we not understand how much he is worth? Why do you belittle men by selling jewellery?"

"Don't say that. The celebrity of men is a woman's principal asset. Where you are great, there we are blessed."

"Let this be the place where they are great. That is what I ardently desire when I look at you. I'll say no more on this subject; we'll talk about it some other time. There are many petty souls in Bengal who are jealous of Amar *babu*. The people of this country are a plague on the wealthy. I beseech you, don't include me among those dwarves. Listen to the great, meritoriously criminal act I have committed—the responsibility of the money raised for the Durga *puja* was placed in my hands. That money I have added to the fund for sending Amar *babu* abroad. I have done this without telling anyone. When it gets known, the devotees of the Mother Goddess will not need to run to the market for a scapegoat. I, an atheist, know what the *puja* really means. They are religious; what do they understand?"

"What have you done, Avik? Is this worthy of what you call your pure atheist creed? This is only betrayal."

"I agree. But let me tell you what weakened the foundation of my creed. My followers had resolved to celebrate the *puja* in a grand way. But the trifling sum raised was not only ridiculous but also mournful. With that, one couldn't even have successfully completed the final act of sacrificing the sacrificial lamb, the red blood of the fifth act of the performance would have faded. I had nothing against that. We had decided that with drum sticks in hand, beating the drum as best we could, with unbearable enthusiasm, we would disembowel some gourd or pumpkin with a scimitar. This was enough for an atheist but not for the faithful. One evening, without my knowledge, one of them dressed up as a fakir and five others as his disciples, and thus, they approached a wealthy widow saying the goddess Jagadamba had instructed them through a dream that barring a puja consecrated in consonance with ancient customs, with the requisite number of sacrificial victims, the goddess would consume the flesh of her son who worked in Rangoon. They wheedled her out of five thousand rupees. The day

I heard of this, that very day I put the money to good use. So, I'll lose my caste, so what? At least, the money was not ignominiously spent. So that is my confession to you. By admitting the sin, I have redeemed it. I have only twenty-nine rupees left. For meeting the expense incurred on pumpkins."

In the meantime, Sushmi came and said, "Bachchu the bearer's fever has gone up, with a cough; the doctor has written something here; take a look."

Grasping Vibha's hand, Avik said, "O benefactresss of the world, you who are engaged day and night in looking after the sick, you do not have time for the wretches who are disgustingly healthy."

"This is no charity, dear; it is to forget one wretch who is healthy that so much work elsewhere has to be fabricated. Leave my hand; let me go, sit for a while and look after my jewels."

"And who will look after my greed."

"Your atheist creed."

There was no news of Avik for a while. No letter, nothing. Vibha's face would have a stricken look about it. She would have no heart to do anything. Her feelings would be all muddled up. What has happened, what might happen, she would have no idea. The days would pass, heavy with a back-breaking weight. She would feel all the time that Avik had gone away, nursing wounded pride. Having left his parents' home, there was nothing to tie him down. Why did he suddenly disappear? Maybe he'll never come back. Her heart would only say, "Don't be angry; come back, I won't hurt you anymore." The more she recalled Avik's childishness, his lack of judgement and his obstinate, unsatisfiable demands, the more tears would stream out of her eyes—Vibha would reproach herself for being an unfeeling block of stone.

Then there was a letter with a steamer's postmark, in which Avik had written—

'I am off to England as a stoker on a ship. I am indeed saying, don't worry, but knowing you, it does make me glad. Nevertheless, let me add that I am now used to being scorched by the engine's heat. I know that you'll be angry, why I did not claim passage from you, the reason being that you don't have a shred of respect for the fact that I am an artist. This is my everlasting regret, but I won't blame you for this. I know for certain that the talented people of that evolved country will accept me with an acceptance that is of authentic value.

'Many idiots have praised my art. Also, many liars have practiced deception. You never tried to ingratiate yourself with me through feigned appreciation. Even though you knew that the slightest praise from you would be like ambrosia for me. I have only gleaned a measureless pain from the implacable truth of your character, but I have laid great store by that truth. A day will come when the world will recognise me, and that day, you will do me the truest honour, and mixed with that honour will be your heart's nectar. And as long as your belief does not arrive at an irrefutable truth, so long you will wait. With this in my heart, I have set out on this very difficult endeavour.

'You will have learnt by now that your necklace is stolen. I just couldn't bear the thought that you were going to sell it in the market. You were bent upon breaking my ribcage in order to burglarise my heart. In exchange for your necklace, I have left a collection of my paintings next to your jewellery box. Don't laugh. You won't get more than torn paper's worth for it anywhere in Bengal. Wait, my little Vi, my queen bee, you won't be cheated, never! Just like the spade suddenly uncovers a hidden treasure, I make this claim, that similarly the priceless radiance of these paintings will emerge suddenly out of nothing. Till then, laugh, because all men are children for all women—those that they love. I am on my way across the seas with my imagination full of your curious laughter. And I take with me from your honey-flavoured room a honey-flavoured ill-repute. I have seen how earnestly you pray to your God. From now on, pray thus—let the immense pain I felt on leaving you be redeemed one day.

'I do not know whether you have ever been jealous of me in your heart of hearts. It is true; I have loved women. I like women, perhaps not as much. They have loved me; I am grateful for that. But you certainly know they are a nebulous cluster, and in the middle of them all, you are the only morning star. They are a preface; you are the truth. All this might sound sentimental. I don't have a choice; I am not a poet. My words are like a raft; when hit by waves, it swing wildly. I know where the pain is deep, there one has to be serious, or else truth has no value. Weakness is restless; you have often laughed at my weakness. Finding traces of it in this letter you will laugh a little and say, 'Well, it reads like something from Avi.' But maybe this time round, you will not laugh. I have been finicky after not getting you, however it would be most unfair to say that you are ungenerous in giving your heart. Indeed, in this life my manifestation besides you could not be complete. Maybe it will never be. This acute dissatisfaction has made a beggar out of me. Which is why whether I believe anything else or not, perhaps I will have to believe in the transmigration of souls. You have not expressed your love to me in clear terms, but from the depths of your silence, what you have given me at every moment, this atheist has been unable to define—he has called it 'unearthly.' Perhaps, in some way, through this very attraction, alongside you, I have returned to your God. I am not certain of this. Maybe it's all a fabrication. But, when, unbeknownst to us, a mighty wound is sustained in a secret chamber of our heart, words have of themselves fabricated, perhaps, a truth such as we have as yet not known.

'Vi, my queen bee, I have not loved anyone more than

you in this world. If one can imagine that that love has a true role to play, and if that is what you all call God, then his blessings and your blessings are united in this atheist. I will return again—and then, my opinion, my faith, all this I will surrender, with my eyes closed, in your hands; deliver it to the last station of your pilgrimage so that with the obstacle of intelligence, I am not separated from you, even for a moment, ever. Being, today, far from you, the unthinkability of love glows bright in my heart. You have transported me beyond the thorny barricade of argumentation—I can see you in all your supernatural glory. So far, I have tried to understand it through intelligence; now I want it through everything I have.'

Your devoted atheist, Avik.

*Ashwin,* 1929

# Laboratory

Nandkishore had graduated as an engineer from the University of London. He was someone who could be considered a god-gifted student, in other words, brilliant. Beginning with his school and right up to the end, he rode in the vanguard through the portal of exams.

His intelligence was broad and his needs unrestrained, but his means were tight.

He had succeeded in insinuating himself into the task of building two bridges for the railways. The revenue and expenditure involved knew highs and lows, but the example was not appropriate. When, in this enterprise, he had not stinted in using both hands, his conscience didn't prick him. The dues and obligations related to the work of an abstract entity called 'the Company', and, therefore, personal losses or gains were not affected. In his own field, his bosses knew him to be a genius; his books were impeccable. He was not given his due remuneration only because he was a Bengali. When Englishmen, his juniors, would shove their hands deep in their well-filled pockets and say, 'Hello, Mr Mullick' while patting his back in an obviously bossy way, he didn't feel good. Especially because when it came to work, it was he, but when it came to pay and name, it was they. The upshot was that he arrived at a private estimate of how much he was worth and devised a shrewd means of satisfying it.

Nandkishore never gave himself any airs about what was due or not due. He lived in a one-and-a-half-storey house in Sikdarpara. He did not have the time to discard his shop-soiled clothes. When somebody made fun of him, he would say, "I dress as a worker should."

But for his scientific collection and testing, he had built himself a grand house. He was so absorbed in his pursuits, he had no time for what people were saying—such a tall building, where was the Aladdin's lamp to pay for it?

There is a kind of passion that takes hold of a man; it is like intoxication, one is unaware that people are pointing fingers. The man was totally free of care; he was crazy about science. While turning over the pages of a catalogue, he would grip the armrest of his chair, and his entire being would jerk and start in fits. From Germany and from America, he would order expensive instruments not available in our local universities, even prominent ones. There was pain in the heart of one greedy for knowledge. In this unfortunate country, we have to satisfy ourselves with the leftovers of the feast of knowledge. The opportunities that exist over there for the use of big machines are denied to our students, who are left with scraps gleaned from textbooks. He would jump up and cry, "We have the brains, but we don't have the pockets. We have to open the highway of science for our boys, and widen it; this is our pledge."

The more he collected expensive instruments, the more unbearable became the religious sense of his colleagues. It was the *sahib* who rescued him from this danger. He had a great deal of respect for Nandkishore's abilities. Besides, he also knew instances of skilful and hefty divergence of funds in railway work.

He had to leave his job. Having procured through the *sahib*'s good offices railway scrap at cheap rates he established a factory. At that time, the market was just heating up due to Europe's first war. Be it his extraordinary skills, he opened new channels and pathways and brought on, in this market, a flood of profit.

Then, another passion took hold of him.

Nandkishore was in the Punjab on a business-related trip. There he found himself a female companion. He was having tea in the morning in the verandah when this twenty- year-old girl, her *ghaghra* swaying, presented herself before him—her eyes were like embers—a smile on her lips, like a blade just sharpened. She came and sat at his feet and said, "*Babuji*, for the last few days I have been seeing you here morning and evening. I am really surprised."

Nandkishore said, "Why? Isn't there a zoo nearby?"

She said, "No need for a zoo. Those who should be inside, are roaming outside. So, I am looking for a human being."

"Have you found one?"

She pointed at Nandkishore, and said, "Here is one."

Nandkishore laughed and said, "What quality have you seen in me?"

She said, "The big merchants here, gold chains around their necks, diamond rings on their fingers, come and surround you—they thought, 'A foreigner, a Bengali at that, would know nothing about business. We've got a good, fat prey.' But I saw, none of their tricks worked. On the contrary, they have fallen into the trap laid by you. But they are yet to realise something that I have realised."

Nandkishore was startled by this. He understood he was dealing with something here—something not easy.

The girl said, "Let me tell you about myself; listen. In our neighbourhood, there is a well-known astrologer. He had read my horoscope and had said, 'One day the world will know about me.' He had said, 'The Devil grazes on my birthplace.'"

Nandkishore, said, "Really! The Devil?"

The girl said, "*Babuji*, do you know that this devil is the most famous person in the world? No matter how many people speak ill of him, he is most true. Our father, '*Bom*

*Bhoothnath*' is always vacant. It's not his job to run the household. Just see, the government *bahadur* has won the world through devilry, not through Christianity. But they are true, the reason why they have been able to hold their sway over others. The day they break their word; it is the Devil who will pinch their ears and put an end to them."

Nandkishore was amazed.

The girl said, '*Daddy*, don't get me wrong. There is the Devil's *mantra* in you, so you will win. I have had several men under my spell, but today I have seen someone who puts me in the shade. Don't leave me *babu*, or else you will be cheated."

Nandkishore laughed and said, "What do I have to do?"

"Being heavily in debt, my maternal grandmother's house is about to be sold. You will have to liquidate the debt."

"How much do you owe?"

"Seven thousand rupees."

Nandkishore was startled by the audacity of her demand. He said, "Okay, I'll pay it off. And after that?"

"After that I'll never leave you."

"What will you do?"

"I will see to it that, barring me, no one else can cheat you."

Nandkishore laughed and said, "Okay, that's good enough. Here, wear, my ring."

She had a touchstone in her heart—and on it appeared the trace of a valuable gemstone. He saw that from within, the girl shone the fierceness of her character—he understood that she knew how much she was worth, and this without the slightest doubt. Nandkishore said, breezily, "I'll give the money."—and he gave seven thousand rupees to the girl's grandmother.

Everybody knew the girl by the name of Sohini. Her face was of the western type, harsh and beautiful. But Nandkishore was not the man to be swayed by beauty alone. He did not have the time to gamble with his heart in the bazaar of youth.

The state from which Nandkishore had brought the girl was not quite proper or secure. But that obdurate, stubborn man set no store for worldly need or the precepts of tradition. Friends would ask, "Have you gotten married?" The answer they got was, "The marriage was one of degree, enough to be bearable." People would laugh when they saw his untiring efforts to cast his wife into the mould of his learning. People would ask, "Is she going to be a professor or something?" Nanda would say, "No, she has to do nandkishory, which is not something meant for any old girl." He would say, "I don't like inter-caste marriages."

"What are you saying?"

"The husband is an engineer and the wife is a pander, this is forbidden by the scriptures. I can see in every house that people of different castes are tying the knot; I am seeing to it that the caste matches. If you want a devoted wife, you must first match their vows.'

## II

Nandkishore died at a relatively advanced age, resulting from an accident brought on by a temerarious scientific experiment.

Sohini closed down all businesses. Fond merchants, having cheated several widows, arrived from all directions. A sprinkling of relatives laid a few legal traps. Sohini came to understand all the loopholes in the law. Besides, she spun a feminine charm in, of all places, the lawyers' locality. She displayed her unscrupulous skill in this art; there was no question of paying heed to custom. She won her cases, one after another, and a distant brother-in-law went to jail for forging title deeds.

They had had one daughter, and she had been christened Neelima. That name, the girl herself changed to Neela. No one should think that the parents had sought, through a gentle name, to smother all criticism with regard to the girl's dark complexion. The girl was in fact strikingly fair. The mother said, their ancestors were from Kashmir—the girl's body glowed as fair as Kashmir's white lotus, her eyes carried a hint of blue lotus, while her hair struck everybody as being yellowish brown.

There was no way to come to any conclusion regarding the girl's caste or clan when the subject of her marriage came up. The only way open was to steal hearts; her magic leapt over the barrier of the law books. There was a young

Marwari, his money old, his education modern. All of a sudden, he fell into Cupid's invisible trap. Neela was waiting for her car near the school's entrance. The boy had seen her there once. After this, he had, on several occasions, taken the same road. With natural feminine wiles, the girl stood at the entranceway before her car would drive up. Not only had Marwari young men from two or three communities developed the habit of taking their constitutional in the vicinity, but among them was also the Marwari who, without looking right or left, leapt straight into the net. He never came back. They got married at the registrar's on the other side of society. For not very long. For him, his wife came first, and their life as a couple was put paid to by typhoid, which, for Neela, resulted in release.

Within and without the created world, the tumult continued. The mother saw her daughter fidgeting. She remembered the burning restlessness of the volcano of her own youth. She grew anxious. With deep absorption she erected a barricade of learning. No male teacher was kept. Instead, she recruited a learned woman for the purpose. She too felt the heat of Neela's youth; it would excite her with an indeterminate, hot, and humid desire. A spellbound crowd would gather here and there. But the door was closed. Those who aspired to friendship would be invited to tea, tennis, or the cinema, but the invitations never reached their destination. In the honey-scented sky, many a greedy soul would roam, but no unfortunate miserable wretch would obtain Sohini's permission. On the other hand, the girl, curious, would seize the opportunity to cast a few glances in all the wrong directions. She read books not approved by the textbook committee, procured pictures which those who favoured schooling in art called deception or mockery. She even managed to make her teachers absent-minded. While returning from the Diocesan school, a boy with a wisp of a moustache and disheveled hair but good-looking, threw a letter in her car. It had caused a tingling in her blood. She had concealed the letter in her dress. But she was caught by the mother. She was locked up without food for an entire day.

Sohini began searching for a suitable boy among the meritorious students to whom her husband had given scholarships. Everybody cast sideways glances at her purse full of money. One of them even dedicated his thesis to her. She said, "Oh my goodness, you have brought shame upon me. Your post-graduation is almost at its term, and yet, a misplaced anointment, coupled with the absence of a well-measured devotion, means no progress can be expected."

For quite some time, Sohini had been looking at a particular boy. She liked him. His name, Revati Bhattacharya. He was already a Doctor of Science. One or two of his papers had already been published abroad.

## III

Sohini was well-versed in the art of socialising. Manmatha Chaudhuri was one of Revati's earliest academic mentors. She got him in her sway. For a few days, she plied him with toast and omelettes, sometimes with the roe of hilsa, and then she put the proposition to him. She said, "You are probably wondering why I am inviting you to tea so often."

"Mrs Mullick, let me tell you that is none of my business."

Sohini said, "People think that we make friends to pursue our own selfish interests."

"See, Mrs Mullick, my opinion on the matter is—the interests matter little; it is the friendship that is a gain. Besides, it is no trifling matter that a poor professor like me serves somebody's purpose. The intelligence of those like me cannot be exposed to the light beyond a certain bookish point and thus fades away. I see that what I say makes you laugh. See, even though I am a teacher, I also have a sense of humour. Please keep this in mind when you call me next for tea."

"Most certainly, and I am relieved. I have seen professors to make whom laugh one has to call a doctor."

"Well said! I see you are of my party. Therefore, let us come to the point."

"You perhaps know that in his life; my husband had just one passion—his laboratory. I don't have a son;

I am looking for someone whom I can establish in this laboratory. I have heard of Revati Bhattacharya."

The professor said, "He is indeed worthy. In his field, one will require some resources to take matters forward."

Sohini said, "My accumulated wealth has grown mouldy. Widows of my age are brokers of gods and goddesses, and thus wait to crack open the gates to the afterlife. It may upset you to learn that I do not believe in these things."

Chaudhuri opened his eyes wide and asked, "What do you believe in then?"

"I want a human being among human beings, someone who fits the description according to my late husband. This is what I consider to be my sacred duty."

Chaudhuri said, "Hurray! The stone floats on water! Peradventure, one final proof of intelligence even among women. I know a B.Sc. idiot who, the other day, touched my feet and started somersaulting backwards, his brains are leaving him like the tufts of a silk-cotton tree. So, you want to install Revati in the laboratory, in your own house? Can't it be shifted to some other spot?"

"Mr Chaudhuri, make no mistake. I am a woman. It is here, in this laboratory, that my husband accomplished what he did. If I can appoint someone in front of that altar, someone worthy, who will switch on the light, then, no matter where my husband is, he will be happy."

Chaudhuri said, "By Jove! I am hearing the voice of

a woman. Not bad, not bad at all. Just know that if you want to help Revati to the fullest extent, then you will have to cross the line of one hundred thousand rupees."

"Even if I do, I will still have a paltry sum left over."

"But the one you want to please in the other world, are you sure he won't lose his temper? I have heard that if they so wish, they can ride your neck and jump up and down."

"You do read the newspapers, don't you? No sooner does a man die than reams of praise start appearing in print, paragraph after paragraph. There is no harm in relying upon the generosity of that dead man. The one who has accumulated wealth, has accumulated along with it a lot of sin. Of what use are we if we cannot lighten the burden of the sins of our husbands? To hell with money; I don't need money."

The professor grew excited and said, "What can I say to you? The gold extracted from a mine is pure, even when other substances are mixed with it. You are an ingot of that gold in disguise. I have understood you. Now tell me what I have to do."

"Obtain the consent of this boy."

"I will try, but the task is not that easy. Anybody else and he would have jumped at your offer."

"Where's the problem?"

"Since he was a child, a womanly planet has occupied his horoscope. His path is protected by a firm unintelligence."

"What are you saying? A man—"

"See, Mrs Mullick, what is there to be angry about? Do you know what a matriarchal society is? One in which women are superior to men. There was a time when the wave of a Dravidian society used to wash the shores of Bengal."

Sohini said, "Those good days are gone. Perhaps that wave still plays in a subterranean way, muddles the mind, but the ship is firmly in the hands of men. They are the ones who whisper the mantra into our ears, which they alone pull. It's almost a matter of tearing out the ear altogether?"

"Wonderful! You know how to talk. If the time comes for women of your ilk, then in a matriarchal society, the laundry list will be in the washerman's house, and we can send the principal of our college to dehusk the rice. Psychologists say that in Bengal there is no matriarchy, outwardly, but in the Bengali novel, there is. Have you ever heard the men outside Bengal crying '*Maa, Maa*'? Let me give you the news: on top of Revati's intelligence is mounted a girl."

"Does he love someone?"

"That would have been understandable; the nerves are beating out life's rhythm. One could say that the fountain of intelligence is nagging the young woman's hands. This is the age for it. But instead of that, he has become a bead in the hands of one who counts her rosary day and night. With what will I save him—youth, intelligence, or science?"

"Okay, can we invite him over for tea here one of these days? Will he agree to have food with unclean spirits like us?"

"Unclean. If he doesn't, then we will cleanse him so that no trace of brahminery will remain in his manhood. Let me also ask you something. It seems you have a beautiful daughter?"

"I do. And the benighted wretch *is* beautiful. Tell me what should I do?"

"No, no, don't get me wrong. Speaking for myself—I like beautiful women. It is a disease with me. But his relations have no sense of humour; they'll take fright."

"No fear. I will marry my daughter to someone of our own caste."

This was a complete falsehood.

"You yourself married outside your caste."

"I have had to put up with a bit of harassment. I also have had to litigate enormously to take possession of the property. Don't ask me what I have had to go through."

"I've heard a bit of it. There were rumours flying around linking your name to the other party's articled clerk. After winning the case, you stepped away; while that man was on the verge of hanging himself. Is it true?"

"How do you think women have survived since time immemorial? Deceit requires quite a bit of skill; she's equal to the tumult of the battle, but she needs to expend some honey in the process. That is the established mode of warfare for women."

"There you go getting me wrong all over again. We are scientists; we are not judges; we observe dispassionately the play of character versus character. Let that conflict resolve itself as it may. In your game the solution was to your liking; I had said you are blessed. I had also thought it was a good thing. I was a professor and not an articled clerk; that saved me. The distance between Mercury and the Sun is just enough for Mercury to survive. That is a mathematical calculation; no good or bad is involved. These things, I think you have learnt to distinguish."

"So I have. The planets succumb to gravitation but also resist gravitation—this fact is one that must be learned."

"I admit one more thing. Just now as I was talking to you, I was doing some sums in my unconscious mind, mathematical sums. Just think, if I had been ten years younger, then today I would have recklessly run a risk. Collision just passed me by a whisker. What else? Yet, a humid tide rises in my breast. Just think, Creation is just a game of mathematics!"

Having said this, Chaudhuri slapped his knees and laughed. He was not aware of the fact that before meeting him, Sohini had, for a duration of two hours, so changed her age that the Creator was completely hoodwinked.

## IV

The next day the professor came and saw Sohini washing a ragged, coatless dog and wiping it clean with a towel.

Chaudhuri asked, "Why such an honour for this disgraceful looking creature?"

"Because I saved his life. He had come under a car and broken his leg; I put a bandage on him and healed him. Now, I have a share in its life-force."

"Seeing his inauspicious appearance every day won't cause you any distress?"

"I haven't kept him to see his face. I feel good about the way he recovered from the point of death. When I satisfy his desire to live, I don't have to run with a billy goat to Kalitala in order to fulfill my religious duties. I have decided to open a hospital to take care of all the blind and lame dogs of your biology department."

"Mrs Mullick, the more I see you, the more I am astonished."

"If you see a little more, you will be relieved. You said you would give me news about Revati *babu*, so let us get started, shall we?"

"He's distantly related to me. So, I have inside information. Revati's mother died soon after his birth. He was brought up all along by his father's sister. She is said to be of a dull sort. The slightest error in her fastidious household chores would raise her hackles. There wasn't a person in the family who didn't fear her. She reduced Revati's manliness to a fine powder. If he was late from school by even five minutes, he would be interrogated for twenty-five."

Sohini said, "As far as I know, it is up to men to chastise and discipline while women shower affection; that is how things even out, don't they?"

The professor said, "It is not up to those with a swan-like grace to even things out. They will bend this way and that. Don't mind my saying so, Mrs Mullick, but even among them are to be found some who, by accident, keep their heads high and walk the straight and narrow. Such as—"

"Say no more. But even in me, there is enough of the shackled woman. Don't you see the tendency in me? The man-grab tendency? Otherwise, why would I have bothered you?"

"You don't have to repeat yourself so often, y'know. Today I have come without being prepared for class. The neglect of duty is so pleasant."

"Perhaps you have a weakness for the fame of the species."

"Not at all impossible. But even within that, there is no great difference. Anyway, we'll discuss that later."

Sohini laughed and said, "Maybe not later either. Please finish what you were saying earlier. How did Revati *babu* make such quick progress?"

"What he is, is nothing compared to what he could have been. He had gotten the opportunity during a particular research project, to go high up in the mountains. He had decided to go to Badrikashram. Disaster struck! The aunt had an aunt; who had to die on the road to Badrika. The aunt said, "As long as I am alive, mountains are out." Therefore, what I was trying to say, I cannot bring myself to say. Let it be!"

"But why put all the blame on the aunt alone? Won't the mother's darling ever grow up?"

"That I have said before. Matriarchy rouses the ego in the blood; and the boys are dumbfounded. I can't express enough my regret. That's number one. After that, when it was decided that Revati would go to Cambridge on a government scholarship, the aunt came howling out. It was her belief that he was going to marry a white woman. I had said, 'So what?' Good lord! I had spoken in jest, but it was taken to be a fact. The aunt said, "If he goes abroad, I'll hang myself." Calling upon which god would ensure the tying of the noose, I, an atheist, didn't know, but the rope was not found in the market. I abused Revati like anything. I called him stupid; I called him a dunce; I called him an imbecile. That was the end of it. Revu is not squeezing out drops of oil from a traditional Indian oil press."

Sohini, disturbed, cried out, "I feel like beating my head against a wall and dying. A woman has drowned

Revati, and another woman will drag him ashore, I swear."

"Let me be clear, madam. You have hands capable of catching a beast by its horns and sending it under—but not ones that you can grab by its tail and lift it out. So now get into the habit. Let me ask you something. what got you so interested in science?"

"My husband was passionate about all kinds of science. His favourite vices were Burmese cheroots, and his laboratory. He got me into the habit of smoking and almost made a Burmese out of me. I gave it up when I saw that men didn't approve. His other vice held me in thrall. Men make fools out of women, but he would keep me enthralled day and night with knowledge. See, Chaudhuri *moshai,* a man's weakness cannot remain hidden to a woman, but I saw no gap in his convictions. When I saw him up close, he was great. Today, I see him from afar; he is greater still."

Professor Chaudhri asked, "Where exactly does he strike you as being great?"

"Do you want to know? Not because he was learned. But because he approached knowledge with pure devotion. He resided in the light and air of prayer. We women, if we don't get to see or feel a thing, our prayer is out of depth. And the lab has become an object of worship for me. Sometimes I feel like burning incense and blowing a conch shell here. I fear my husband's hatred. His daily worship consisted of all these devices and instruments and college students milling around him, getting to know things from him, and I, too, would sit amongst them."

"Could the students concentrate on the science?"

"Those who could were chosen. I have seen students who were true renunciates. I have also seen those who, in the guise of taking notes, would write letters next door and discuss literature."

"How did it feel?"

"To tell you the truth, it didn't feel bad. My husband would go off to the office and the ones with imagination would hang around."

"If you don't mind my saying so, I am in the habit of studying psychology. Let me ask you, did they get any results?"

"I don't like saying so, dirty old me! I got to know one or two, thinking of whom wrenches my heart even today."

"One or two?"

"The heart is greedy; the fire of this greed is hidden in the pith of the flesh and, given a prick, it bursts into flames. I had sunk my reputation at the very beginning; to tell you the truth, I have no compunction about it. We are not eternal ascetics. Women spend their lives putting on a show. Draupadi and Kunti have to dress up as Sita and Savitri. Let me tell you one thing, Chaudhuri *moshai*, remember that my sense of right and wrong was not clear right since childhood. No guru ever taught me that. So, I jumped into bed without thinking twice and came through unscathed. My body bore a few scars, but my mind was unaffected. Nothing clung to me. Anyway, when he went away, he put a torch to my attachment on the pyre of his burning body; the accumulated sins are being reduced to ashes, one by one. The fires of that ritual are burning in this laboratory."

"Bravo! To tell you the truth, what courage you have shown!"

"It is easy to tell the truth when you have someone who can coax it out of you. You are so easy and so truthful."

"Those boys, who wrote letters and received your divine offerings, do they still hover around you?"

"It is precisely why they have effaced all the filth in my heart. I saw they were more interested in my chequebook. They thought, a woman's infatuation doesn't want to die; they'll break in through love's burglar hole and lay hands on my safe. They didn't know I was not that interested. My dry Punjabi heart. I can ignore the laws and customs of society to satisfy my body, but I'll die rather than betray somebody. They couldn't get a penny out of the lab. My life force, turned into flint, has sealed off the treasure of my god. They don't have it in them to melt that stone. The one who had chosen and brought me here, was not mistaken."

"I salute him, and if I find those boys, I'll teach them a lesson or two."

Before leaving, the professor made a round of the lab, accompanied by Sohini. He said, "It is here that womanly intellignence has turned into illicit liquor, that the tree on which hung an evil spirit has been felled and there has emerged a true spirit."

Sohini said, "No matter what you say, fear stalks my heart. Womanly intelligence is one of God's most ancient creations. When one is young, the will is strong, then it hides in the shrubbery. No sooner does the blood run cold than the aunts of ancient faith come out. I hope to die before that happens."

The professor said, "Not to fear, you will die with your eyes open."

## V

A white *sari*, and some powder on her salt-and-pepper hair imparted to Sohini's face a becoming glow of purity. Accompanied by her daughter, she made her way, via the motor-launch, to the botanical gardens. The girl was wearing a bluish-green Benarasi *sari*, with a pink corset visible. Drops of kumkum on her forehead, a hint of kohl in her eyes, a bun bunched up and falling casually on her shoulders, and a pair of sandals of black leather with embroidered red velvet lining.

Sohini had ascertained beforehand the row of margosas under which Revati spent his Sundays and caught up with him there. She offered her respect to him, placing her head right on his feet. Revati made a fuss.

Sohini said, "Please don't mind, my son, you are the son of a Brahmin and I a daughter of Kshatriya. You might have heard of me from Chaudhuri *moshai*."

"Indeed. But where will I offer a seat to you here?"

"On the fresh green grass right here, where else would one get such a seat? You are probably thinking what am I up to over here. I have come here to fulfil my vow. I won't find another Brahmin like you."

Revati, taken aback, said, "A Brahmin like me?"

"What else? My guru says, "This is the age where knowledge is above all things; those who master it are true Brahmins."

Revati, flustered, said, "My father used to be a priest much given to rituals, I don't even know a single mantra."

"What are you saying? The mantra you know has brought the whole world to its knees. You must be wondering how has a woman learnt to talk like this. From a man among men. He was my husband. Give me your word, son, that you will come to the place he considered sacred."

"Tomorrow I have the morning off. I shall go."

"I see that you are interested in trees. I am very pleased. When my husband had gone to Burma in search of trees; I accompanied him."

Accompanied him, true, but not to deal in science. She could not remain without making sure that the dross that arose within her, her husband's character too, was subject to it. Suspicion ran through her innermost being. Once, when Nandkishore was in agony, he had told his wife, "My only comfort in death is that you will not be able to find me and brng me back."

Sohini had replied, "Can I go with you?"

Nandkishore had laughed and exclaimed, "Good lord!"

Sohini told Revati, "On the way back from Burma, I had brought some saplings with me. The Burmese call it *kwaitamiyeng*. It gives lovely flowers—but I just could not save them."

Sohini had discovered the name rummaging through her husband's library that very morning. She had never seen the tree. She wanted to entice the scholar into a net of knowledge.

Revati was amazed. He asked, "Do you know what it is called in latin?"

Sohini answered with much ease, "It's called Millettia."

She added, "My husband wouldn't accept anything easily; even so, he blindly believed that whatever is there in nature, fruit or flower, was beautiful. Women who, in a specific circumstance, turned their attention to it, their children would turn out to be beautiful. Do you believe so too?"

Needless to add, this was not Nandkishore's opinion.

Revati scratched his head and said, "I haven't gathered sufficient proof of that as yet."

Sohini said, "I have at least one proof in my own

house. Where did my daughter get her extraordinary beauty from? As if spring's array of flowers—let it be, you'll understand when you see her with your own eyes."

Revati was eager to see. No theatrical manoeuvre had been ignored.

Sohini had disguised her Brahmin cook as an officiating priest. He wore a *cheli*, forehead smeared with sandlewood paste, and a sacred thread rubbed with wood-apple paste hung around his neck. Sohini called him and said, "*Thakur*, it's time; call Neelu."

Neela had been made to cool her heels in the steamer. She was to emerge, a wicker tray containing presents in hand, and would be seen for quite a while in the morning's bright shade.

In the meantime, Sohini began examining Revati intently. Silky dark complexion, with a touch of yellow, with a broad forehead, the hair brushed over with fingers. His eyes not big, but inflamed with the power of vision, the thing that struck most people when they looked at his face. A mouth of effeminate softness. Out of all the information she had gathered about Revati, one thing stood out the most. He was loved by his schoolmates, by a sentimentality, to the point of tears. There was a weak gentleness about his face, which brought out an attachment in boys.

Sohini sensed something wrong. She believed that a man needn't be good-looking in order to hold on to a woman's heart. What was needed was male animal magnetism. That was akin to a wordless, wireless communication between his nerves and his muscles. It shows regularly in the audacity of his desires.

She recalled the headiness of her own first flowering. The one she attracted or was attracted by had neither looks nor knowledge nor a proud lineage. But there was an invisible radiance of energy whose imperceptible presence made her experience his manliness with all her body and mind. She grew restless at the thought that a similar, compelling thrill would begin taking hold over Neela. It is the final condition of youth, which is its most dangerous condition; it was then that Sohini had been mesmerised with untiring dealing with knowledge. But as things were, the ground of Sohini's heart was naturally fertile. However, all girls are not susceptible to the attraction of impersonal knowledge. No light reached Neela's soul.

Neela made her way through the banks of the river. Sunlight played on her forehead, on her hair. The gold embroidery sparkled on her Benarasi *sari*. Revati's gaze took her in in one glance. He averted his gaze at the next moment. That was what he had been taught since his childhood. The beautiful girl who puts on a spectacle of great illusion and steals our hearts, she ought to be kept out of view as per his aunt's dictums. Therefore, when one got such an opportunity, the nectar of sight had to be consumed in one gulp.

Mocking him in her heart, Sohini said, 'Look, just look at her once."

Revati, startled, lifted his gaze up to her.

Sohini said, "Look, you Doctor of Science, how the colour of her skin matches so marvelously with the colour of the leaves."

Revati said, a little hesitantly, "Marvelous indeed."

Sohini said to herself, 'Well, what the hell.' And then she said, "The orange is peeping out from behind with greenish-blue on the outside. Which flower does it go with? Let's see..."

Encouraged, Revati took a good look. He said, "I am reminded of a flower, but the outer part is not exactly blue, but brown."

"Which flower?"

Revati said, "Melina."

"Oh! Okay. It has fine petals, of which one is bright yellow and the other four are dark coloured."

Revati was taken by surprise. He said, "How is it that you know flowers so well?"

Sohini laughed and said, "Shouldn't I have known! All flowers, excepting those used for puja, are like alien beings to us."

Neela approached slowly, tray in hand. The mother said, "Why are you standing there all huddled up? Come touch his feet."

"No-no, it's alright", said Revati, flustered. Revati was

sitting cross-legged; Neela had to feel around for his feet. A frisson ran through Revati's body. On the tray was a bouquet of rare orchids; on a silver plate were placed sweets made of almonds, others of pistachios, and yet others of rice flour, moulded condensed milk, cream *barfis*, and steamed curd cut into squares.

Sohini said, "All of this Neela has prepared with her own hands."

It was a complete falsehood. In all this, Neela had neither hand nor heart.

Sohini added, "You have to taste some, son; it has been made at home especially for you."

They were all made, on request, by a well-known confectioner from Burra Bazar.

Revati folded his hands and said, "I am not used to eating at this hour. Give me permission to take them home."

Sohini said, "Well, it was against my husband's principles to force somebody to eat. He used to say, a human being is not a python."

Sohini packed all the food into a tiffin carrier. She told Neela, "Arrange the flowers on the tray, dear, and see that you don't mix them up. And cover the flowers with that silk handkerchief tied around your bun."

The scientist's gaze had a thirsty look about it. This was a thing beyond the measure of the natural world. Neela's shapely fingers were beating out various rhythms among the flowers as she arranged them—Revati had to turn his gaze away. From time to time, he would steal a glance towards Neela. On the one hand, the contours of her face were outlined by a single necklace encrusted with rubies, pearls, and emeralds, which draped over her hair like a rainbow; on the other, the dash of colour of her bodice. Sohini was packing the sweets, but she had a third eye. The magic that was being performed before her, did not escape her eyes.

According to the experiment of her husband, Sohini had a clear idea that the barricaded field of science and knowledge was not one on which any old cow could graze. Today she realised that the barricade was not fortifying to the same degree for everyone. She didn't like that.

## VI

The following day, Sohini sent for the professor. She said, "By calling you to secure my own ends, I am perhaps hurting you. Maybe it disrupts your work too."

"I beseech you to call me more often. If I am needed, good; if not, even better."

"You know that when it came to acquiring expensive instruments and equipment, my husband had no sense of proportion. He would play fast and loose with his employers to satisfy this selfless greed. He insisted stubbornly that such a laboratory should be found nowhere else in the whole of Asia, and his stubbornness had worn off on me. He had kept me alive in this spirit; otherwise, would blood such as mine have fermented as to spill over in all directions? See, Chaudhuri *moshai,* you are the friend to whom I can mention unhesitatingly the bad that is there in my character. The mind is relieved to find an open way to unburden itself of its shame."

Chaudhuri said, "It is not necessary to hide the truth from those who can see everything. A half-truth is a thing of shame. It is we who see the whole, we scientists."

"He used to say, man wants desperately to save his life, but life is never saved. Which is why he searches around to satisfy his urge to save his life for something that is more than life. That rare thing he found in his laboratory. If I cannot keep it alive then, only then will I have killed him as a slayer of a husband. I need a guardian for this, and that is why I was looking for Revati."

"Did you try?"

"I did, I hope to hold the fruit in my hand, but it won't endure."

"Why?"

"When his aunt hears that I have drawn Revati towards me, she will swoop down on him and snatch him away. She will think that I have laid a trap to marry my daughter off to him."

"I see nothing wrong in that; if it happens, all the better. But you were saying you wouldn't marry your daughter outside her caste."

"I did not know your mind then, as I had wanted to very badly. But I have given up on that."

"Why?"

"I have understood; my daughter is a disrupter. Whatever falls into her hands, she won't leave it intact."

"But she is *your* daughter."

"Indeed, which is why I know her to the core."

The professor said, "But how can you forget that women are capable of inspiring men?"

"I have not forgotten. Even meat can be fed to men, but wine is the cause of their downfall. My daughter is not unlike a cup of wine, filled to the brim."

"Well, then say what you want to do."

"I want to donate my laboratory to the public."

"By bypassing your only daughter?"

"My daughter? If I give it to her, I don't know what utter ruin it will come to. I'll make Revati the president of my trust. To that, the aunt won't be able to object."

"If I could grasp the logic behind a woman's objection, then why would I be born a man? But I don't understand one thing: if you don't want to make him your son-in-law, then why make him president?"

"What will I do with the machines? I need men to breathe life into them. The other thing is—since my husband passed away, not a single device has been purchased. Not for want of money. In order to buy, you have to first set a goal. I have news that Revati is working on magnetism. Let the collection advance along those lines, no matter how much it costs."

"What can I say? Had you been a man, I would have carried you on my shoulders and done a jig. Your husband stole money from the rail company, and you have stolen his male consciousness. I have never seen such an astonishing pen-wielding mind. It is surprising, that you should think it necessary to seek my advice."

"That's because you are so true you know how to say the right thing."

"You make me laugh. I am not a complete dunce to say the wrong thing to you and get caught. So, let's get to work—there are a lot of formalities, such as drawing up a list of things required, ascertaining the cost, engaging a good lawyer to determine your title-deed, laying down rules and regulations, etc."

"All this is your responsibility."

"Only in name. You must know well, I say what you want me to say and do what you want me to do. My gain is only this, that I'll be able to meet you twice a day. You do not know with what eyes I have seen you."

Sohini got up from her seat and, swiftly catching hold of Chaudhuri's neck, planted a kiss on his cheek and moved away, sitting down again like a demure, innocent being.

"I say, this is the beginning of my ruin."

"If there had been even a soupçon of that, I would not have ventured thus far. This allocation will accrue to you from time to time."

"You mean it?"

"I mean it. I have nothing to lose and looking at your face I do not see you have much to gain."

"In other words, this is the lumberjack's blow to dead wood! I am off to the lawyer's."

"Will you come by tomorrow, to this locality?"

"To do what?"

"To give heart to Revati."

"And to lose my own?"

"Are you the only person with a heart?"

"Don't you have any heart left in you?"

"There is plenty left over."

"Enough to make many monkeys dance."

## VII

The next day, Revati presented himself at the laboratory at least twenty minutes ahead of schedule. Sohini was not ready, and rushed to the room wearing a crumpled sari. Revati understood he had committed an error. He said, "My watch is not working properly."

Sohini replied curtly, "Indeed."

At one point, when Revati started at a slight noise and looked towards the door, Sukhan the valet entered the room with the keys to the glass case. Sohini asked, "Would you care for a cup of tea?"

Revati thought he should say yes. He said, "No harm in that."

The poor fellow was not in the habit of drinking tea; at the hint of a cold, he would have wood-apple leaves boiled in warm water. He was convinced that Neela herself would serve the drink.

Sohini asked, "Do you prefer your tea strong?"

On the spur of the moment Revati replied, "Yes."

He thought in these circumstances this was the done thing. The tea was served, and it was certainly strong. As black as ink, as bitter as a margosa leaf. The tea was served by a Muslim chef. This too, was meant to test him. He couldn't find the word with which to articulate an objection. Sohini did not like this shy mindedness. She said to the chef, "Why don't you pour him the tea, Mubarak? It's getting cold."

Revati had not presented himself twenty minutes early in order to be served by a Muslim chef.

Only the Almighty could gauge the distress with which he was putting the spoon to mouth, and so could Sohini. A woman after all, she noticed Revati's discomfiture and said, "Put that cup aside. I'll pour you some milk, and you should have some fruits, too. You've come early; perhaps you haven't had breakfast."

That was true. Revati thought there would be a reiteration of the Botanical Gardens episode. There wasn't even a hint of it, only a bitter taste in the mouth and the bitter experience of a hope belied.

At this point, the professor made his entry. No sooner had he entered than he slapped Revati on the back and said, "Well, how are you, everything seems to have gone cold. You are sitting like a toddler and quaffing milk, I see. What you see around you is not *Khokababu*'s toy shop. Those who have eyes have seen, the disciples of the Infinite come here to do their dance of destruction, the *tandav.*"

"Why are you scolding him? He had left his house without having a bite. When he arrived, he was looking famished."

"Aunty II! Aunty I will give a slap on one cheek, and Aunty II will plant a kiss on the other. And the boy in the middle will be reduced to mush. To tell the truth, nobody notices when the goddess of wealth comes on her own; those who track her down through seven continents, they alone appreciate her worth. There is no way of not getting wealth other than by not wanting it. Okay, tell me missus—away with all missuses; I'll just call you Sohini, whether that makes you angry or not."

"God help me; why should I be angry? Call me Sohini by all means, and if you call me Suhi, I will be even gladder."

"Allow me to let out a secret. There is another word that resembles the name of Sohini, and its meaning is very true. No sooner do I rise from bed in the morning than those two go '*hini hini kini kini*'. With these two words I beat the tambourine in my heart."

"You are used to squaring your equations in chemistry research; it's an offshoot of that."

"There are people who die in the process of squaring. You shouldn't fiddle around too much; it's highly inflammatory."

And he laughed heartily after saying this.

"No, but we shouldn't engage in this discussion in front of this young fellow here. He hasn't begun his apprenticeship in this explosives factory. His aunt protects him under her wing and that wing is non-combustible."

Revati's feminine face was going red.

"Sohini, I was going to ask you, have you administered a dose of opium to him this morning? Why is he dozing off?"

"If I have, it's without knowing it."

"Rebu, get up, I say get up. You shouldn't be so shy in front of women. That only makes them more audacious. They look for the weaknesses of a man as if it were a disease; the slightest opening, and they raise the temperature skywards. I know the subject; I just have to warn the boys. People like me, who have been wounded but not killed, you have to learn from us. Rebu, my son, don't you mind anything. Those who do not talk, those who remain silent, they are the most terrible. Let us go, shall we? I'll show you around. Here are the two galvanometers, absolutely state-of-the-art, a high vacuum pump, and this is a microphotometer, not a device to get students to pass the exams. Let's see, you come here and take your seat. I want to see that bald professor of yours—don't want to take his name—blanche when he sees this. When you had first started acquiring knowledge from me, didn't I tell you that there is a thing called 'future' dangling in front of your nose? Don't make it hollow by taking it too lightly. If my name be inscribed in a corner in small letters, in this, the first chapter of your life, that will make up for everything."

In a twinkling of an eye, the scientist woke up. His eyes grew bright. The face underwent a transformation from within. Sohini, enthralled, said, "All those who know you, they all expect you to make the kind of progress that is not of one day but is forever. But as great as is the hope, so are the obstacles both within and without."

The professor gave another resounding slap on Revati's back. The latter felt his spine tingle. Chaudhuri said, in his loud booming voice, "Look Rebu, the great future whose vehicle should have been Airavat, the divine elephant, a miserly present embarks him on a bullock cart; he lies in the mud, immobolised. Do you hear, Sohini, Suhi? No fear, I will not slap you on the back. Isn't it that I have found the right turn of phrase?"

"Wonderfully."

"Write it down in your diary."

"I will."

"Have you understood the meaning of what I said, Revi?"

"I think I have."

"Remember, great talent is also a great responsibility. That it is nobody's personal property. One has to answer for it before the Eternal. Do you hear Suhi, do you hear? Tell me, how did this sound?"

"Well said. Had there been a king of yore, he would have taken off a necklace—"

"They are all dead, but—"

"This is a small thing, but it shall not die; I shall remember."

Revati said, "No fear, you won't find me weak in anything."

He made as if to touch Sohini's feet. Sohini quickly stopped him.

Chaudhuri said, "But what are you doing? Not to perform a virtuous act is a mistake, but to prevent one from being performed is an even bigger mistake."

Sohini said, "If you have to do it, then do it there—"

She pointed at a bust of Nandkishore on a pedestal. A few incense sticks were burning away; there were flowers heaped on a plate.

She said, "I have read in the scriptures about Pataki's redemption. I was redeemed by that great man. He had to stoop really low, but in his final years, he was able to look up—it would be a lie to sit next to him when under his feet would be more appropriate. He has initiated me into the path of knowledge as a means of saving souls. He told me not to love the precious gems of his life to increase the vanity of a son-in-law. He said, "There I have preserved my own beatitude and the beatitude of my country."

The professor said, "Did you hear that, Rebu? This is going to be trust property, and you shall be put–in charge."

Revati, flustered, said, "I am not worthy of this office. I cannot take this responsibility."

Sohini said, "You cannot! Is this spoken like a man?"

Revati said, "I have been a student all of my life. I have no experience in this sort of work."

Chaudhuri said, "A duck never swims before the egg hatches. Today, the shell of your egg is about to crack."

Sohini said, "Don't be afraid. I will always accompany you through everything."

## VIII

Revati went away, relieved. Sohini stayed back, looking at the professor.

Chaudhuri said, "There are many kinds of fools in this world; a male fool is above all fools. But remember, the ability to shoulder a responsibility is born with the giving of the responsibility. He is a man who has a pair of hands, but given a pair of hooves, he immediately grows a tail to thrash about. Have you seen hooves instead of hands on Revati?"

"No, I don't like it. Those who have been brought up

by women never lose their milk teeth. My misfortune! Why did I think of others when you are around?"

"Happy to hear that. Might you elaborate a little on what virtue you have seen in me?"

"You have absolutely no greed."

"That's ill-spoken! I am not greedy for a thing like greed? I do—"

Sohini interrupted him by placing a kiss on each of his two cheeks.

"In which account is this deposited, Sohini?"

"What I owe you I can never repay. I am paying only the interest."

"On the first day, I got one, today two. Will it go on increasing?"

"Of course it will. At compound interest." Chaudhuri replied, "Sohini, you have made me the officiating priest in your husband's last rites. My goodness! What a responsibility! I have to please someone whose being I can no longer touch! This is not a custom-bound fee that—"

"You are no custom-bound *guru* yourself. Your word will be law. You have made arrangements for the fee?"

"I have been working on it these past few days; I have visited heaps of shops and bazars. Provisions have been laid out in the big room downstairs. Any earthly soul who would like to purloin them will be fully satisfied without doubt."

Going downstairs with Chaudhuri, Sohini saw various

devices, models, expensive books, microscope slides, and biological exhibits meant for students of science. Each item was marked with a name and address. Scholarship cheques had been made out for two hundred and fifty students. No expense had been spared. It had surpassed what is usually set aside for Brahmin-feeding at the last rites of the wealthy, even though the congregation was not visible.

"How much should I give to the officiating priest; you did not say."

"Your pleasure is my payment."

"With pleasure I have kept for you this chronometer. My husband had procured it from Germany; he used it regularly while doing research."

Chaudhuri said, "I cannot express what I feel. Don't want to spoil the occasion; my priestly task has been accomplished."

"There is someone else, that I cannot forget today—the widow of our Manik."

"Who do you mean? Manik?"

"He was my husband's head mechanic. He had an amazing pair of hands. He had worked with hair-breadth precision when it came to the most subtle tasks; and he had an unfailing eye for instruments. My husband treated him like a close friend. He would take him in his car to show him how things were done in big factories. On the other hand, he was a drunkard; his assistants would often abuse him. My husband would say, 'What is there in him is not the result of training; it is something more.' His respect for him was absolute. From this you can understand why he honoured me right till the end. My faults were insignificant compared to the value he saw in me. Where he had this impossible trust in a woman gathered from nowhere, there I never betrayed it, not even in trifles. Even today, I defend that trust with my life. He wouldn't get so much from anyone else. Where I was small, he didn't notice me; but where I was big, there, he gave me all his respect. If he hadn't gauged my worth, then where would I have gone, tell me? I am very bad, but I myself say I am very good because otherwise he would not have put up with me."

"See Sohini, I am proud to say that right from the beginning I saw you were good. Had yours been a cheap lustre, it would have been extinguished at the first whiff of scandal."

"Anyway, let people say what they want; the respect he gave me remains to this day and will remain till the end."

"Sohini, the more I see you, the more I know you are not the easy type of woman who will melt at the mere mention of a husband's name."

"True, I am not. I saw a power in him. I knew from the start that he was human; the gem was worth something only for the necklace that rolled around his neck, not on anyone else."

At this point Neela entered the room. She said,

addressing the professor, "Sir, please don't mind, I want to have a word with my mother."

"Don't bother about me, dear. I am going to the lab. I want to take a look at what Revati is working on."

Neela said, "No fear, the work is going on well enough. There are days when I have seen through the window that he has his head down, writing something, taking notes, thinking with a pen between his teeth. I am forbidden entry lest Sir Isaac's gravitation be upset. The other day, *maa* was telling someone he was working on magnetism. Anyone, especially a woman passing by, makes the needle swing."

Chaudhuri laughed heartily. He said, "My dear girl, the laboratory is inside; work on magnetism is in progress. Those who make the needle waver, they have to be feared. They lead you astray, that's why. I am off."

Neela said to her mother, "For how much longer do I have to be tied to your *sari*-end? You won't be able to keep me confined forever. You'll come to grief."

"Say what you propose doing about it."

Neela said, "You know that a movement is on to throw open higher studies for women; you have given them all of the money. Why don't you employ me there?"

"Because I am afraid that you'll go astray."

"Is stopping me from walking the only way to keep me on the right path?"

"No, I know that; that is what worries me."

"Instead of doing the thinking for me, why don't you, for a change, let me think. You have to, anyway. I am not a little girl anymore. You think that in all these public places lots of people come and go; it's dangerous. It's not as if people won't go about their business in the world just because of you. And the law that will stop me completely from getting to know them is not in your hands either."

"I know everything; I fear I will not be able to control the causes of my fear. So, you want to be admitted to the higher studies circle?"

"Yes."

"Okay, so be it. I know you will, one by one, plunge their male teachers into hell. You have to give me your word on one thing. Under no circumstances will you get close to Revati. And you will not enter his lab."

"*Maa*, I don't know what you think of me. Do you think I have such poor taste as to want to get close to your little Isaac Newton? Not even if I die."

And she mimicked the way Revati squirmed when he was ill at ease. She said, "That kind of person doesn't suit me. He should be left wholly to those women who like to groom old boys to adulthood. He is not the kind of prey worth hunting."

"You are overstating your purpose, which I suspect is not what is in your mind. Well, feel what you like about him; if you try to destroy him, that won't be good for you."

"I don't understand your whims and fancies, *maa*. You

dressed me up as a doll in order to marry me off to him; you think I don't understand that? Is that why you are warning me against hovering around him, lest his polish rub off through close contact with dross?"

"Listen Neela, let me make it known to you that it is impossible for you to marry him."

"So, if I marry the prince of Motigarh?"

"If you want to, go ahead."

"It's convenient; he has three wives, so my burden will be lighter, and he staggers about drunk in nightclubs— I'll have lots of time on my hands."

"Okay, fine, that is perfectly all right. But I won't allow you to marry Revati."

"Because I might addle the brains of Isaac Newton?"

"I don't want to get into that argument with you. Just remember my words."

"What if he starts slobbering all over me?"

"Then he will have to leave this neighbourhood— feed him yourself; he won't get a penny of your father's funds."

"Good lord! I wash my hands of your Sir Isaac Newton."

And that was the scene in brief that day.

## IX

"Chaudhuri *moshai*, everything is going well. It is only about my daughter that I cannot make up my mind. I don't understand what she is up to."

Chaudhuri said, "Well, who all are up to what regarding her is worth thinking about too. Meanwhile, the rumour is rife that your husband had left lots of money to preserve the lab. The amount keeps increasing from mouth to mouth. People are laying bets in the bazaar on this kingdom and its princess."

"The princess will sell for mud, I know. But as long as I am alive, the lab will not sell cheap."

"But people have begun gathering. I suddenly saw one of our own professors, Mazumdar, walk hand in hand with Neela out of a cinema hall. He turned away no sooner than he saw me. The fellow goes around making speeches on good topics and waxes eloquent on the welfare of the country. But his averted gaze the other day made me worry for the country."

"Chaudhuri *moshai,* the doorlocks have burst open."

"Indeed, they have! Now this poor wretch has to watch out for his meagre possessions."

"A plague on Mazumdar's neighbourhood, my fears are about Revati."

Chaudhuri said, "There's nothing to fear as of now. He's immersed in work. He is making wonderful progress."

"Chaudhuri *moshai*, his danger is his science; no matter how great a master he may be, he is an ignorant when it comes to what you call matriarchy."

"You are right there. He has yet to be inoculated. Once he contracts the infection it will be difficult to save him."

"You will have to come and see him at least once every day."

"Let him not contract the disease from somewhere. In the end, I hope I won't have to die. Don't fear; even though you are a woman, I hope you can take a joke in the right spirit. I have crossed the neighbourhood of the epidemic. The contagion won't spread to me. But there is one difficulty. Day after tomorrow I have to set out for Gujranwala."

"Is this another joke? Have mercy on this poor woman."

"It is not a joke, my co-pilgrim, Amulya Auddy, was a doctor there. He had a practice of twenty-five odd years. He has built up some assets. He died of heart failure, and is survived by a widow and children. I have to square off his accounts, sell off land and property, and bring them out of there. I can't say how long that will take."

"What can I say?"

"In this world, words are of no use, Sohini. Say without fear, whatever will happen, will happen. Those who accept fate do not fear. We scientists say that the ineluctable cannot be moved as much by a hair's breadth. As long as you can do something, do; when you can no longer do anything, then just call it a day"

"All right then."

"The Mazumdar I spoke about is not the most dangerous of the lot. He is kept in the group as a face-saving ploy. Those that I have heard of are such that even if we were to follow Chanakya's opinion and keep them at arm's length, there would still be cause for concern. There is the attorney Banku Bihari giving shelter to whom it is like embracing an octopus. All these people like the warm blood of a rich widow. Keep this in mind. If you can, do something. Remember my philosophy at all times."

"Listen Chaudhuri *moshai*, keep your philosophy to yourself. I will not accept what you call destiny nor the infallible laws of causality when it comes to someone laying their hands on my lab. I am from Punjab; a dagger can appear most playful in my hands. I can murder someone whether it be my daughter or someone aspiring to be my son-in-law."

She had a sheath tied hidden away under her *sari*. In a flash, she took out a dagger, and held it briefly to the light. She said, "He had chosen me—I am not your everyday Bengali girl to sit and weep over love all the time. I can give my life for love. I can take it too. My lab and my life force, in between lies this knife."

Chaudhuri, said, "I could write poetry once upon a time; today it seems to me that I can do so once again."

"If you want to write poetry, you can. But retract your philosophy. What cannot be accepted, in the final analysis, I won't accept. I'll fight alone. And will say with pride, 'I'll win, I'll win, I'll win.'"

"Bravo! I recant. I'll now beat a drum in honour of your triumph. For now, I will take your leave for a few days. I won't be tardy in returning."

The surprising thing was—Sohini's eyes welled up in tears. She said, "Please don't mind." And she threw her arms around Chaudhuri's neck. She said, "In this world, no ties survive; this too is momentary."

And she fell on her knees to touch the professor's feet.

## X

What the newspapers call 'circumstances' arrive in a crowd. The story of life is often suspended over ups and downs. Suddenly, there is a collision in the final chapter; and everything comes to a standstill. The Creator weaves his story slowly and finishes it off with one blow.

Sohini's maternal grandmother lived in Ambala. She got a telegram saying, "If you wish to meet, make haste."

She was Sohini's only surviving relative. It is from this person's hands that Nandkishore had bought Sohini.

Her mother told Neela, "You too are coming with me."

Neela said, "That can never be."

"Why not?"

"They are organising a felicitation for me."

"Who are they?"

"Members of the Jagani Club. Don't be scared; they are gentlemen. Take a look at the members list, and you will understand. Very exclusive."

"What are your intentions?"

"Difficult to be clear. The intention is in the name itself. A lot of spiritual, literary and artistic meaning is hidden in the name. Nabakumar *babu* has explained it brilliantly. They have decided to approach you for a donation."

"But I see that they have exhausted the funds previously raised. You are completely in their hands. They've got what I have forsaken. They can get nothing more from me."

"*Maa*, why are you so angry? They only want to work selflessly for the good of the country."

"Right, let's stop this discussion. I am sure that, meanwhile, you have informed your friends that you are free?"

"Yes, I have."

"The selfless have let you know that funds allocated for your husband you can use as you like."

"Yes, they have."

"I have heard that they are preparing themselves to probate the will?"

"True. Banku Bihari is my solicitor."

"He has given hopes and counsel in addition?"

Neela gave no reply.

"I will straighten out your Banku Bihari if he even so much as crosses my line of vision. If not within the law, then without it. I'll be coming back via Peshawar. I am posting four Sikh guards outside the lab, day and night. Before going away, I want to show you something—I am a Punjabi woman."

No sooner had she said this than she took the knife out of its sheathe. She said, "This knife does not know who my daughter is, nor my daughter's solicitor. This memory is your responsibility; if there is reckoning to be done when I come back, so be it."

## XI

There was a lot of vacant land all around the lab to ensure that no noise or tremor reached the place of work. This tranquillity helped Revati in applying himself to his work. He would often come by at night to work.

The clock downstairs struck two. Revati, for a moment, was looking at the sky outside his window and thinking.

A shadow was cast on the wall. He looked around and saw that Neela had come in. She was dressed in a sheer silk chemise. Startled, he was about to get up from his chair. Neela came and sat on his lap and put her arms around him. An uncontrollable tremor took hold of Revati's body; his chest began rising and falling rapidly. Overcome, he began saying, "Go away, get out of this room."

She said, "Why?"

Revati said, "I cannot bear it. Why have come into this room?"

Neela tightened her embrace and said, "Why? Don't you love me?"

Revati said, "I do, I do, I do, but please leave this room."

Suddenly, a Punjabi guard entered the room. In a contemptuous tone he said, "*Maiji*, this is shameful; get out of here."

Revati, unknown to his conscious mind, had pressed the calling buzzer.

The Punjabi spoke again, "*Babuji*, don't be dishonourable."

Revati pushed Neela away with foce and got up from his seat. The guard said to Neela, "Please go outside or else I'll have to follow my boss' orders."

In other words, I will evict you by force, and it will be humiliating for you. While going out, Neela added, "Do you hear, Sir Isaac Newton? You are invited to our house for tea tomorrow at 4:30pm sharp. You can't hear? Have you fainted?"

An evanescent voice replied, "I've heard."

Through her nightdress, Revati could not help glimpsing at the perfectly sculpted body that arose before him in unprecedented splendour. Neela went away. Revati's face remained glued to his table. He couldn't have imagined such an amazing beauty. A shower of electricity had penetrated his nerves; and was circulating within like a stream of fire. Clenching his fist, Revati made himself say, "I won't go to tea tomorrow." He was trying hard to bind himself to a firm pledge, but no words escaped his lips. He wrote on the blotting paper, 'I Won't go, won't go, won't go.' Suddenly he noticed, lying on the table, a dark red handkerself; the name 'Neela' was embroidered in one corner. He pressed the handkerchief to his face; his head filled up with perfume, and an intoxication coursed through his entire body.

Neela came back to the room. "There is a piece of work I forgot about."

The guard made to stop her. Neela said, "Not to worry, I am not here to steal something. I just need a signature—I want to make you president of the Jagani Club, you are known throughout the country."

Constricted, Revati said, "I know nothing about this club."

"You don't have to know anything. Excepting that Brojendro *babu* is the patron of the club."

"I don't know who Brojendro *babu* is."

"All you have to know is that he is director of the Metropolitan Bank. Darling, be a good boy now; it's not for an autograph."

Then she put her right hand around his shoulder and took his hand in her grasp with the left and commanded, "Sign."

And he signed as if in a dream.

As Neela was folding up the paper, the guard said, "I'll have to look at the paper."

Neela said, "But you won't understand anything."

The guard said, "No need to understand."

He snatched the piece of paper and tore it into little

pieces. He said, "If you want to draw up a contract, do so outside. Not here."

Revati felt relieved. The guard told Neela, "Let me see you off."

He took her away.

After some time, the Punjabi guard came back to the room. He said, "I close the doors on all four sides. You have opened it from inside to let her in."

What suspicion! What an insult!

Revati said, again and again, "I did not, I did not."

"Then how did she get into the room?"

Indeed. The scientist set out to inspect all the rooms. Finally, he found, facing the road, a large window with a latch. Someone had opened the latch during the day.

The guard had little respect for Revati's cunning. An idiot immersed in study, that's all. He slapped his forehead and said, "Woman! Wicked by nature!"

Of what remained of the night, Revati spent telling himself, he wouldn't go for tea the next day.

A crow cawed. Revati went home.

## X

The following day, he was punctual as usual. At exactly 4.45 pm, Revati presented himself for tea. He thought the meeting would be a private one between Neela and him.

He had no sense of fashion. He was dressed in a dhoti

and kurta, freshly laundered, a carefully folded shawl thrown over his shoulder. He came and saw that the meeting was being held in the garden. His heart sank at the sight; he felt a desperate urge to hide. When he tried sitting in a corner, everybody got up and said, "Come, come Dr. Bhattacharya, your seat is here."

An upright, high-backed chair right in the middle of the circle. He understood that he was the cynosure of all eyes present. Neela came and garlanded him and put a mark of sandalwood paste on his forehead. Brojendro *babu* proposed that he be sworn in as the president of the Jagani Club. He was seconded by Banku *babu*, paeans resounded on all sides. The author, Haridas *babu* dwelt at length on Dr. Bhattacharya's international repute. He said, "Setting Revati *babu*'s name as a sail the ship of Jagani Club will ferry us to the shores of the great Western seas."

The organisers of the meeting went and whispered into the ears of reporters, "See to it that all the rhetorical flourishes are reported accurately."

When the speakers began speaking one after the other, "After such a long time, Dr. Bhattacharya has placed a sign of victory for science on the forehead of Mother India," Revati felt his chest expand with pride, and saw himself manifested in the middle of the sky of the civilised world. In his heart, he protested against all the negative rumours he had heard about the Jagani Club. When Haridas *babu* said, "The amulet of Revati *babu*'s name has been hung around the neck of this gathering as an amulet of protection and from this you can gauge the loftiness of our intention," Revati experienced clearly the honour and responsibility surrounding his name. His heart cast off the rind of reservation from itself. Women put away their cigarettes and leaned over his chair, laughed sweetly and said, "Pardon us for bothering you, but you have to give us an autograph."

Revati felt—as though all this while he had been in a dream and the beads of his dream had unravelled and a butterfly had emerged from its cocoon.

One by one, people took their leave. Neela grasped Revati's hand and said, "You are not going away."

A fiery wine was poured into his veins.

The day was coming to an end.

In the middle of the arbour, the darkness of a green evening.

The two sat on a bench close together. Placing Revati's hand on top of her own, Neela said, "Being a man, why do you fear women so much."

Revati, full of audacity, said, "Fear? Who? Me? Never!"

"Don't you fear my mother?"

"Why should I fear her? I respect her."

"And me?"

"Certainly, I fear you."

"That is good news. *Maa* has said that under no circumstances will she marry me off to you. Then I'll commit suicide."

"I will not accept any constraints. We shall certainly get married."

Neela placed her head on his shoulders and said, "You probably don't know how much I want you."

Drawing Neela's head closer to his chest, Revati said, "There is no force on earth which can take you away from me."

"Caste?"

"To hell with caste."

"Then you'll have to notify the registrar tomorrow itself."

"I will, tomorrow itself."

Revati had began displaying male pride.

The results did not tarry in coming.

## XI

The grandmother was displaying symptoms of paralysis. She was expected to die. As long as she was alive, she would not let go of Sohini. Seizing this opportunity with both hands, Neela's impassioned youth was stirred and excited in good measure.

Under the influence of his scholarship, the taste of masculinity had gone flat in Revati's mouth—Neela didn't like him enough. But it was safe to marry her, even though he didn't have the strength to contain post-marital disorder. Not only that, but the question of greed that was mixed up with the laboratory was not insignificant.

His well-wishers said no one else was as capable as he of taking responsibility for the lab. Intelligent wags guessed that Sohini wouldn't let him go at any cost.

On the other hand, meekly accepting the taunts of his assistants, Revati allowed the newspapers to publish the news of his presidency of the Jagani Club. When Neela said, "You are scared, aren't you?" he retorted, "I don't care." He was beset with the resolve to not have anyone doubt his masculinity. He said, "I have a regular correspondence with Eddington; one day I'll invite him over to the club." The members of the club said, "Amen."

Revati's actual work had come to a stop. All his thinking was scattered abroad. His heart awaited the arrival of Neela, looked forward to the moment when she would creep up from behind and cover his eyes with her hand. She would sit on the arm of the chair and throw her left arm around his neck. He would reason with himself by saying that his work had stopped only temporarily and once things stabilised, it would miraculously be joined just short of rupture. There were no immediate signs of stability. There was not the slightest tinge of remorse in Neela's heart that the stopping of his work was a loss to the world; she considered the whole thing to be a farce.

Day after day, he was enmeshed in the net. Jagani Club had taken hold of him in earnest, was turning him into a complete male. Now the unspeakable would never be uttered by him, but listening to the unlistenable would elicit uproarious laughter. Dr Bhattacharya had become a jolly good fellow for them.

From time to time, Revati would be seized by jealousy. Neela would light a cigar with the bank director's cigar. It was beyond Revati to imitate this. His head would spin when the smoke hit his throat, but this sight would render his body and mind sick. Besides, when all kinds of pushing and shoving occurred he would not resist objecting. Neela would say, "We have no attachment to this body, why give it so much importance—what is really valuable is love how could I not spread it all around?"—and she would take hold of Revati's hand. Revati would then consider the others to be unfortunate wretches—satisfied with the husk, unable to obtain the kernel.

The guards were mounted day and night around the lab but inside there was interrupted work and no one to supervise it.

## XII

Neela was leaning on a cushion with her feet up on the sofa in her drawing room. Revati was seated on the floor with his head resting on Neela's feet, a sheaf of foolscap paper with scribblings on it in his hand.

Revati turned his head and said, "The language is somehow too colourful, it wouldembarrass me to read such a high-flown piece of writing."

"So, you understand language too, do you? This is not a chemistry formula—don't be so choosy; just memorise it. Do you know this has been written by our litterateur Promod Ranjan *babu*?"

"It will be very difficult for me to memorise these long sentences with so many big words in them."

"Difficult, you say?" Even I have already memorised it just by having to drill it into your ears—'when Jagani Club adorned me in Amravati's *Mandarmalya*, that was the most auspicious day of my life—' grand. No fear, I'll be next to you; I'll prompt you as you go along."

"I don't know Bengali literature, but I feel as if the entire thing is making fun of me. It would be much simpler if I said it in English— 'Dear friends, allow me to offer you my heartfelt thanks for the honour you have conferred upon me on behalf of the Jagani Club—the Great Awakener' etc. Just two simple sentences like that and we are done—"

"No, that won't do; Bengali from you will be so much more amusing—especially when it goes— 'O youth of Bengal, O you independent charioteers of the chariot of independent governance, O vanguard on the path with ruptured chains'—is there really any way of putting that in English? To hear that from a man of science such as you, it would have young Bengalis dancing like cobras with their hoods deployed. There is still time; let's read it aloud together."

Carrying his significant frame noisily over the staircase, dressed formally like a *sahib*, the bank director, Brojendro Haldar, came to a crunching halt before them. He said, “No this is unbearable; whenever I come, he’s got Neela tied up in something. He has nothing better to do than to separate Neela from the rest of us like barbed wire.”

Revati, a bit stricken, said, “Today I had to attend to something out of the ordinary, so—”

“It is precisely on the assurance of your being busy that I came along. Today you have invited the members; I thought you’d be occupied, so I managed to squeeze out half an hour to quickly come over. And here I am, hearing that he is here on work. Astonishing! When there is no work, he is found vacationing here. And when there is work, he is still to be found here. How do working professionals like us keep up with leeches like him? Is this fair, Neela?”

Neela said, “The problem with Dr Bhattacharya is that he doesn’t know how to get to the point. It’s not true that he has come here on work, rather, he cannot restrain himself from coming here, so he’s here; this is worth listening to, and it’s true. He has stubbornly been taking up all my time. This is the man in him. All of you have to admit defeat in front of this *bangal*.”

“‘Okay, good, in that case, we too must display our manliness. From now on, the members of the Jagani Club will take up the discussion on the subject of the abduction of women. We will revive the age of myth."

Neela said, "It sounds like fun. Abduction of women is better than the nuptials of women. But what will be the procedure?"

Haldar said, "I can show it to you."

"Right now?"

"Yes, right now. '

And he lifted Neela into his arms from the sofa with both hands.

Neela laughed out loud and put her arms around his neck.

Revati's face grew dark. His problem was that he lacked the strength to either imitate or stop this. He grew more and more angry with Neela for indulging these uncivilised ignoramuses.

Haldar said, "The car is ready. I'm taking you to Diamond Harbour. I will drive you back this evening. I had some work at the bank, but to hell with that. A good deed will be performed. I am creating a quiet environment for Dr. Bhattacharya to work in. It is better to remove a big nuisance like you; he will thank me for it."

Revati saw that there was no attempt on Neela's part to struggle to release herself; on the contrary, she felt at ease with where she found herself. She remained wrapped around his neck as if entranced. Her parting shot was, "No fear, dear scientist, this is just a rehearsal—I am not crossing over to Lanka yet; I will return to your invitation."

Revati tore up the piece of writing in his hands.

His pride in his knowledge had proved itself worthless before Haldar's physical strength and uncivilised assertion of male right.

The dinner that day was in a well-known restaurant. Revati was the host; Neela occupied the honoured seat next to him. A famous actress had come to sing at the function. Banku Bihari had gotten up to propose a toast; paeans were being sung to Revati and, by association, to Neela. The women were puffing away furiously to prove they were not altogether women. Those a little older wore the mark of youth, made hints and gestures, laughed shrilly, and pinched each other's cheeks, all in a race to outpace in jollity their younger counterparts.

Suddenly Sohini entered the room. A sudden hush descended upon the guests. Looking at Revati, Sohini said, "I can't recognise you, Dr. Bhattacharya. I presume you had called for money, which I had sent last Friday. I clearly see the funds were adequate. You will have to get up; I want to check the lab list against the supplies delivered."

"You are mistrusting me?"

"I have trusted you thus far. But if you have any decency left, please don't mention the word 'trust' ever again."

Revati was about to get up when Neela caught him by his sleeves and forced him down beside her. She said, "He has invited his friends over today; let the others leave first, then he shall leave."

There was a cruel twist to Neela's retort. Sir Isaac was a darling of her mother; there was no scientist as big as him; that is why, to the exclusion of all others, the responsibility of the lab had fallen on his shoulders. To drive the nail in further, Neela said, "You know, *Maa*, there are sixty-five guests here today, counting not only those in this room; there is another bunch in the next room—can't you hear them go 'ho ho ho'? It is Rs. 25 per head, you have to count the liquour, even if it is not consumed. The fine on empty glasses is not insubstantial. Anybody else would have shrivelled up at this. Seeing his generosity, even the bank director is stunned. Do you know how much we had to pay for the film singer? She charges Rs. 400 per night."

Revati's heart was flopping around like a decapitated catfish in its death throes. His throat was dry; he could not utter a word.

Sohini asked, "What is today's gathering in honour of?"

"You don't know? It's out in the Associated Press: he is now the President of Jagani Club, and this feast is in his honour. He will pay the Rs. 600 fees for lifetime membership later, at his convenience."

"It might not be convenient soon."

Revati's heart was caught under a steamroller.

Sohini asked him, "So it won't be convenient for you to get up now?"

Revati looked at Neela. Her ironic gaze roused the

man in him. He said, "How do I leave? The guests are—"

Sohini said, "Okay, I'll sit and wait here. Meanwhile, Nasrullah, please man the door."

Neela said, "That won't do, *Maa*, we are going to have secret consultations; it won't be appropriate for you to stay."

"Look, Neela, don't be too clever by half; I can play that game better than you. As if I don't know what your consultation is about. I am telling you; I am the person needed the most for this consultation."

Neela said, "What have you heard and from whom?"

"The art of being informed lies, like a snake in its hole, in a bagful of money. There are three lawyers here, whose job is it to find out whether there is a loophole in the laboratory fund. Isn't that so, Neela?"

Neela said, "To tell you the truth, it is not natural that the daughter should have no share in her father's inheritance. So, everyone suspects—"

Sohini got up from her chair. She said, "The source of this suspicion is situated further back in time. Who is your father, and a share of whose property do you want? You are the daugheter of such a man that you should be ashamed of uttering such things."

Neela jumped up and said, "What are you even saying, *Maa*?"

"I am telling the truth. He knew everything, everything. What he had to get from me, he got in full measure will get even today; he did not expect anything else."

Barrister Ghosh said, "Why should we take your word as proof?"

"He knew that. He has mentioned everything openly in a sworn affidavit."

"Hey friends, it's getting late, let's go.'

In the face of the mother's Peshawari posture, all of the sixty-five guests vanished.

At this point Chaudhuri presented himself, suitcase in hand. He said, "I had to rush here after your telegram—how are you doing, Revi, your face is white as a parchment—Where is the child's milk bowl?"

Pointing to Neela, Sohini said, "The one who is procuring it, is sitting over there."

"Have you become a milkmaid, my child?"

"She's more into catching milkmen, and there's the prey sitting next to her."

"Who? Our Revi?"

"This time round, it's my daughter who has rescued the lab. I am not a judge of people, but my daughter understood that I had turned my lab into a cowshed—it just managed not to drown in a lake of dung; the whole thing."

Chaudhuri said, "My dear, since you have discovered the creature, then you have to take charge of this simpleton. He has everything except brains. If you stay with him, people might not notice it. It's easy to lead stupid men by their noses."

Neela said, "So, Sir Isaac Newton, the registrar's office has been notified. Would you like to withdraw the notice?"

Revati thrust out his chest and said, "Not even if I have to die."

"The marriage will take place at an inauspicious hour."

"Most certainly, it will."

Sohini said, "Miles away from the lab, if you please."

The professor said, "Dear Neelu, the idiot is not altogether incapable. Let him get over his intoxication; you won't have to bother about feeding him."

"Sir Isaac, you will have to get yourself a new set of clothes; otherwise, I'll have to cover my head in front of you."

Another shadow fell on the wall. The aunt had arrived at the scene. She said, "Revi, come along."

Revati meekly followed after her, not looking back even once.

*Ashwin,* 1940

# The Last Word

In the turbid, random colours of life's flow when, all of a sudden, the story takes on its true form, the identity of its principal male and female characters seems to have been woven much, much before. One must obey the dictates of this prologue. So, I'll take some time to clarify the exact same thing. But I'll have to falsify names and places. Else I won't be able to answer for them to my immediate circle. I'm thinking about what name to give. A romantic name would mean imposing the fifth note of the Basanti *raag*, which I don't want. I think the name Nalinmadhab will do. One could have washed him of his dark complexion and turned him into Nabarun Sengupta. But it wouldn't have rung true, the story would have lost adherents through the inflation of the name, people would have thought he had donned a *jamewar* shawl and had come to stake a claim on the *babu* class in a literary gathering.

I number among the revolutionaries in Bengal. The

mighty British Empire had pulled us close to the shores of the Andamans. Through diverse paths and detours, I had avoided the dragnet of the C.I.D., and had reached Afghanistan. I finally got to America as a sailor. I was full of the stubbornness of the East Bengali; I did not forget for a moment that I would have to file away, day and night, and as long as I lived, at the chains that bound the hands and feet of India. However, having spent some time abroad, I understood—that the process through which we had begun this episode of revolution was like striking a match to our store of gunpowder. That had only burnt our own foreheads, leaving no stain on the face of British might. It was the flame that drew the moth into its fatal embrace. When, arrogantly, we jumped in, we didn't understand that we were not setting afire the powder kegs of history but only our own humble funeral pyres. Meanwhile, we saw Europe's great armies wear an apocalyptic aspect accompanied by elaborate arrangements—and with it, disappeared the audacious hope that we would be able to install this epoch-changing, all-ervasive destructiveness on the altar of our humble abode. We didn't even have the means of calling a conference to commit suicide. I understood clearly—if we had to live, it wouldn't do to use the primitive nails on the fingers of our ancient ancestors. In our age, machine must fight machine; it is easy to die in any old way, but to die as Vulcan's worshippers is not easy. No use in getting impatient; we had to begin from scratch—we had a long way to go, we had a formidable enterprise on our hands.

I took initiation into engineering. I somehow got myself into the Ford Motor factory in Detroit. I was trying my hand at it but didn't feel I was getting anywhere. I don't know what struck me one day; I felt that if I made Ford understand that I was not interested in just my own progress but in freeing my country, I thought that that magician of a wealth-creator in freedom-loving America would be happy, that he would make my way straight. Ford smirked and said, "My name is Henry Ford; it's an old English name. Our cousins in England are out of work; I'll think of them first—this is my resolve." I had thought he might have been enthusiastic about making Indians work.

I understood one thing: those who had money, had sympathy for only those like themselves. And I saw that on the circular path of manufacturing money my learning could not advance further. Because of this, my eyes were opened in one respect: I had to go deeper into my study of engineering. I had to learn how to collect what was needed to make machines. The world had stored its minerals in its womb for the mighty of the earth, and with this they conquered all, and for the poor was reserved the harvest of its upper layers, their ribs sticking out, their stomachs caved in. I devoted myself to the study of mining. Ford said that the English were dysfunctional, and India was its proof—they had put their hands to cultivating indigo one day and tea the next—a bunch of civilians had gone to office to arrange for so-called 'law and order,' but they could not inaugurate the exploitation of India's vast and hidden resources, whether natural or those of the human spirit. Instead, they sat and sucked the blood of jute farmers. I saluted Jamshed Tata from beyond the seas. I have decided that my job is not to chuck firecrackers. I would rather burgle the underground city through its stone walls. I won't chant the name of the Mother like the bunch of old fools who cling to their mother's sleeve, and I would not make a mantra out of the notion of 'holy poverty' in the name of the helpless, hungry, illiterate mass of the poor. In my youth, I had played this game quite a bit—I had shed copious tears in front of the glittering idol made by those who swore by self-rule in their mud houses and of whom the poet had sung. Having come to this enlightened country, I have learned to call a spade a spade and to roll up my sleeves and get to work. Now I will set out, shovel in one hand, a spade in the other, and hammer on in search of hidden treasure—this, the disciple of the poet's effusive tone will not be able to recognise as worship of the Motherland.

After leaving Ford's factory, I studied mines and minerals for about nine years. I toured many places in Europe to gain hands-on experience; I have invented a couple of devices myself and have been encouraged by my professors; I learned to believe in myself and despise the earlier entranced failure that I was.

The link between these lofty attitudes and my short story is not essential—I could have left it out; indeed, it might have been better to leave it out. But, on this matter, one thing has to be said, so let me just say it. When, in the beginning, the colourful auroras occur in the epicentre of life due to the magnetism of feminine influence, I was absent-minded, absolutely absent-minded. I was an ascetic, a *karma yogi*—and with these words I had tied a tight knot on the loose ends of my mind. When those interested in giving away their daughters in marriage were coming and going, I made it clear that the girl's father should get in touch only if untimely widowhood figured in the girl's horoscope.

In the western continents, there is no way of avoiding female company. On that score, I was expected to have a tough time. I was a handsome man: in my country, women had no other way to convey this except through the mute language of the eyes, which is why this fact lay outside my consciousness. Just as I had discovered abroad that my intelligence was out of the ordinary, so it was discovered that I was good-looking. I could tell many stories to arouse the jealousy of readers in this country, but I swear that I never allowed my heart to be caught up in the sorcery of emotions. Perhaps I was made of sterner stuff' Not sentimental and soft like the men of taste in Bengal, I had locked up my resolve in a safe made of stone. It was also against my principle to play romantic games with women and then let drop the whole thing at the opportune moment. I knew for certain that the stubbornness with which I had sought shelter in my pledges, the slightest slip would mean being crushed to death under my broken pledge because of its very stubbornness. There was no way of cheating my way out of it. Besides, I couldn't get rid of my old-fashioned inhibitions about girls of a different background. Therefore, I ignored those who boasted about the love of women.

I had obtained a good degree from abroad. Knowing that I would be worthless in a government job here, I had taken employment with a *raja* of the moon clan—let's say in the court of Chandravir Singh, of the Chotnagpur plateau. Fortunately, as it turned out, his son, Devika Prasad, had studied for a while at Cambridge. Incidentally, I had met him in Zurich, and he had heard good things about me. I had explained my plan to him. Enthused, he put me to work on the geological survey of his state. The higher bureaucracy was cross that the job hadn't been given to an Englishman. But Devika Prasad was a fierce customer. The old king was swayed for a while, but I hung on.

Before coming here, my mother had said to me, "Dear son, now that you've got a good job get married and fulfil my long-held expectations."

I said, "In other words, ruin my prospects. The work I do doesn't go well with marriage."

The firm resolve—my mother's request went abegging. I packed all my equipment and came away to the jungle.

Now, on the potential horizon of my exploits before my countrymen, a small story shows us what had—what could have—been a maze of delusion or of hope.

I roam in the forests, questioning the stones, in search of some ground. The sky is an intoxication of *palash* flowers and the *manjari* flowers are on the *sal* trees, and swarms of bees buzz around—Businessmen busy collecting lac. *Tussore* silk cocoons are being collected from the mulberry. The *Santhals* are gathering ripe mahua flowers. A slender stream dances its way with a faint gurgle; I had named it Tanika. This is not a factory floor or a college classroom; this is the kingdom of sweet evenings, where, finding a solitary heart, the great illusion, Nature displays its colours—as it is wont to do at sunset every day.

The heart was in rapture. The pressures of work had slowed down a bit; I was slightly upset with myself; I had been applying pressure to the oar. I was thinking I had been caught in the web of tropical weather. Since birth, the hand fan's unceasing rhythm, like the beads of a rosary, had been driving our blood in the diabolical tropics—its sweat-drenched magic has to be avoided.

It was late. The river forked into two after hitting a sandbank in the middle of its course. On that sandy island sat quietly a group of herons. At the end of the day, this sight would indicate to me that it was time to wind up my work. Carrying soil and rocks in my bag, I was walking towards my bungalow, where I would test them in my laboratory there. The barren land lies unused between afternoon and evening; it is difficult for a solitary individual to while away that time of day. Especially in a wild forest devoid of human beings. That is why I had chosen that time for my experiments. I switch on the electricity and the lights on my dynamo—I sit with my scales, my microscope, and my chemicals. There are days when I work late into the night. Today, at a certain place, I had detected traces of manganese. Therefore, I quickened my pace in enthusiastic anticipation. The crows flew home, cawing against the saffron sky.

Suddenly, the path to my workplace was obstructed. On it lay a clump of five *sal* trees and on a slight incline if someone sat in that enclosure, he or she would be visible only through a single gap. It would be most normal to suddenly avert one's gaze. That day, there was a peculiar radiance bursting through the clouds. In that gap in the forest, within the shadows, a bright light seemed to have broken through the knots of the god of horizons and spread like a fistful of gold. In that light, sat the girl leaning against a tree with her legs drawn up against her chest, writing away, focused, in a diary. In a moment, there was manifested to me an amazing marvel. Such things happen but rarely in life. A surging wave summoned by the full moon began lapping against my breast, pushing against it with the force of a high tide.

Hidden by the trees, I gazed on. An astonishing picture began imprinting itself in the chambers of everlasting memories of the heart. In my wide experience of the world, my mind had come across several unexpected, charming doors. I skirted around them. Today, I felt myself in front of one of life's ultimate bends. I am not used to feeling like that or speaking like that at all. The blow that strikes one, unknown to one, a wonderful nature opens the latch and flows uninhibited; how could such a blow strike me? I have always stood rock solid, inert as a mountain. From within came cascading down a waterfall.

I wanted to say something, but I couldn't figure out the first words to pronounce in life's greatest conversation. It is among the first words of the Bible—'Let there be light,' let the unexpressed be expressed. At a certain point—the girl—I learnt her real name later on, but I won't use that. I named her Achira. What does it mean? It means the one who, like lightning, expresses herself in an instant. That name remains—seeing her face, I thought Achira was aware that someone was present but hidden. Presence has its own mute signal; at one point I thought of saying, 'Excuse me—' Excuse what? What was the crime? What was there to say? I stepped away a little, took out my short English shovel. I pretended to stab the earth with it; I put something—I know not what—into my bag that was really bad. After that, I trained my eyes on the ground with a scientific vision and went away. But I knew in my heart of hearts the one I had tried to fool had not been fooled. She had, no doubt, received many times over, the proof of the weakness of entranced masculinity. I hoped that, in my case, she had, in her heart, enjoyed this. If I had had to jump over an obstacle slightly easier than this then, then I don't know what would have happened. Would she have been angry or feigned anger? As I wound my way to the bungalow with a heart in turmoil, my eyes happened to notice an envelope torn in two. This is not a geological sample. Nonetheless, I picked it up and looked at it. It was addressed to Bhabatosh Majumdar, ICS, address Chhapra, written in a woman's hand. It had a stamp, but without the seal of the post office. Like the hesitation of a maiden. In my scientific mind, I understood clearly that inside the envelope lay the scar of a tragedy. From the fragments of the earth, it is our task to extract the history of its revolutions. Then and there, my research-honed hands determined to discover the mystery behind this torn envelope. Meanwhile, I was thinking, the mystery of my mind was unprecedented. To be in contact with a certain situation, what is that emotion that we can see in all its detail on a new shape, and one is struck by its identity. The mind, which, through sheer perseverance, had gone in search of the goal of life from town to town, I had understood that mind with utmost clarity. I had thought that that was its true nature, that I could swear on the integrity of its conduct. But it was for the first time I saw that outside the governance of its intelligence, a fool lay hidden within it. Was caught the forest-dweller who would listen not to reason, but to desire. The forest has its aura, the silent conspiracy of foliage, the chant of an ancient spirit. You can hear, all day long, the rigorous strains of its noble tune; deep into the night, its grave melody hums with the consciousness of creatures and surrounds the intelligence with the deepest inspiration of an antique vitality.

This forest-dwelling aura was working inside my geological activity—I was looking for radium, looking to see if I could wrest it from the grip of miserly earth—when I had seen Achira blossom within the confines of the shadows of the *sal* trees. I had certainly seen Bengali women before this. But I hadn't had the opportunity of seeing one so independent of everything else and in such a singular fashion. Here the foliage of the jungle added its own words to the dark softness of her body. I had seen many foreign beauties in my time and had been appreciated by them. But this was the first time I had seen a Bengali woman exactly there, where she can be seen in her completeness. In this dense forest, she was not mixed up with its various elements, familiar and unfamiliar; seeing her, one wouldn't get the impression that she went to the diocesan school, swinging her plait, or had a degree from Bethune College or served tea to uproarious laughter at Kaliganj's tennis parties. The songs of Horu Thakur and Ram Bose that I had heard and forgotten many years ago as a child, these songs do not play on the radio and do not resonate through a gramophone in the neighbourhood. I don't know why, but the preface of that Bengali beauty was written in the easy compositions of those songs—'Let the heart's pain, o friends, remain in the heart.' That there was a melancholy picture in the melody of this song took form and floated up to my eyes clearly. This too was made possible. As a geology student, I knew that a powerful earthquake could bring to the surface the burning lava within the bowels of the earth, and I saw within myself turbulent things lying at the bottom, in the lower darkness, exposed to the light of day. I had never hoped to see this topsy-turviness within the firm soul of the stern scientist Nalinmadhab.

I can understand that every evening, as I returned to my place of work, she would see me, and—oh absent-minded me! I had not seen her. After going abroad, I had grown proud of my looks. 'Oh, how handsome'—my ears had grown used to this phrase. But I had heard from those among my friends who had gone abroad that Bengali girls had a different taste; they looked for soft, effeminate features in masculine beauty. As the saying went—as handsome as Kartik. Whatever else a Bengali Kartik might be, he was not a male commander of an army of gods. In Paris, I had heard from one lady friend,

'The colour white is an absence of colour;, the colour drawn on an oriental's body by a warm sky is the true colour, that colour of shadows that is the colour we like.' This utterance probably does not hold true this side of the Bay of Bengal.

Thus far there had been no occasion for such discussions to arise in my mind. For a few days the question made me think. My sunburnt complexion, long and lively my body, strong my arms, quick my gait, and my gaze sharp—or so I have been told—the nose, the forehead, the chin, all made for a clear and powerful face. Epstein had wanted to sculpt my face in stone but didn't find the time. But I know Bengalis to be their mother's son, and the mothers liked to see the treasure in their lap as wax dolls. Thinking about these thoughts, I would grow angry. I was prematurely arguing in my imagination with Achira. I was telling her, 'What you think is handsome is, but a god meant for immersion; without your panegyrics, he won't last very long.' I was telling her, 'I, who had been present at debutante balls in big countries, and had refused many a hand extended towards me, and you will ignore me?' This fabricated quarrel was so juvenile, so full of overfamiliarity with the other, that I laughed at my own anger. On the other hand, the scientist's logic was doing its work within me. I tell my heart, this is no mean thing, that she sat beside the path that I took coming and going—if she had only prayed for solitude, she would have shifted elsewhere by now. At first, I had cast sideways glances at her, as if pretending not to see her. Recently we have locked eyes—as far as I understand, this was not taken to be a fatal accident involving two pairs of eyes by her.

An even more extraordinary test had taken place. Previously, I used to, laden with soil and stone samples, go at the end of the day only once, homewards. Of late, my toing and froing had been more frequent. Achira was old enough to understand that this was not just about geology. My daring increased by leaps and bounds, especially when I saw that awareness of this deliberate ploy had not evicted the young girl. There were days when, suddenly looking back, I would see Achira following my quick pace, and quickly shifting her gaze back to the diary and when caught doing so. I suspected the speed at which she wrote in her diary had slowed somewhat. In my scientist's intelligence arose a discussion on the mysteries of the heart. I understood that she had taken a vow of penance for some man, his name Bhabatosh, assistant magistrate at Chhapra, a job he has been doing since his return from abroad. Previous to this, when he was in the country, they loved each other dearly. Before taking up the job, a radical change had come over. What this could be, I had to find out. Which was not too difficult since Bankim, my Cambridge classmate, was teaching at the University of Patna.

I sent a letter by post: 'Bhabatosh was in the Bihar

Civil Service. In the circle of guardians of marriageable daughters, Bhabatosh was a suitable boy. One of my friends had asked me to help him lay a conjugal trap for him for the sake of his daughter. I would be grateful if you could let me know, in full detail, whether the road is clear or not. I also want to know something about the man's character.'

The reply came. 'The road is closed. And if you are still interested in his character then read on.

'When I was in college, I was a student of Professor Anil Kumar Sarkar—his name combines many letters of the alphabet. His erudition was as out of the common, as his simplicty was childlike. If you saw his granddaughter, the only light in his household, you would think that satisfied with his penance, not only has Saraswati, goddess of learning, sprung up in the world of his intelligence but also has her beauty nestled in his lap. That devil, Bhabatosh, had entered this paradise. His intelligence was sharp and his conversation fluent. First the professor was taken in, and then his granddaughter. Our hands would itch for action when we witnessed their unbearable intimacy. But we couldn't say a thing; the marriage had been fixed, and it was only a question of the boy going abroad and coming back. His passage and all his expenses were arranged by the professor. Bhabatosh was susceptible to contracting a cold. The rest of us would pray twice a day to a deaf god that may he die of pneumonia before his marriage. But he did not die. He passed his exam. And then he married the daughter of a high official of the Government of India. Angry and ashamed, the professor left his job, and no one knows where he and his granddaughter have vanished, without a trace.'

I read the letter. I decided that I would rescue this girl from her shame and dishonour.

Meanwhile, I grew restless trying to figure out a way to strike up a conversation with Achira. If I had been a literary man instead of a scientist, or a denizen of western Bengal instead of being a *bangal*, then I wouldn't have been at a loss for words. But I was scared to talk to a Bengali girl, I felt I didn't know sufficiently about them. I had this idea that Hindu women were unapproachable for unfamiliar men. If I went to talk to her just like that, she might deem it inappropriate. The word 'custom' is blind. Before joining work here, I had spent a few days in Calcutta—I had seen, among friends and family, painted women who frequented the cinema and the theatre, women of the race of friends and companions, their—but let them be. However, without even knowing Achira, I could tell she belonged to a different race— and outside this type stood a pure, dignified girl, too sensitive to touch. I was turning over in my mind how to start a conversation with her.

At this time a couple of dacoities had taken place in the environs. I thought, in this context, of telling Achira, 'I'll tell the king to arrange for some guards for you.' An English girl would have treated this benign overfamiliarity as audacious, would have shaken her head and said, 'That's my business.' But I had no experience to indicate to me how this Bengali girl would take it. Having spent a good deal of time away from Bengal, my mind had grown accustomed to English ways and manners.

It was almost the end of the day. It was time for Achira to go home or for her grandfather to take her for a stroll. At that moment, a North Indian country yokel suddenly snatched Achira's bag and diary from her hands and made off with them. I stepped out of the clearing and said, "You have nothing to fear."

And then I ran after the man and pounced on his neck, at which he dropped the bag and diary and ran away. I restored the proceeds of the crime to Achira.

Achira said, "Thankfully, you—"

I said, "Don't mention it, thankfully that man came along."

"Meaning?"

"Meaning, thanks to him, I was able to address my first words to you. All these days I couldn't think of what to say to you."

"But that man is a dacoit."

'No, he is not a dacoit; he is my wingman."

Achira lifted the loose end of her sari to her face and laughed merrily. Her laughter was as sweet as the melodious cascade of a waterfall.

She stopped laughing and said, "It would have been

much more fun had he been a real dacoit."

"Much more fun for whom?"

"For the one who was looted. I have read a story like this."

"And what would have happened to the rescuer?"

"I would have taken him home and offered him tea."

"And what will happen to this make-believe rescuer?"

"He is not in need of anything. He only wanted the first words of an introduction—he has got the second, third, fourth, fifth words as well."

"Will the numbers run dry?"

"Why should they?"

"Tell me, had it been you, what would your first words have been?"

"For me, I would have said, 'Why are you going about collecting pebbles and stones on the roads like a child? Haven't you grown up?'"

"Why didn't you?"

"I was afraid."

"Afraid? Afraid of me?"

"You are a wealthy man. I have heard from my grandfather. He has read your article in a foreign newspaper. Whatever he reads he tries to explain to me."

"This too?"

"Yes. But confronted with a ring of Latin words. I begged off and said, "Let me fetch the book on quantum theory."

"That you understand?"

"Not a bit. But *dadu* is of the conviction that everyone can understand everything. And I don't like breaking that conviction. He has another amazing notion—in ordinary intelligence, women are sharper than men. So, I go in fear of having to listen to his explanations on the scientific connectedness of "timespace", this time around for sure. Actually, he has infinite compassion for women. When my grandmother was alive, she would shut him up as soon as he began his lofty discourses. So, he got no proof from grandmother of how far a woman's sharp intelligence could go. I can't disappoint him. I've heard a lot, understood nothing, will hear a lot and understand nothing."

Achira's face was shining with affection and curiosity. I did not wish for this intercourse with a pleasant voice to come to an end quickly. The light of day grew faint. The evening light had come on over the *sal* forest. *Santhal* women were headed homewords after having collected firewood from the forest, one could hear them singing at a distance.

A voice was heard saying, "My child, where are you? It's dark! The times are not good."

"Indeed *dadu*, which is why I have appointed a bodyguard."

No sooner did the person appear than I took the dust of his feet. He was unprepared for this. I introduced myself, "My name is Nalinmadhab Sengupta."

This cheered up the old man. He said, "Did you say you are Dr. Sengupta? But you are just a boy!"

I said, "Absolutely! I am no more than 36 years old."

Again, that melodious laughter from Achira's mellifluous throat was like double the resonance of a sitar. She said, "To *dadu* everybody in the world is a boy and *Dadu* is Agarwala to all of them."

The professor said, "Agarwala? A new word has been imported into Bengali. From where?"

"From that dear Marwari student of yours, Kundanlal Agarwala. He used to get me mango chutney in a bottle; I had asked him what Agarwala meant. He had replied, 'a pioneer.'"

The professor said, "Dr. Sengupta, now that we have met, you have to come over once."

"You don't have to say anything, *dadu*, he is impatient to leave. He has heard from me that you have collected data from everywhere and are ready to expound, perched on Einstein's shoulders."

I said to myself, 'Good lord! What a mischievious person!'

The professor encouraged, said, "You too, think that timespace—"

I was a bit flustered and said, "I understand nothing of timespace. Trying to explain all that to me would be a waste of time."

The old man grew solicitous, "Time! Where is the lack of time here?! Okay, do one thing: why don't you have dinner with us today, eh?"

I was going to jump on that and say, "Right now?!"

Achira spoke up, "*Dadu*, I don't call you juvenile for nothing. You invite whoever you like and put me in a bind. Where will I get a Firpo's here in Dandakaranya. They are used to English dinners and eat all sorts of meat—why do you want to give your granddaughter a bad name? We will have to arrange for some *bhetki* and some lamb."

"All right, all right, say when would it suit you?"

"Tomorrow itself. But I don't want to distress Achira *debi*. I have to tour dense forests, mountains, and caves. I usually carry some rice flakes in my bag and a bunch of bananas, imported eggplant, chickpeas, and peanuts too. I'll bring along my provisions of vegetables, Achira *debi* can mix it with curd with her own hands. If you agree to this, then there is no problem."

"*Dadu*, don't trust these people. You had written an article on the role of vitamins in Bengali cuisine for a monthly magazine, so he's trying to please you with his list of bananas and puffed rice."

I thought to myself, 'She has put me in jeopardy; it was never possible for me to read an article on vitamins in a Bengali journal, an article authored by a doctor. But how to admit it? Especially, when he asked me, his pleasure showing, "Have you really read it?"'

I said, "Whether I have read it or not is not the point; the real thing—"

"The real thing is he knows that if we invite him tomorrow, then he won't want for fowl or beast on his plate. Which is why he's chanting praises to the English eggplant. Just take a look at his physique, will anybody think he feeds on spinach alone? *Dadu*, you are so gullible everybody takes you for a ride, even I. Which is why I don't dare pull your leg once in a while."

We were chatting and proceeding towards their house when Achira suddenly said to me, "Now it is time for you to return home."

"But why? I thought I would see you off at your door."

"The house is in a mess. You might say, Bengali girls are untidy. Tomrrow, I'll put the house in order in such a way that you will be reminded of English ladies."

The professor said, "Dr. Sengupta, don't think that my granddaughter Achira talks too much, that is not her nature. In this desolation , she keeps me distracted with her constant chatter. And she is now used to this. When she is quiet, my house feels haunted, and I feel lonely. She knows that. I fear somebody may misunderstand her."

Achira put her arms around the old man and said, "Let them, *dadu*, I don't want to be blameless; that is so uninteresting."

The professor said with pride, "Do you know, Dr. Sengupta, my granddaughter can talk? I haven't seen anyone like her."

"*Dadu*, you haven't seen anybody like me, and I

haven't seen anyone like you."

I said, "Before I go, dear professor, you have to give me your word on one matter."

"Fine."

"Every time you address me formally, I bite my tongue. If you address me as you would someone younger than you, I will feel truly honoured, and held in affection. Your granddaughter may be of some assistance in addressing me informally."

"Good lord! I am just a mere granddaughter; I won't be able to touch those heights' You are a big man. What I say is, let a few days go by, and if I can forget your degree-bearing form, then all will be possible. But *dadu* is free. Start straightaway, *dadu*. Say, "Please come over for a meal tomorrow; if my granddaughter puts too much salt in the fish curry, then put up with it like a man and say, 'Wonderful! May I have another helping?'"

The professor placed a friendly hand on my shoulder and said, "My dear, if you had seen my granddaughter a while back, you would have understood she is really of a shy sort. That is why when she thinks it her duty to get to know someone, she forces herself to talk too much."

"Do you see Dr. Sengupta, how gently *dadu* admonishes me? As if, wielding a sugar cane stalk. He could have said, 'You are rude, and your loquaciousness is irritating.' But you will defend me, won't you? What will you say?"

"I won't say it in front of you."

"Because it will sound too harsh?"

"You know what I'm talking about."

"Alright then, let us call it a day; now go home."

"I have one more thing to say. The invitation I have for tomorrow is for my rechristening. From tomorrow, Dr. Sengupta will no longer be a part of Nalinmadhab. Just like a comet loses its tail in the vicinity of the Sun, leaving intact only its head."

"In that case, it would be a chopping off of the name; why call it a rechristening?"

And there ended my first big day.

The pacific beauty of old age, its tranquil shape. The eyes seemed to be showering blessings. A polished walking stick in his hand, a folded shawl around his neck, a dhoti carefully pleated, a *tussore* silk upper garment, and hair grown scarce on his scalp though neatly combed, nevertheless.

It was plain that his appearance and his lifestyle both bore the artistic imprint of his granddaughter. He put up with the torment of being spoilt just to please his granddaughter.

My scientific nosing around was outpaced by the need to keep myself informed about them. I will use the professor's name, Anil Kumar Sarkar. A PhD from Cambridge University of the previous generation. A few months ago, he had quit as the principal of a suburban college, and had rented an abandoned bungalow belonging to the postal department in this princely state, and had it refurbished and renovated at his own expense. This was as far as history went. The remaining details I could match with Bankim's letter.

The prehistory of my story ends here. There is not much that separates the beginning and the end of a short story. I'll resist the temptation to prolong and elaborate; I don't want to spoil its nature.

The time to speak clearly with Achira came shortly. That day, we were picnicking on the banks of the Tanika.

The professor, all of a sudden, asked me, child-like, "Nalin, are you married?"

The question was so clearly significant that anybody else would have avoided asking it altoghether. I answered, "No, not yet."

Nothing escaped Achira's notice. She said, "*Dadu*, that "not yet" is meant to console anxious parents; it has no specific meaning."

"How are you so certain that it is entirely meaningless?"

"It's a mathematical problem. Though not what one understands when one says higher mathematics. We have already heard you are 36 years old. I am making a calculated guess; your mother has already told you six or seven times, "Son, I want a daughter-in-law in the house." You must've said, "Before that I want to bring money to put into an iron safe." Your mother had wiped her tears and stood silent. After that, in the interim, you've got everything; only you need to be hanged. In the end, when you got a position in this princely state with a fat salary, your mother must have again said, "Son, you must marry now, I have only so many days to live." You had answered, "My life and my science are one, to be dedicated to the country. I will never marry." In despair, she again wiped the tears from her eyes. Tell me, whether I have gone wrong in working out the sum of your 36 years of existence."

Talking carelessly with this girl was not without risk. A few days previously something had occurred. The subject had been broached, and Achira had told me, "In this country, you get women to be companions in your household. Those who don't need a woman in their house, for them women are wholly unnecessary. But those who practice science abroad find suitable female practitioners, just as Professor Curie got Madame Curie. Haven't you come across a woman like that when you were there?"

I recalled Catherine. We had worked together in London. Indeed, her name had appeared alongside mine in one of my research books. I had to accept the truth of Achira's assertion. She said, "Why didn't you marry her? Was she not willing?"

I had to say, "Yes, indeed, a proposition had come from her."

"Then?"

"My work was in India. It was not about science alone."

"In other words, a successful love was not desirable

for a hermit like you. For women, their highest goal is personal; yours are impersonal."

I had no immediate answer to this. Seeing me silent, Achira said, "You don't read Bengali literature, do you? There is a poem about Kach and Debjani. The poem deals with the subject I just mentioned, that a woman's duty is to bind men, and a man's duty is to break through those bonds. Towards immortality. Kach had set out ignoring Debjani's prayer, and you have ignored your mother's plea. It's the same thing. In this eternal conflict between men and women, you have emerged victorious. May your maleness triumph. Let women cry; those tears are but ritual offerings in their worship of you. The offering is meant for the god, but the god is not bound by it."

The professor understood nothing of the main purpose behind this discussion. He said with some pride, "How profound truths are uttered effortlessly by my granddaughter, if someone heard her—"

He was perennially afraid that other people wouldn't understand her.

Achira said, "Other people can't put up with a woman's impudence; don't waste your time thinking about them. It's enough that you understand me."

Achira says serious things lightly, but today, she is so earnest. I, for my part, sensed one thing: Bhabatosh had given her to understand that like the wife he had plucked out of the illuminated sky of the higher bureaucracy of the government of India, her aim, too, was lofty and unselfish. He could gather force in the service of his country from the storehouse of British administration. It was not that easy to fool Achira. That she had not forgotten was proved by the envelope torn into two.

Achira spoke again, "Do you know Nalin *babu* the dire prediction Debjani made about Kach?"

"No."

"She had said, "You will not be able to use for yourself that fruit of your search for knowledge, nor will you be able to pass it on to someone else." I find this astonishing. If this dire prediction had been made by someone with regard to Europe, then that someone would have been saved. By using the resources of the world as their own, they are dying out of unseemly greed. Isn't it true, *dadu*?"

"Very true, but the astonishing part is, how did you think up all this?"

"Not at all by myself. I have heard you say similar things many times. You have a great quality: you are forgetful. What you say, you entirely forget. That leaves us with no fear of putting our own seal on stolen goods."

I said, "The art of stealing is a high art. Whether it is wealth or the nation, the bigger the emperor, the bigger the thief. Only those who get caught just before putting their stamp on it come to be known as petty larcens."

Achira said, "So many of his students have copied out his utterances and made a name for themselves by getting them published. And then, surprised by what they've written, he praises them. He has no means of knowing that he is praising himself. It is my immense fortune that I often receive such praise—if you ask Nalin *babu*, he shall readily admit that he has begun consigning the tales of my originality in his notebooks, the very ones in which he writes of the Bronze Age. Do you remember, *dadu*, many years ago, when you were at the college, you had recited the poem about Kach and Debjani to me? Ever since, I have held men in high esteem in my heart, but never admitted it verbally."

"But, my dear, I have never diminished the esteem of women in any of my utterances."

"You? You, who are a blind admirer of women, I laugh, secretly, at your high praise of women. Women accept everything shamelessly. Reaping praise at very little cost to themselves has become a habit with them."

The conversation that day was not just a bit of fun. It was the beginning of a war. There were two sides to Achira's personality, each of which sought its own refuge— one was their house, and the other was the grove in the forest. By the time we had established an easy rapport, I had decided that in the enclosure of *sal* trees, amidst laughter and play, I would tell her of the crisis-ridden nature of my life and would somehow drive it towards some sort of a conclusion. But the road was closed. Just as, on the first day of our acquaintance, the first words would not come easily, so the Achira here had no first word. In this confrontation, I could not find a way to the innermost confines of her heart. Near her house, her humour and outspokenness would stop me in my tracks, while in the shade of the forest, she would contain my restlessness with a stubborn and wordless silence. On certain days, invited for tea, on a certain horizon, there would be an opportunity to open my heart; Achira would understand that I was approaching the danger zone, and on that very day, she would shower me, unnaturally, with a profusion of piercing words. There wouldn't be so much as a crack left open, and winds blew contrary. My mind grew fretful; there were so many obstacles in the performing of the task that I was secretly ashamed. At the budget meeting, there was a proposal to sanction more funds for my research division; the report related to the subject remained more than half unfinished. Meanwhile, I had been listening to a discussion on Croce's aesthetics over the past few days. The subject was well beyond my competence and appreciation. Achira certainly knew this. She encouraged her grandfather, and had a good laugh over it in private. Of late, the professor had been explaining all the arguments against behaviourism. The misery of this theoretical discussion was that Achira would take leave at a certain point and remove herself to the garden by saying, "I have heard these arguments before." I would remain seated like an idiot, casting occasional glances at the door.

One advantage was that the professor wouldn't ask me whether I understood an obscure aspect of the argument or not. He felt everything was crystal clear.

But this wouldn't do anymore; I had to seize the opportunity sooner or later. During a picnic, when the professor, seated on the steps of a terracotta temple, was reading a recently imported book on the new chemistry, Achira, ensconced in a clump of ebony trees suddenly said to me, "In this ancient forest there is a blind and active force, and I fear it increasingly."

I said, "Astonishing. I have written something similar in my diary."

Achira went on, "Just like in an old building, in one of its crevices, surreptitiously a sapling of a fig tree takes root and destroys it, so is this jungle. It is this that I was speaking about with *dadu*. *Dadu* had said, "If you stay away from human intercourse for long, then your consciousness grows weak under the influence of nature, and primitive vital forces take root." I had said, "What should one do under such circusmtances?" He had replied, "We bring our consciousness along with us—it is, indeed, away from the crowd and in solitude that we get to cultivate it, just like my books." It is easy for *Dadu* to say this, but the same medicine doesn't work for everybody. What do you think?"

I said, "Okay, you must understand what I say correctly. I think that in such a place one must have the company of a person in its entirety, within and without, under whose influence human nature can be held together as a whole. As long as you don't have that, blind force will continue to defeat us. Had you been an ordinary girl, then I would not have dared to state the truth so clearly, in the end."

Achira said, "Say it, please; don't hesitate."

I said, "I am a scientist; what I have to say, I will say impersonally. There was a time you loved Bhabatosh dearly. Do you love him as much even today."

"Take it that I don't."

"I have displaced your heart."

"That may be so, but it is not only you; there is also the terrible blind force of the jungle. Which is why I don't respect this displacement. I feel ashamed of it."

"Why don't you respect it?"

"Man has long striven to build his ideas through soul-force, and they are broken by blind life forces. My feelings for you are a result of the assault of that blind force."

"Being a woman, you reproach love thus?"

"I do, precisely because I am a woman. The ideals of love are things we use in our worship. That is what is called the quality of being a *Sati*, an ideal woman. This thing is not of nature, of the forest, or otherwise; it is womanly. In this wilderness, all this time, I was worshipping this ideal despite all injury, despite all deceit. If I can't defend that, I will be rendered unclean."

"Can you respect Bhabatosh?"

"No."

"Can you go to him?"

"No. But he and my life's first love are not the same thing. Today, that love of mine is impersonal. It requires no basis."

"I am not being able to follow you."

"You won't be able to follow. Your asset is your knowledge—at its peak, that knowledge is impersonal. A woman's asset is her heart. Were she to lose everything outwardly—that which can be seen, touched, and enjoyed—even so remains the ideal of her love, which is incapable of being expressed through language. In other words, impersonal."

I said, "See, there is no time for an argument. You might have read in the local papers that my work here is finished. The assistant geologist has said that prospecting must begin some distance from here, but—"

"Why didn't you go?"

"From you—"

"You want to hear the last word from me, having previously extracted the first word."

"Indeed."

"Then let me be clear. Ensconced in this wood, I have observed you without your being aware of it. You have worked tirelessly throughout the day, defying extreme heat. You didn't need anyone. There were days when you seemed in despair at not being able to obtain what you had sought. But the very next day, you began digging again indefatigably. A strong heart rides in a strong body. I have never seen anybody so dedicated to science. Even from a distance, I was filled with devotion."

"And now—"

"No, let me speak. As we got to know each other more and more, the feebler grew that dedication. Your work was hampered by a thousand petty occasions. Then I feared myself—this woman, fie on me for having brought this seed of defeat. Even though I had my own devotion, my own contemplation. That would purify my life, illuminate it, I knew for certain. I saw myself sliding back—the restlessness that had taken hold of me, its inspiration was, from inside the breath of this shaded forest, of its ancient life force. At times, enveloped by this demon night I have felt that there are demons who could snatch me away from my grandfather. Its venomous arm was coming closer and closer to me, day after day. Then, I would leave my bed, run and throw myself into the waterfall and bathe myself."

No sooner did Achira say this than she called out, "*Dadu*!"

The professor left his book, approached us and said with gentle affection, "What is it, my child?"

"Weren't you saying the other day that Man's truth has become evolution, through his devoted quest—that evolution is not biological?"

"Yes, that is what I say. On earth, barbarians are at

an animal stage. Only through devoted efforts, has he become knowledgeable. There is more such effort ahead; he will have to forsake matter; only then will he become a god. Gods have been imagined in the *Puranas*, but in the past, there were no gods; god is in the future, in the last chapter of human history."

"*Dadu*, let us reconcile your and my argument. It has been causing much turbulence in my mind of late."

I stood up to go, "In that case, I must go."

"No, do sit down. *Dadu,* that office of principal that you had in college has fallen vacant once again. The secretary has written earnestly requesting you to come and reclaim it. You showed me all your letters, but you didn't show me this one. Suspecting your intentions, I stole it."

"It was unfair of me."

"It wasn't unfair. I have dragged you from your seat. We are there only to bring you down."

"What are you saying, my child?"

"The truth. Without creation, the creator is empty-handed, as you are without students. Tell the truth."

"It's because I have always been a teacher—"

"And you shall be one, once again. You are a born teacher; you are a preceptor. Your quest for knowledge is not for yourself; it is to be given away to others. Haven't you seen, Nalin *babu*? No sooner does an idea strike him than he's after me, mercilessly. I don't understand three quarters of it. Or else he's after you, which is even worse.

He doesn't know where your mind is; he thinks it is after pure knowledge. *Dadu,* you absolutely need students but select them carefully."

The professor said, "It is the student who selects the teacher; it is he who is interested."

"Alright, we'll come to that later. Recently I have become aware that I have been turning the teacher into a bookworm. This is how I disrupt his meditation in my own selfish interest. You have to take up the job; you must go back there at this very moment."

Flabbergasted, the professor stared at Achira. Achira said, "Oh, I know you are thinking what will happen to me. You are my destiny. O innocent one, if I do not please you, then we'll have to procure Grandmother the Second, sell off your library, and get a few ornaments made, and I'll run off somewhere. If you are not an overweening egotist, you have to acknowledge this fact: that you can't do without me even for a day. In my absence, you mistake the 15th of *Ashwin* in the Bengali calendar for the 15th of October in the English. The days when your assistant professor is invited over, on those very days you shut the door of your library and devote yourself to some really difficult equations. You get into the car and give the chauffeur an address where a construction is yet to begin. Nalin *babu* thinks I am exaggerating."

I said, "Absolutely not! Having known him for a few days, I am now certain that what you say is the unalloyed truth."

"Why are such inauspicious utterances coming out of your mouth today? Do you know Nalin? He has lately been showing symptoms of loose talk?"

"All symptoms will disappear; you just get back to work. The pulse will become normal. All this delirious scolding will stop."

The professor looked at me and said, "What is your advice, Nalin?"

It's because he was such a learned man that he trusted in the intelligence of a geologist. I was silent for a while and then said, "Nobody can give you truer advice than Achira *debi*."

Achira got up and touched my feet; I was embarrassed and took a step backwards. Achira said, "Please do not be embarrassed; compared to you, I am nothing. That will become apparent one day. And let me say my farewell, here. We won't see each other before leaving."

The professor was surprised and said, "What are you saying, my child?"

"*Dadu*, you know a lot of things, but there are many things about which my intelligence is sharper than yours; please humbly accept this."

I took the dust off the professor's feet. He embraced me and said, "I am certain that before you lie famous deeds."

Here my short story ends. The next few words belong to the geologist. Back home, I consulted again my working notes and records. I suddenly felt a joy in my heart—I understand this is what is called release. In the evening, having finished the day's work, I came to the verandah and felt—the bird had flown the cage, but a chain still remained attached to its feet. It tinkles when I move.

*Falgun,* 1939

# Letter From a Wife

Dear Husband,

It's been fifteen years to the day since we've been married, and I haven't written a letter to you since. I've been by your side all the while—you've said words, many words, and so have I; yet, I haven't had so much as a pretext to write to you.

Today, I'm on a pilgrimage in this holy land, and you are in your office. Your relationship to Calcutta is like that of a snail to its shell; it is attached to your body and soul. So, you didn't apply for leave. It must be the wish of the Almighty; He has approved my application for leave.

I am the *Mejobou* to your family. It is now after fifteen years and on this seashore that I realise that I have another relationship with this world and its Creator. It is thus that I am picking up the courage to write to you, but it is not a letter from the *Mejobou*.

When only the one who had written the link to your

family on my forehead, only he and no one else, knew of this possibility, I and my brother came down with typhoid. My brother died, but I survived. The girls in my locality began saying, 'Mrinal was saved because she was a girl; had she been a boy— 'Yama, the god of death, must've in the past, been a master in the art of thievery; he lusts only after the most expensive things.

No dying for me. It is to explain this as best as I can that I have sat down to write this letter to you.

When your distantly related uncle came with your friend Nirad to look at the prospective bride, I was only twelve. Our house was in the remote countryside, where the jackals howl in the day. You have to travel in a bullock cart up to a distance of eight *kos,* and then cover the remaining three miles of unpaved road in a palanquin to reach the village. They must have felt awful. And then our East Bengali cuisine— your uncle must still remember the farce around that meal.

It was your mother's stubborn desire to compensate for the lack of looks of the wife of her eldest son, *Borobou,* with the wife of the middle son, *Mejobou;* otherwise, why should they have taken the trouble to travel to our village? And then in Bengal, nobody has to search for the ailments of the spleen, the liver, and the stomach or for marriageable daughters; they come unbidden and don't let go of you.

My father's heart began pounding in his chest; *maa* chanted the name of Durga. How would the priests of an obscure village appease the gods from the city? They relied on the beauty of their daughter, but the girl wasn't vain about her looks; she would consider herself worth whatever price the one who had come to see her was willing to pay. That's why, despite all their looks and their virtues, girls are never rid of anxiety.

The terror that had seized the entire household, indeed, the entire neighbourhood, sat like a stone upon my chest. It was as if all the light in the sky that day, along with all the powers of the world, were bent upon acting as minions of the two examiners and their pair of eyes by holding up a twelve-year-old village girl to their gaze firmly and strongly—I had nowhere to hide.

A flute played, making the entire sky whimper—as I came to stay with you people. The wives, after having finished enumerating all my shortcomings, finally agreed on the conclusion that, on the whole, I was pretty. Hearing this, my elder sister-in-law's face grew serious. I wonder, what was the need for my beauty? The thing called beauty, if it had been moulded out of the clay of the Ganges, by a pundit of yore, would have been considered worth taking care of, but since my beauty had been fashioned by the Creator for his own amusement, it had, in your religion, no value.

You didn't take long to forget that I was beautiful. But that I had brains, that you had to remember every step of the way. This intelligence was so natural to me that even after having spent years as a housewife, it is intact. *Maa* was very anxious because of this intelligence of mine; for a woman, it is the cause of woe. Someone who has to negotiate obstacles if that someone goes by her intelligence alone, then she will break her forehead through beating it against those very obstacles. But what could I have done? The Creator had given me, in a moment of distraction, far more intelligence than was needed to be a wife in your household, and to whom should I return this surplus? You called me an impudent woman twice every day. Bitter words are the consolation of the impotent; therefore, I forgive you.

I had something outside of your world of wives; none of you even learnt of it. I used to hide and write poetry. It may have been rubbish, but there the walls of the inner quarters did not loom as large. There was my release; there I was what I was. You didn't like in me all that went beyond the *Mejobou* of the family; you didn't require her, you didn't catch on, in the last fifteen years that I was a poet.

Among the oldest memories of your house, the one that comes to mind now is that of your cowshed. Your cows lived next to the staircase that leads to the inner quarters; apart from the front yard they have no room to move. In a corner of the front yard, there was a wooden trough containing fodder. In the morning, the attendant had plenty to do, and the hungry cows would lick the corners of the trough clean and then proceed to chew bits and pieces out of it. My heart would cry out. I am from a village—when I first came to your family house, those two cows and their calves looked to me like the only creatures I could relate to in your entire city. As long as I was newly married, I would go hungry and feed them instead in secret. When I grew older, seeing my open sympathy for the cows, my relatives began suspecting the soundness of my lineage.

My daughter died no sooner than she was born. She had called out to me to accompany her when she went away. Had she lived, she would have furnished all that would have been great and true in my life; from *Mejobou,* I would have become a mother. Mothers belong to the world as much as they do to a household. I felt the pain of being a mother but not the liberation.

I remember that the English doctor was annoyed when he saw our inner quarters and, annoyed still, gave us a scolding upon seeing the labour room. You people have a bit of a garden outside the front room. The room doesn't lack decoration or furniture. The inside is like the backside of a woolen artefact. There is no shame left in that, no beauty, no decoration; on that side, the lamp glows dimly. The wind enters like a thief; the rubbish in the front yard does not want to move, and the grime of the wall and the floor reign pristine. But the doctor had made a slight mistake; he believed that this troubles us day and night. Just the opposite; the little cared-for thing is like ash, and that ash hides its fire in its bosom but conceals its heat from everybody. When self-respect diminishes, then things not cared for do not seem unfair. There is no trouble in it. That is why women are so ashamed of feeling pain. That is why I say, if your commitment is such that women have to suffer, then, as far as is possible it is better to let them remain uncared for; care only enhances the degree of sorrow.

No matter how you keep us, it never occurs to us to remember that there is such a thing as sorrow. When Death came and stood at the head of the bed in the labour room; there was no fear in my heart. What is life to us that we should fear death? Only those who have been cared for and for whom life's attachment is strong fear death. That day, if you had caught and tugged at me then as grass is uprooted from loose soil, so I would have been uprooted. Bengali girls wish for death at the slightest word. Where is the courage in dying then? One is ashamed to die; it is so easy for us.

Like the evening star, my daughter sank back into my womb in an instant. I went back to my routine and my cows. I would have spent my life rolling on like this, and there would have been no occasion for me to write you this letter. But the wind carries a seed to the hard floor of the courtyard, and there sprouts an *ashwattha* tree; from that humble beginning, it breaks through the rib cage made of stone and wood. I don't know from where a mote of life came and settled on the surface of my solid routine, and then the fabric of my life began tearing up.

After the death of her widowed mother, the younger sister of my elder sister-in-law, Bindu, unable to bear the torture inflicted upon her by her cousins, sought refuge with her elder sister; that day you all thought, 'What kind of a bother is this?' What to do? It's my damned character—I saw you all were irritated by the incident, and so my mind was made up to stand resolutely by the side of this unfortunate girl. Seeking shelter with another against their wish—nothing could be more dishonourable. Forced to accept her circumstances, one could just shove her aside.

I saw the plight of my elder sister-in-law. She had taken pity on the girl and had brought her here. But when she saw her husband was unhappy about it, then she pretended that this was a big burden for her to carry, that she would be relieved if Bindu were driven out somewhere. She did not have the guts to openly hold this orphan sister in affection. She was an obedient wife.

Seeing her situation, my heart cried out. I saw that my elder sister went out of her way to show everybody that she had made very summary arrangements for the girl's food and clothing and that the girl had been shown her place among the servants and maids of the house, and I felt not only awful about this; but also ashamed. My elder sister-in-law was eager to prove to everybody that, through a trick, Bindu had been got at a very reasonable rate. She did a deal of work with very little expense involved. The family of our elder sister-in-law on her father's side had little except lineage to recommend itself; it had neither the looks, nor the money to show for it. You know well how one had to plead with my father-in-law to marry her off to this family. She had always considered her marriage into this family a crime. Which is why in all matters she adopted, as far as possible, the lowest profile and occupied as little space in your household as possible.

But this noble example caused a lot of problems for us. I cannot belittle you in every way. It is not in my character to judge a thing that I consider good for one to be bad for another—you've had enough of that.

I took Bindu to my room. Your elder sister-in-law said, "*Mejobou* is out to spoil this girl of poor origins." It was as if I had conjured up a great danger for everyone, as she went around telling everybody in the family. But I knew for certain that she was relieved. Now, I would carry most of the blame on my shoulders. Her burden was lightened in this way: the affection she could not show her sister was now my responsibility to show. My elder sister-in-law would try to snip off Bindu's age by a few years. But she was not younger than fourteen; it would not have been unfair to conceal this fact. You know that she wasn't pretty to look at; she was so ugly that had she cracked her skull by falling on the floor, people would have been more bothered about the condition of the floor. So, not having parents, she could not be given away in marriage and how many men would have had as stout a heart as to marry her?

Bindu had come to me very scared. As if I wouldn't be able to bear her touch. There seemed to be no point in her having been born in this world; therefore, she skirted around people, avoiding their gaze. In her father's house, her cousins hadn't left a corner for her such as would accommodate a useless object. Useless garbage easily finds a place around the house, because garbage can be easily forgotten; but a useless girl who is on the one hand useless, and on the other cannot be forgotten, doesn't find a place even in a rubbish-heap. Even though it would be difficult to assert that Bindu's cousins were eminently useful. But they're doing fine.

So, when I called Bindu to my room, she came with a trembling heart. I felt very bad noticing her fear. I told her with a lot of gentle kindness that she had a place in my room.

But my room is not just mine. So, my task was not easy. After a few days with me Bindu broke out in a reddish rash. Either it was prickly heat or something else; you people said smallpox. Because you see, she was Bindu. A quack in your locality came and said one had to wait for one or two days before a diagnosis could be pronounced. But who was going to wait another two days. Bindu almost died of shame for having contracted an illness. I said to myself, let it be smallpox; I would stay with her in the labour room; no one else needed bother. When all of you became aggressive towards me on this issue and even my elder sister-in-law feigned irritation, and you all were preparing to send the unfortunate wretch to the hospital, it transpired that all the rashes on her body disappeared. Upon this, you people grew more agitated. You said, "Certainly the smallpox has set in." Just because she was Bindu.

There is one immense advantage in growing up without love and affection; the body grows hard and robust. It refuses to fall ill; the principal routes through which death may penetrate are firmly closed. The disease made fun of her; but nothing happened. Yet, one thing was understood: it was difficult to give shelter to the most insignificant creature on earth. The more they require shelter, the harder it becomes to provide any.

No sooner had Bindu got over her fear of me than she was seized of another malady. She began loving me in such a way that I took fright. I had never in my life seen love like this. I have read about it in books, but that was between men and women. It had been a while since I had been reminded of the fact that I was beautiful—after all those days, this ugly girl was infatuated by my looks. She would devour me hungrily with her eyes. She would say, "Sister, no one but me has been able to see this face." On days when I would do my own hair, she would sulk. She liked taking the mass of my hair in her hands and shaking it this way and that. Except when invited out, I had no need to dress up, do my hair, put on make-up. But Bindu would pester me and do some make-up on me every day. The girl was crazy about me.

In your inner quarters, there is not even an inch to spare. On the northern side, next to the gutter, along the wall, had sprouted a mangosteen tree. The day I would see fresh new leaves on that mangosteen tree; I would know that spring was here. And the day I saw the soul of the unwanted child in my care take colour, that day I understood that there is a spring breeze even in the affairs of the heart—it comes from heaven, not from the street.

The unbearable wave of Bindu's love had made me restless. I admit, at times, I would be angry, but through her love I saw in me something that I had not seen in my life before. She was my true and free nature.

You people thought I was going too far in showering my love and affection on a girl like Bindu. There was no end to bickering and fault-finding because of this. The day my bracelet went missing from my room, you were not bashful in conveying to me that Bindu had some sort of a hand in this theft. When the daring *swadeshi* people's houses were searched, you easily jumped to the conclusion that Bindu was a police informer. There was no other proof for this, but that she was Bindu.

Your servants would refuse to do anything for her—if

one requested them to do some work for her, that girl would cringe and stiffen all over.

For these reasons, my expenses over her went up. I specially kept a maidservant just for her. You people didn't like that. You, my dear husband, were so enraged by the kind of clothes I gave Bindu to wear that you discontinued the money you gave to me for my private expenses. From the next day onwards, I started wearing a coarse, unbleached *dhoti* costing one rupee and four annas. And when Moti's mother came to take away my plate after meals, I told her not to. I would go to the tap in the courtyard, feed the calves with the leftovers, and then wash the plate. You were not happy when you suddenly surprised me in the act. It would not do to make me happy while you people *had* to be made happy. This piece of wisdom never made sense to me.

As your people's anger went on increasing, so did Bindu's age. At this natural occurrence you were unnaturally confused. I am still astonished about the thing. Why didn't you drive Bindu out of the house forcibly? I well understood, deep within, that your people were scared of me. God had given me intelligence, and your people could not escape acknowledging this fact.

Unable to evict Bindu by main force, you ultimately threw yourselves at the feet of the Creator. A husband was found for Bindu. Elder sister-in-law said, "Thank God, Mother Kali has saved our family from disgrace."

I did not know what husband you all had found for Bindu; from you people, I gathered that he was good in every respect. Bindu clasped my feet and wept. She said, "Why on earth am I to marry?"

I tried explaining to her, "Don't be afraid, Bindu, I've heard your husband is a good man."

Bindu said, "If he's good, why should he choose me, I who have nothing?"

The husband's family did not even take a look at Bindu. Elder sister-in-law was mighty relieved at that.

But Bindu wept inconsolably day and night. I knew what she was going through. I had fought many battles on Bindu's behalf, but I could not muster the courage to stop her marriage. On what basis could I do so? If I did, who would look after her?

One, she was a girl; and two, she was dark; what house she was off to, to meet what fate, better not to think of such things.

Bindu said, "Sister, five days to go before my marriage; I shall die before that."

I scolded her, but the One Who Knows All knew that if in any easy manner Bindu could die, I would have been relieved.

The day before her marriage, Bindu went and told her sister, "Sister, I will stay in the cowshed; I will do what you tell me to, but please don't abandon me like this."

For some days, elder sister-in-law had been quietly

shedding tears. She shed some more. But in this world, having a heart is not enough; there are scriptures too. She said, "You know, Bindi, a husband is the be-all and the end-all for a woman. If your fate is unkind, nobody can do anything about it."

The truth is, whichever way one turns, there is no way open—Bindu had to be married off, and then let devil take the hindmost.

I had wanted the marriage to take place in our house. But you people insisted that it take place at the groom's house—it was the tradition in their clan.

I understood that if Bindu's marriage entailed expenses for your people, your domestic gods wouldn't put up with it. So, I had to shut up. But one thing you people didn't know. I wanted to inform my elder sister-in-law; in the end I couldn't, because she might have died of fright—I had secretly made up Bindu with some of my own ornaments. I sense that that was noticed by my elder sister-in-law, but she pretended otherwise. For God's sake, forgive her for that.

Before going away, Bindu hugged me and said, "Sister, so you too have abandoned me summarily?"

I said, "No, Bindi, no matter your condition, I will never abandon you."

Three days went by. The lamb presented to you by a subject of your fief, I saved it from your terrible hunger and gave it shelter in the cowshed on the ground floor. I would personally feed it first thing in the morning; I have tried your servants; they were more interested in eating it than in feeding it. Then, one day, in that room, I entered and saw Bindu cowering in a corner. Upon seeing me, she fell at my feet and started crying silently.

Bindu's husband was mad.

"Are you telling me the truth, Bindi?"

"How can I tell such a lie to you, sister? He's mad. My father-in-law was against the marriage—but he is mortally scared of my mother-in-law. He went off to Benares before the marriage. The mother-in-law willfully married off her son to me."

I sat down on the heap of coal. Women don't take pity on women. The mother-in-law said, "She's nothing but a girl. So, what if my son is mad? He is still a man."

One could not, at a glance, make out whether Bindi's husband was mad or not, but there were days when he had to be locked up in a room. On the wedding night, he was okay, but not having slept at night because of the bustle, the very next day he went completely insane. Bindu had sat down for the afternoon meal when, all of a sudden, her husband took her brass plate full of rice and threw it into the courtyard. Why? Because he thought Bindu was Rani Rashmoni, the servant had surely stolen the Rani's golden utensils and given her, her own ordinary plate. He was furious. Bindu nearly died of fright. On the third night, when her mother-in-law asked Bindu to sleep in her husband's room, Bindu went all dry inside. Her mother-in-law was terrible; angry, she would become unconscious. She too was mad, all the more frighteningly for not being completely so. Bindu had to go. The husband was calm that night. But Bindu was scared stiff as a log. When her husband finally dozed off late at night, Bindu used all her wits to flee. I need not describe in detail why.

Your people said, "Bindu is lying."

I said, "She has never told a lie."

Your people said, "How do you know?"

I said, "I know for certain."

Your people tried intimidation: "You'll be in trouble, if her in-laws go to the police."

I said, "They used deceit to marry off a madman; I am sure the court will want to listen."

Your people said, "Oh, do we have to go to court over this? Why? What is at stake for us?"

I said, "I'll sell off my ornaments and do what I can."

You people said, "Are you going to run to a lawyer?"

There was no answer to this. I could only slap my forehead. What more could I do?

Besides, Bindu's elder brother-in-law had landed up and was creating a ruckus. He said he would inform the police.

I don't know what strength I had—but I just wouldn't accept that the cow that had run away from the butcher and sought refuge with me, I would have to return it to the butcher, pursued by the police. I defied them and said,

"Let them inform the police."

Having said this, I thought to myself, I would take Bindu to my bedroom and keep her with me and lock the door. But then I searched for Bindu and couldn't find her. While I was arguing with you people, Bindu had quietly slipped away outside and had surrendered to her elder brother-in-law.

She had understood that were she to remain in the house, she would be putting me at risk.

By running away in the middle of everything, she had made things worse for herself. And her mother-in-law's argument was that her son was not eating her up alive. Bad husbands weren't rare. Compared to them, her son was a nugget of gold.

My elder sister-in-law said, "It's her wretched fate; what can anyone do about that? He may be crazy, but he's the husband after all."

Before your conscience lies the image of the virtuous, saintly woman, who had carried her leper husband on her lap to drop him off at the brothel. This story is of the most degraded cowardice; you men have not had the least prick of conscience in propagating it, which is why, having been born humans, you people could get angry over Bindu's behaviour, *and* you still kept your heads high.

My heart broke for Bindu, but for your people I just felt infinitely shameful. I was a simple girl from the country; on top of that, I had washed up in your house. God knows by what sleight of hand he gave me this mind of mine. I just couldn't stand you people talking of religion.

I knew Bindu would never return to the house even if her life depended on it. But I had, before her marriage, given her my word that I would never leave her at the mercy of the world. My younger brother, Sarat, was studying in a college in Calcutta. You all know that due to his involvement in all kinds of volunteer work, killing rats in plague-infested localities, and running to rescue people when the Damodar broke its banks; he was so enthusiastic about all that, that failing his FA exams twice had not fazed him. I called him and said, "See to it, Sarat, that I get news of Bindu. However, don't dare write to me. I won't receive any letters."

Instead of assigning him this duty, if I had asked him to abduct Bindu or smash her lunatic husband's head, he would have felt happier.

I was talking to Sarat when you suddenly entered the room and said, "What mischief are you up to now?"

I said, "Only the ones I had hatched right in the beginning when I came to live with you people—But that is your own doing."

You asked me, "Where have you hidden Bindu now?"

I said, "Had Bindu come, I would have surely hidden her. But don't be bothered, she won't come."

Seeing Sarat with me stoked your suspicions even more. I know that you people did not take kindly to

Sarat's comings and goings in the house. You were afraid that the police might have an eye on him—when and in what political circumstances he would become entangled and would take all of you down with him, who could tell? Which is why I would send my blessings for *Bhai Fota* through someone else instead of calling him home.

I heard from you that Bindu had run away again, and therefore, her elder brother-in-law had landed up at our house again. Hearing the news, my heart was as if pierced by a dart. I understood the miseries undergone by that unfortunate girl, but there was no way one could do anything about it.

Sarat hurried away to gather information. He came back in the evening and said, "Bindu had gone to her cousins' house, but they flew into a rage and took the trouble of returning her to her in-laws. And the sting of the trouble and the expenses that that entailed is still fresh in their minds."

Your grandmother, waiting to go on a pilgrimage to the holy land of Puri, had put up at your house. I told your people, "I too will go."Seeing my sudden attachment to religion gladdened all of you, and you all raised no objection. You were also conscious of the possibility that if I stayed on in Calcutta, I could raise a new fuss over Bindu at any time. Great difficulties where I was concerned. On Sunday, it was decided I would leave on Wednesday. I called Sarat and told him, "Do whatever it takes, but see to it that Bindu boards the train for Puri, Wednesday."

Sarat's face brightened up at once. He said, "Not to worry, my sister, I will put her on the train and accompany her up to Puri—I will use this opportunity to go and visit Lord Jagannath."

The same evening, Sarat came to me. My heart sank when I saw his face. I said, "Sarat? You couldn't manage it, could you?"

He said, "No."

I said, "She wouldn't agree?"

He said, "She doesn't need to any longer. Yesterday she set fire to her clothes and committed suicide. I learnt this from the person I had befriended during *Bhai Fota.* She had left a letter addressed to you. But her in-laws have destroyed it."

Thank God, peace at last.

You all said, "It was just a big show."

But you people never stopped to wonder why the spectacle always involves the saris of the womenfolk and never the dhotis of our valiant men.

Bindi's fate was that of an accursed wretch indeed. As long as she lived, she was known neither for beauty nor for any domestic skill—even while dying it did not occur to her to die in such a novel fashion that the menfolk of the country break into spontaneous applause. Even in death she made people angry.

My elder sister-in-law had wept, hidden in her room.

There was consolation in her tears. No matter what, there had been a resolution. She had not died for nothing, had she gone on living, God knows what might have happened.

I am on my pilgrimage. Bindu didn't need to come, but I needed to.

What people understand when they say 'sorrow', didn't exist for me in your world. In your family's house there is no dearth of food or clothing. I can't speak for your elder brother's character, but there was never anything in your character for me to blame God for. Even if your character had been like that of your elder brother, I would, perhaps, have spent my days as I have until now and like my saintly, virtuous sister-in-law, I would have tried to blame not my husband, the god of my life, but the Creator of this world. Therefore, I do not wish to lodge any complaint against you—that is not why I am writing this letter to you.

But I will never return to that house on 27, Makhan Boral Lane. I have seen Bindu. I know what it means to be recognised as a woman in a household. I don't need that anymore.

Subsequently, I have also seen that God did not forsake her despite her being a woman. No matter how much force you were all to exert on her, there is a limit to that force. You thought that you could, according to your will and your custom, keep her suppressed under your feet for life, forever. Your feet are not so big. Death is bigger than you. Even in her death, Bindu is greater—there she is not just another Bengali girl, not a sister to her cousins, not just the cheated wife of a nameless madman. There, she is infinite.

The day Death's flute played through the broken heart of this girl, on the shores of my life's river, that day, for the first time, an arrow pierced my breast. I had asked God, 'Why is it that only those things that are most petty in the world are also the most difficult? Why is that this gloomy fortress in the middle of the lane, why should its gloomy effervescence be such a formidable obstacle? In your wide world, no matter how the receptacle of the six seasons calls out, I cannot cross the threshold of your inner quarters even for a moment. In this world of yours with this life of mine, why must I expire within that petty brick and mortar structure, bit by bit? How petty is my way of everyday life, how petty are its fixed rules, its fixed practices, its fixed ways of speaking, and all its fixed ways of dying—but ultimately it is the snake-noose of that indigence that will win—and will be defeated the world of joy created by You.'

But Death's flute played on—O where is the mason's wall, O where is the barricade of thorns put up by our laws! In what misery, in what humiliation, it can make one a prisoner! There! You can see the victory flag of life flying in Death's hand. O *Mejobou,* you need not fear; it won't take more than a moment to strip off your *Mejobou*'s shell!

I fear not your lanes anymore. In front of me lies the

blue sea, and above me the clouds of *Ashaar*.

You all had covered me with the darkness of your habit. For a moment, Bindu had succeeded in piercing the veil and seeing me for who I am. It's that girl who, by dying, has torn apart this fabric of illusion to shreds. Today I came out and saw that I have no place left for my pride. She is the one who had liked my uncared-for beauty, it is she who looks upon it through this beautiful sky. It is your *Mejobou* who has died.

You think I am going to die—no, no need to fear, I won't play such an old prank on you all. Meerabai was a woman like me; her chains were as heavy; she didn't have to die in order to live. In her songs, Meerabai had declared, "Leave father, leave mother, leave all, Meera persists, O Lord"—let what may happen, happen.

This persistence is called life.

I will live. I am saved.

Yours shelterlessly,
Mrinal
*Shravan*, 1914

# Damnation

It is as if the month of *Shravan* has gone bankrupt overnight. There is not a shred of cloud anywhere in the sky.

What is surprising is that my morning is being spent like this. In my garden, the leaves of the rain tree at the edge of the henna bushes are glistening, and I am looking on. When this mid-river catastrophe was as yet at a distance, how many winter nights I had spent drenched in sweat, how many summer days my hands and feet had gone clammy and cold, just imagining it. But today, I am spared all these fearful thoughts such that I notice even the rock-still chameleon, poised in front of its prey, on a branch of the custard-apple tree.

What is hard is not that I will lose everything and be thrown out into the streets—what made me sick with shame was that the famous tradition of truthfulness, three generations-old in my family, was going to be shattered to bits on the slippery slopes of my life. I have often had thoughts about committing suicide. Now that the curtains have parted, now that, like black worms, my infamy has left the cavernous depths of registers and books and is finding its way out, through the courts into the world of the press, a tremendous load has been taken off my shoulders. I won't have to drag around with me the remains of my ancestors. Everybody knows I am a swindler. What a relief!

The lawyers will fight it out, and everything will come out. Only the greatest shame of it all will not have the chance of making it to court—because, barring religion, it has no court of appeal left to it. Which is why I have picked up the pen today to bruit it abroad.

My great-grandfather, Uddhav Dutta, saved his master, in the latter's moment of distress, by giving away his own property. This is why we have been proud of our impoverished condition, prouder than some are of their wealth.

My father, Sanatan Dutta, was a student of Derozio. He was as fond of truth as he was of liquor. *Maa* had, one day, told us the story of the barber; hearing this, my father had forbidden us from going to the inner quarters of the house in the evenings. We slept in the schoolroom. There, the maps on the walls would tell us the truth; they would tell us nothing of the wilderness, of fields and meadows, and would hang by a noose the story about the seven seas and the thirteen rivers. As far as the truth was concerned, my father was no less finicky than his forebears. There was no end to the explanations sought from us. One day, a hawker sold something to my elder brother. We were playing with one of the strings of the packet in which it was wrapped. I was made by my father to run out into the street after the man to return the string to him.

We were in a prison of holiness, behind the bars of truthfulness. To call us human would have been an exaggeration—excepting us, everyone was human; we were, for our part, an example to ordinary humanity. Our games were hard, our jests few, and stories uninteresting, our laughter modest, and conduct perfectly becoming. The great lacuna that was introduced, by virtue, into our childish lives was filled with public praise. From our teacher to our grocer, everybody agreed that the sons of the Dutta family had somehow lost their way here; they belonged to the Age of Truth.

Even roads, which have been rendered lifeless by stone, may have gaps that Nature could exploit to plant the green flag of its life-force, victorious, in it. In my youth, all dates were auspicious, or so it seemed. But, in them, I had, in the rituals of fasting, tasted nectar.

Akhil *babu's* house was among those we were not forbidden to visit. He was an adept of the Brahmo Samaj. Father trusted him. He had a daughter, Anusuya, six years my junior; I had taken up the job of disciplining her.

I still remember the lids of her brown eyes. In the

shades of those lids, all the harsh light of the earth would grow mellow. With what tender affection she would gaze at one's face. I also remember the plaited hair that fell on her back, and I remember her hands—I don't know why, but it seemed that her long fingers were waiting, with complete trust, to be grasped in someone's fist.

It would be saying too much if I said that I saw her thus that day. But we still understand a lot in not understanding fully. Unbeknownst to us, many pictures painted in our minds and hearts remain invisible—until a sudden illumination by a ray of light makes us see them.

The door to Anu's heart was not heavily guarded. She would believe any rubbish. And what she had learnt about the world from the old maid who looked after her was not worth a place even in the rubbish heap of our school room with its maps. And then, on top of this, there was no counting the number of things she would conjure up out of her imagination. Here, I would only have to discipline her. I only had to say, "Anu, all these are lies, you know, it's sinful." Upon hearing this, a pall of fear would cover the dark eyelids of the girl. When Anu would make up outrageous things to stop her younger sister from crying—or to induce her to having her milk, by saying there was a bird where there was no bird, or some such fanciful thing, spoken in a loud voice, I, putting on my most fearfully serious face, had to warn her saying, "God is listening to all the fibs you are telling her, you should say sorry to Him immediately."

She always submitted to all my efforts at disciplining her. The more she considered herself guilty, the happier I was. Given the opportunity to do good, by severely disciplining someone, the discipliner is also served and rewarded. Consequently, Anu thought that I was a better person than not only her but the better part of humanity as well.

In due course, I grew up, finished school and went to college. Akhil *babu's* wife nurtured the fond hope of marrying Anu off to a good boy like me. I too, felt the same, I was not one to evade the eyes of the father of a daughter of marriageable age. But, one day, I heard that Anu was betrothed to a fresh *munsiff* with a Bachelor of Law degree. We were poor—I had been given to understand that was why we were precious. But the process of the bride's father's calculations was independent.

The idol was immersed. In what hidden corner of life had it fallen? The person whom, since childhood, I had known best, that person had, within a day, disappeared into the billowing waves of a sea made up of hundreds of thousands of unknown people. Only the heart knows what rang out within it. But, had I understood even after immersion, the idol of my deity? No. Wounded pride had multiplied the fury of those waves. I had always seen Anu as my junior; she grew even smaller that day compared to my worth. That my excellence was not worshipped that day— that was what seemed to me to be the biggest misfortune in the world.

I understood that in the world, it is not enough just to be good. I swore that I would make so much money that Akhil *babu* would be forced to say, "Destiny has played tricks with me." I threw myself into becoming a man of work.

The most tangible asset for a working man is an unbound faith in oneself, in which I was never very deficient. This quality is infectious. One who has faith in himself is more likely to attract the faith of others. That my practical intelligence was natural and extraordinary, everyone began believing so.

'How To' books and papers began crowding my shelves and tables. Renovation of the house, installation of electric lights and fans, how much X or Y product costs, the solid facts behind the rise and fall of markets, the mysteries of the stock exchange, planning, estimation— on all these subjects and more, I had acquired a mastery that was recognised by many.

But I spent many days talking of work and not doing any myself. Whenever my disciples would propose that I join this or that native company, I would give them to understand that whatever was thorough in the planning, they were, in fact, all deficient in execution—besides, there was no way one could be involved in them and remain honest. No business can run without at times playing fast and loose with the public, would say one of my friends, and that would be sufficient reason for our relations to sour.

I could have maintained my reputation intact till my dying day by drawing up perfect plans and estimates. But going against custom, I left making plans and got down to work instead. One, with the death of my father, the responsibility of running the house fell on my shoulders; to that was added another calamity. I'll speak of it now.

Prasanna used to be my classmate. He was as outspoken as he was caustic. He had found an opportunity to have a go at our ancestral reputation for honesty. My father had named me Satyadhan, or 'True Wealth'. Prasanna, noticing our poverty, had said, "Your father gave you false wealth but named you 'True Wealth'; he would have done better to give you true wealth and a false name." I used to fear Prasanna's utterances.

I hadn't seen him in years. Meanwhile, he had been working in all sorts of jobs in Burma, Ludhiana, and Srirangapatnam. Unexpectedly, he came back to Calcutta one day, and sought me out. There was some comfort to have received respect from one whose jest I had always feared.

Prasanna said, "Brother, I am telling you, mark my words, if one day you don't become a second Moti Sil or Durgacharan Laha, I'll rub my nose all the way from Burra Bazar crossing to Bagbazar crossing."

Those who hadn't sat in the same classroom with Prasanna couldn't have appreciated the import of this grand utterance coming from him. Plus, Prasanna had seen the world; his words were worth something.

He said, "Brother, I have seen lots of people who know what they are doing—those are the most dangerous lot. They want to check-mate the world through their intelligence alone, they forget that religion is above everything else—but you are destined for wealth. You hold on firmly to religion and then you understand business too."

It was an age infatuated with starting a business. Everyone had concluded that without trade and commerce, the country could not be free. And everyone understood that once you lay your hands on capital, you could set up roaring practice in all kinds of things such as the law, medicine, the teaching profession, and that students or even their progenitors could set up in business within a day.

I told Prasanna, "My stars are not good."

He said, "Precisely! You have your ancestral wealth."

Then suddenly I felt that Prasanna had been, all these days, making fun of me.

Prasanna said, "Not a joke brother! Honesty is the golden lotus of the goddess of wealth, Lakshmi. Businesses run on trust, not on money."

From the time of my father's generation, certain widows in our neighbourhood had accumulated some money and they were not expecting interest; they knew that women could be cheated at will everywhere else, excepting in our house.

With that money, I started a native agency. Cloth, paper, ink, buttons, soap: no matter what I stocked would get sold, buyers would line up in droves.

There is a saying—the more knowledge increases, the more one knows that one knows nothing. The same thought applies to money. The more money you have, the less you feel you have. In this circumstance, Prasanna said, well, he didn't exactly say it himself, but he got me to proclaim that: "To give one's life to petty shopkeeping would be tantamount to wasting it. Doing business with the world is real business. The money circulating within the country is like the bull who turns the oil press; it doesn't go forward but turns round and round."

Prasanna was so effusive, as though he hadn't heard anything so profound ever in his life before. Then I showed him the nationwide figures for trade in linseed for the last seven years. How much linseed goes where, how far does it go, how much do the prices go up, how much do they come down, how much does it cost in the field, how much in the shipping; how much profit is there in buying it from the farm and selling it straightaway overseas—at times with a line drawn underneath, sometimes accounting in percentages, sometimes in serial order, at other times in reverse, in red and black ink, in clear handwriting on foolscap sheets, some seven or eight of them. When I handed it all over to Prasanna, he was ready to take the dust off my feet.

He said, "I thought I understood some of this, but from today onwards, I am your disciple."

And then he protested a little. He said, "O constance abandoned—do you remember? I don't know; there might be an error in the calculations."

That made me obstinate. That there was no error, the proof grew stronger from page to page. Even taking into account all possible losses, the profits could not be less than twenty to twenty-five percent.

In this way, when plying the narrow canal of shopkeeping, I finally reached the ocean of business; it appeared to me to be a result of my obstinacy—or such was my attitude. The responsibility was mine.

There was the Duttas' reputation for honesty, and then greed for interest; the accumulated funds grew exponentially, and women began selling off their jewellery to give me money.

Having entered the field, I was slightly lost. What had been divided, on paper, into the plan, by red and black lines, on the ground the division couldn't be found so easily. The plan was not satisfactory; I was not happy in my work. The inner self understood clearly; I did not have the capacity for work, nor was I able to admit this. In due course, the work went to Prasanna, even though to Prasanna I was the head of the business, its creator. His intention and my signature, his capabilities and my ancestral reputation—these two combined such that I just couldn't comprehend where this beast of a business was running off to, on its four legs.

Over time, I reached a point where I couldn't find the flat ground nor see the shore. At that point, if I had let things go and told the truth, then honesty would have been saved. But a reputation for honesty cannot be defended. So, I started collecting interest on capital but not from the profits. And I kept on pushing up the rate of interest and thus the corpus of the accumulated funds.

I've been married for a long time. I thought my wife was only interested in running the house. Then, all of a sudden, I saw that, like Agastya, the desire to multiply her wealth had taken hold of her. I don't know when this wind emerging from within me, started blowing within my entire family. My servants, my maids, even my gatekeeper—everybody was investing in the business. Even my wife caught hold of me. She wanted to sell some of her ornaments and invest in the business. I refused to accept her demand with scorn. I advised her that there was no vice worse than greed—I didn't take my wife's money.

There was another, whose money I couldn't take.

Anu had been widowed after having had a son. Her husband was known for his wealth and his miserly ways. Some said that he had put away a hundred thousand rupees in savings; some said even more. People said, in miserliness, Anu was her husband's equal. I thought, that must be so. Anu had no education or company to be otherwise.

The money that she wanted to send me, it was to invest. There was greed and necessity too, but, out of fear, I did not go to see her even once.

Once when a large bill of exchange became due, Prasanna came and said, "It's time to take Akhil *babu's* daugher's money."

I said, "I might be in a situation where I have to break into somebody's house, but I won't take that money."

Prasanna said, "Ever since your confidence is gone, the business has been running at a loss. When the head hits the obstacle, it becomes more solid."

I wouldn't budge.

The next day, Prasanna came and said, "A famous *Marathi* astrologer has come from the south. Show him your horoscope."

Horoscope! For someone who belonged to Sanatan Dutta's family! In times of yore, in moments of weakness, this was a way for the ignorant to regain some strength. When the visible is frightening, then one clings desperately to the invisible. When I could draw no comfort from trusting my intelligence, I took refuge in stupidity. With my hour of birth and its date, I went to see the astrologer. I was told I was on the brink of catastrophe. Jupiter was favourable—he would, by means of some woman's wealth, procure for me untold riches.

I could have suspected that Prasanna had a hand in this. But I didn't feel up to it. When we had come back home, Prasanna handed me a book and said, "Open it." On the page I opened were written, in English, the words: 'Extraordinary success in business.'

I went to see Anu that day itself.

Following her marriage, Anu had moved to a small town with her husband. She used to be afflicted with malaria so often that doctors were afraid she was stricken with consumption. Asked to shift to another better place, she said, "I'll die, if not today, then tomorrow, why should I waste the money meant for Subodh?"—Thus, she was defending, with her life, both Subodh and the money meant for him.

I went and saw that Anu's illness had nearly removed her from this world. It was as if I were seeing her from a great distance. Her body had grown pale, as if she was glowing. Her substance had wasted away, and she was standing at death's gate, bathed in heavenly light. And there were the dense, dark lids of her sad eyes. There were dark rings under her eyes, as if the shadows of the dusk of her life had fallen over her vision. My mind went still; she seemed to be a goddess.

Seeing me, a tranquil joy spread over Anu's face. She said, "I have been thinking about you ever since my condition worsened last night. I know my days are numbered. Day after tomorrow is *Bhai Fota;* and on that day I want to anoint you as my brother for the last time.'

I said nothing about the money; I called for Subodh. He was seven years old. He had his mother's eyes. He seemed to be wrapped entirely in some kind of transience, as if he had never been given his full share of breast milk. I took him in my lap and kissed his forehead. He remained silent, gazing at my face.

Upon my return, Prasanna asked me, "What happened?"

I said, "There wasn't enough time today."

He said, "The bill is due in the next nine days."

Having seen Anu's face, the lotus that blooms in the lake of death, ruin didn't seem all that frightening to me.

It had been some time since I had stopped looking at the accounts. I couldn't see how we could navigate through the situation, so I kept my eyes closed. I signed everything, desperately, without trying to understand anything. On the morning of *Bhai Fota*, taking a summary of the books of account, Prasanna sat me down forcibly and explained the current situation of the business. I saw that our capital had been entirely eroded. Now, if we didn't throw some ballast off the ship, through loans, it would sink.

Going to the *Bhai Fota*, I was constantly thinking of how to artfully bring up the topic of money. It was a Thursday. Half-witted that I was, I was obliged to even fear Thursdays. An unfortunate wretch trusts everything but his own intelligence. Setting out, I felt dejected.

Anu's fever had gone up. I saw her lying prostrate on the bed. On the floor sat Subodh, silently cutting pictures out of an English picture book, and pasting them in a separate exercise book.

I had come much too early to avoid the inauspicious hours. I was supposed to take my wife along. But I knew that in a corner of her heart, my wife was jealous of Anu, which is why she found a pretext for not accompanying me, nor did I press the matter.

Anu asked, "*Boudidi* didn't come?"

I said, "Not feeling well."

Anu exhaled briefly, she didn't say anything.

The little gentleness that I had once displayed had been melted in a glow of gold, and that glow was now spread over the patient's bed by the autumn sky. So much came to the surface. All those petty matters had, going beyond my impending ruin, acquired today such an enormous dimension that I forgot about the state of my business.

I ate the *Bhai Fota* meal. That traveller who walked the road of death, applied the auspicious mark, praying for my longevity on my forehead, and took the dust off my feet. I wiped my tears as discreetly as possible.

When I had taken a seat, Anu brought out a tin box for me. She said, "This is all that I have put aside for Subodh, and I am putting Subodh too under your care. I can now die in peace."

I said, "Anu, please understand, I can't take the money. I will not fail in my duty towards Subodh, but keep the money with someone else."

Anu said, "There are many waiting to lay their hands on this money. Are you telling me to give it to them?"

I did not utter a word. Anu said, "I have overheard the doctors say that given Subodh's symptoms, he may not live long. I am living in the constant fear of dying too late. Today, I can die with the hope that the doctors might well be wrong. Forty-seven thousand rupees have accumulated in the Company's books—there are other sums from here and there. This money will be more than enough for Subodh's maintenance and treatment. And should God call him to Himself early, then you can use the money for some good purpose."

I said, "Anu, I do not trust myself as much as you trust me."

This made Anu laugh. It sounded like false modesty.

When I was taking leave of her, Anu took the company papers out of the box along with a bundle of notes and explained everything to me. I saw written in her will, if Subodh were to die without an heir or as a minor, the property would come to me.

I said, "Why did you mix up your property with my interests?"

Anu said, "Because I know that my son's interests will not hurt yours."

I said, "It's not our custom to trust anybody so much." Anu replied, "I know you, and I understand *your* customs."

There was jewellery in the box. Anu showed them to me and said, "If Subodh survives and marries, then give these to his wife with my blessings. And give this emerald necklace to your wife, and say that it is my wish that she accepts it."

Saying this, Anu fell to the floor and touched my feet, her eyes welling up with tears. She got up quickly, turned her face, and went away. This was the last time she touched my feet. Just two days after this, in the evening, she stopped breathing and passed away—she didn't even have the time to inform me. When, after *Bhai Fota*, I took a carriage home and got down with the tin box in my hand, I saw Prasanna waiting for me. He asked, "Good news, brother?"

I said, "No one is to touch this money."

Prasanna said, "But—"

I said, "No buts—let what is to happen happen, this money will not be required for my business."

Prasanna said, "Then they will be required for your last rites."

After Anu's death, Subodh came to live with us, and found a companion in my son Nityadhan.

Those who read novels think that big changes occur in a man's life but gradually. A charcoal fire takes time to catch, but big fires catch easily and spread quickly. If

I say that in my heart, over a period of time there grew in me an animus towards Subodh, then everyone will ask for an elaborate explanation. Subodh was an orphan; he was feeble; he was good-looking, and above all, Anu was Subodh's mother—but his way of talking, of going about his business, of playing, everything about him seemed irritating to me.

Truth be told, times were bad. I had pledged not to touch Subodh's money, yet I couldn't do without it; such were the circumstances. One day, finding myself in great difficulty, I took some money out of Subodh's funds. With this, the mechanism of my heart went out of kilter such that I feared showing my face to Subodh. At first, I would avoid him, and then I started losing my temper with him.

The principal reason for my anger was his nature. I am a busy man myself; I do everything in a hurry. But Subodh had a peculiar temperament such that when, for example, I asked him something, he would suddenly be rendered speechless—it's as if he wasn't where he was; he was elsewhere. He would spend hours gazing out of a road-facing window, clutching at its bars, seeing what, thinking what, only he knew. I found this unbearable. Subodh had been ill for a long time, brought up by his mother. He didn't have playmates of his age and thus, had played by himself in his own mind. The problem with such boys is that when there is cause for grief, they know neither how to cry nor how to forget their grief. This is why when one called for Subodh, there would be no response, and if one asked him to do something, he would often forget. He would keep losing his things and when scolded, would stare at one's face—as if staring was his way of crying. I began saying, "He's setting a bad example for my son." The difficulty, however, was that Nitya had taken a liking to him the moment he saw him; however, since they were opposed in character, the attraction was correspondingly greater.

To correct somebody's character was a family calling; in this I supplemented skill with energy. Since Subodh was not inclined to work, I began piling more and more work on him. If he made a mistake, I would every time make him rectify it.

He had another habit; one he got from his mother—he would imagine himself and his surroundings in many different ways. He had given a funny sort of name to the star-apple tree in front of the window; my wife told me he would stand alone in front of the tree and talk to it. I had on many an occasion, tried to have him confess that turning the pillows into cows and treating the bed as a meadow was acting out a lie—he wouldn't even answer. The more I attempted to discipline him; the more faults I found with him. He would get flustered upon seeing me; he was unable to understand my plainest speech. It was simply this: when the heart begins to get angry and finds no obstacle outside, to bump up against, and restrain itself, then that anger intensifies itself on its own, even without new reasons to excite it. If you call such a man a fool three or four times to which he makes no answer, then those three or four occasions create the first occasion for saying so to his face, no other instruments are required. Being irritated by Subodh had become such a habit with me that I had no means to break it.

Five years went by—Subodh was twelve. The company papers and jewellery had meanwhile melted away, and had been transformed into some sums in my books of account.

I reasoned with myself that Anu had left the money with me in her will. In between there was Subodh, true, but he was just a shadow, as good as gone.

The money I was sure to get there was no sacrilege in spending it.

I had suffered from gout since I was young. Of late, the condition had worsened. Those I had kept as my employees would get on everybody's nerves over this. For that time, my wife, my son, Subodh, my servants, no one had any peace.

On the other hand, some of the widows I knew, widows who had kept their savings with me, had their interest pending for a few months. I had never allowed such a thing to happen previously. So, they were anxiously clamouring for their money. I importuned Prasanna, and he just kept postponing the dates. Finally, on the appointed day, everybody who was owed anything was waiting since morning, and Prasanna was nowhere to be seen.

I told Nitya, "Please call Subodh."

He said, "He's sleeping."

I flew into a rage and said, "Sleeping?! It's eleven 'o' clock and he's still sleeping?!"

Subodh, frightened, came and stood before me. I told him, "Go and fetch Prasanna from wherever he can be found."

Having complied with my whims and fancies all along, he had become adept at this sort of thing. He knew everything about finding whosoever, wherever they were to be found.

The clock struck one, two, and then three, but there was no sign of Subodh. The language of those waiting for their dues grew sharper and more heated. I could do nothing about Subodh's lackadaisical attitude. His ways got looser as days went by. These days he wouldn't stand if he could sit, he took seven days to get going. One day, I had found him lazing in bed at five in the evening. He had to be woken up in the morning by force, and he would drag his feet as he walked. I used to tell Subodh that he was a born laggard, with a magna cum laude in laziness. If it could be avoided, Subodh never cried in front of me, but that day the tears just flowed from his eyes. He could put up with blows and abuse, but scorn always touched him to the quick.

The hours went by. The night fell. Nobody lit a lamp

inside the house. I called out to my people; but no one responded. I was angry with everyone in the house. Suddenly, the suspicion took hold of me that Prasanna had probably handed over the money to Subodh, who had run away with it. That Subodh was not at ease in my house, I knew well. Even as a child, I was taught that comfort was a sin, especially for young boys. Therefore, there was no remorse in me on that score. But I abused Subodh inwardly for having had the audacity to run away with the money, a consequence of my rigour. If he had started stealing at this age, what would become of him later? How could he do such a thing after having lived in my house with someone like me? There was no doubt in my mind that Subodh had taken the money and run away. Soon I felt I should run after him and catch him wherever he could be found and, being myself in a parlous frame of mind, give him a sound thrashing.

While I was thinking all this, Subodh entered my unlit room. I was so angry that no matter how I tried, words wouldn't come out of my mouth.

Subodh said, "I couldn't find the money."

Why did he say that? I hadn't asked him to fetch the money. He must have stolen it and hidden it somewhere. It is such goody-goody boys who turn out to be sneaky devils in the end.

With some difficulty, I cleared my throat and said, "Come out with the money."

Provoked, he said, 'No, I won't; do what you want.'

I could no longer control myself. There was a stick at hand; I brought it down aimed at his skull. He fell over. I took fright. I called him by his name; but he wouldn't answer. Nor had I the strength to approach him. I could not get up. As I fumbled around, I realised the rugs were wet. Blood. The blood was spreading. The blood kept oozing out, soaking the place I stood in. Through my open window I could see the evening star; I quickly looked away. It suddenly struck me that the evening star was like the auspicious mark of sandlewood paste that sisters apply on their brothers' foreheads for *Bhai Fota*. The malicious and unjust rage I had nurtured against Subodh for a long time vanished in a trice. He was the treasure of Anu's heart; he had strayed from Anu's lap in search of a path to my heart. What had I done?! Dear God, why did you take away my wits? What need had I of money? I would have saved myself by letting my business go adrift and devoting myself religiously to this sickly boy.

I was afraid that someone might come and catch me. I was desperate that no one should come, that no light should penetrate, that this darkness must not be dispelled even for a moment, that the sun must not rise the following day, that the world be rendered a lie, and envelop the boy and me in a dense, deep black fog forever.

I heard footsteps. I thought to myself, 'Who had informed the police?' I tried to quickly think up an explanation for the deed, but my mind could think of nothing.

The door opened with a bang, and somebody entered the room.

I had woken up with a start. I saw it was still light. I had dozed off; and it was when Subodh had entered the room that I woke up.

Hatkhola, Burra Bazar, Beliaghata, throughout the day, Subodh had been to every place in the city where Prasanna could have been found. Subodh's face had gone pale at the thought of the offence he had committed in not finding Prasanna by whatever means he could employ. After all these years, I saw that his face was truly beautiful, and his eyes truly sad.

I said, "Come, my dear boy Subodh, come and sit in my lap."

He couldn't understand. He thought I was making fun of him. He stood staring at me, wide-eyed, for a few moments, and then he fainted and fell.

In a flash, my gout vanished. I got up quickly, took him in my arms, and laid him on the bed. There was water in the earthen pitcher; I sprinkled a few drops on his face and his forehead, but he did not regain consciousness.

I called for the doctor.

The doctor came and was astonished at Subodh's condition. He said, "He is tired beyond all limits. How did this come about?"

I said, "He has had to, for some reason, exert himself all day today."

The doctor said, "This is not a result of one day's work. He has been wasting away for quite some time; nobody seems to have noticed."

After plying him with stimulants and prescribing a treatment, the doctor tried to bring him back to his senses and then went away.

Before going, he said, "He might survive if he is taken care of meticulously, but his life force is very nearly exhausted. For the last few days, he must have been moving around on willpower alone."

I forgot about my ailments. Giving up my bed for Subodh, I nursed him day and night. I didn't have the money for the doctor's fees. I opened my wife's jewellery box, I took out the emerald necklace and gave it to my wife, saying, "You keep this." The rest I pawned.

But a human cannot survive on money alone. I had oppressed and squeezed the life out of Subodh. I had deprived him, day after day, of the nourishment of affection; and today when I had come to him with my heart full of it, he was in no state to receive it. Empty-handed, he had returned to his mother.

*Bhadra,* 1914